THESE SILENT BONES

A KATE REID NOVEL
BOOK 17

ROBIN MAHLE

HARP HOUSE PUBLISHING, LLC.

Published by HARP House Publishing
September 2024 (1st edition)

Cover design: Ampersand Book Cover Designs

1

Dragging the lifeless body back to shore became a grueling task as a tenuous grip on the victim was about to slip away. It wasn't supposed to go down like this, but in an effort to save himself, the fool had jumped from the boat before it had beached near the shoreline.

"For a smart guy, you're a real dumb ass, you know that?" he whispered.

Death, however, came swiftly after that. He'd succumbed to his many injuries, which had been inflicted by the man who now had to take him back to the boat. He darted his gaze, peering through the bare trees, keeping a close watch for headlights on the road that led to the lake.

The precautionary effort served to distract him from the large stone in his path. He stumbled, letting the body slip through his fingers. It landed on the unyielding earth, the thud momentarily masking the soft lapping of the lake's shoreline.

"You're a heavy son of a bitch," he cursed under his breath.

He was fortunate, however, in that the Lake of the Ozarks was in the middle of its off-season. Winter held at bay many tourists, who would otherwise have been on raucous jet skis and speed-boats whizzing by, regardless of the time of day. Instead, the night air was crisp, the atmosphere, quiet except for his own grunts as he struggled with his cumbersome cargo.

Wading into the shallow water, the buoyant corpse finally offered some relief, but now, to raise it onto the vessel. Hooking the body onto the ladder, he climbed aboard and grabbed the nearby rope. Shimmying down the first few steps, he secured the rope around the man's chest and once onboard, hoisted up the body.

Out of breath, he almost collapsed as the lifeless figure dropped onto the floor of the stern. The exertion was enough to cause sweat to form on his brow, even in the wintry air. While most of the heavy lifting was over, this task was far from finished.

Turning the key, the boat's engine hummed. He jumped off the edge of the bow and pushed the boat away from the shore before quickly climbing aboard again and setting off into the lake. He knew these waters just as he knew the lines on his face. A piece of knowledge passed down through generations, going as far back as when the lake was first formed. Back when the govern-ment condemned a community that now lay dormant at the bottom.

Now, he motored on, cutting through the misty air that coated the windshield. The sound of the boat's engine echoed over the water, but amid the shadowy trees, no lights burned. No tourists. No residents. Not here. Only the life below him accompanied him on this journey.

Slowing to a stop, his vessel now swayed in the deep, and he dropped the anchor. This would be the final resting place for his lifeless companion.

Descending into the cabin compartment, he was careful not to slip on the blood underfoot or leave fingerprints amid the splatters on the walls. Inside, he donned gloves, reaching for the saw. "Sorry it had to be this way." And he set to work. "You should've let it go."

They say this lake is cursed. Strange occurrences—all too common. So, what was another dead body in its depths?

~

THE SEPARATE ENTRANCE offered Dr. Shane Fuller's clients privacy when they came to his home. The converted garage had served as his office for the past five years. Before that, he'd maintained an office near the business district, but it had been taken away, much like everything else in his life.

Sandra Dawes, one of his regular clients, had just arrived. Fuller rounded his desk, catching a glimpse of his reflection in the wall mirror. Contempt at his deepening lines masked his face. But when he smoothed down his thick brown hair, a slight air of authority quickly replaced it. "Good morning, Sandra, how are you?" He offered his hand and a friendly smile.

"I'm doing okay, Doctor Fuller. Glad to be here today, though. I've been feeling like I need a good talk."

"Well, come on in. You know the drill. Take a seat." He gestured to a small loveseat before grabbing a bottle of water from the fridge under his credenza. Returning to her, he offered it. "Here you go. Care for any coffee?"

"No, better not this morning. Thanks for the offer."

"Of course." Fuller sat down across from her, where he'd set up a small seating area a few feet from his desk. Behind Sandra was a picture window covered in sheer curtains. Hazy morning light filtered through them, illuminating her strawberry blond hair.

He set his gaze on Sandra Dawes, his patient of nearly six months. The young wife and mother seemed to always strive for perfection. In her appearance, her lifestyle. It couldn't have been easy, given her husband and family were of modest means. But looking at her now, her hazel eyes glossed over, she looked like she carried the world on her shoulders, and he was the only one who could remove the burden.

Fuller picked up his leather-bound notebook and pen from the side table. "What is it you'd like to talk about today, Sandra?"

Her eyes softened, and a vulnerability shone through that made her appear younger than her thirty-four years—almost childlike.

"You know you're safe here," he said, hoping she'd find the words that seemed to lay at the tip of her tongue.

She peered at her feet and in a low tone, continued, "I've made a terrible mistake."

Fuller sighed. "You judge yourself too harshly. None of us is perfect, not even me." He let out a soft chuckle as a means to break the tension. "Go on."

"About a month or so ago, ...Tim was working late." Sandra dabbed a tissue under her now watery eyes. "The girls were at a sleepover, so I went out. I don't know why. I was bored, I guess."

She went quiet for a moment. He knew better than to interrupt with some mundane phrase, so he waited for her to continue.

"Long story short, I ended up sleeping with another man." Tears streamed down her cheeks now. "It was so stupid. I can't even blame the alcohol because I'd only had a couple of drinks. It was like...I wasn't myself, you know?" Her brow knitted as she tried to reconcile her actions. "I'd never done anything like that before, but now...what do I do? I've been struggling with this for weeks. I can't tell Tim. He'll leave me and take my girls. I'm so ashamed."

Fuller jotted in his notepad. *Guilt. Shame. Regret. Beauty.* "First of all, Sandra, I understand your feelings of shame. But it serves no purpose other than to prevent you from finding forgiveness for yourself. It's time you reexamine your relationship with Tim and determine the root cause of your decision. This was not taken lightly—your choice to go out—to seek out another partner."

"Then why?" she pleaded.

Fuller leaned back in his chair, steepling his fingers, superiority growing inside him. "I can't tell you why, Sandra. Only you hold the truth. But let's examine the possibilities. In our past sessions, you've mentioned your marriage had become stale, and boring. Then, with your daughters away, your husband working late again." He shrugged. "An emptiness pervaded your evening, and so you sought to fill it."

Fuller knew all too well that feeling of emptiness. Sandra nodded as he went on. "You've also implied a longing for passion in your marriage. The flame, which once burned brightly, is now barely a flicker. Tim provides stability and security, but not excitement. Maybe that's what you were seeking."

Excitement brewed in him even now, yet his was derived from something else...Sandra's need for his help. She hung onto his every word in search of absolution. *His* absolution. "In your restlessness, you craved intensity, thrill, danger even. This stranger represented escape and risk-taking. He was the polar opposite of your husband." He paused, regarding Sandra. "But affairs leave scars, on both the betrayer and the betrayed."

Sandra crumpled, fresh tears streaming down her face. "I never meant to hurt him. I just wanted to feel desired."

He knew that feeling all too well and a deeper bond began to stretch between him. She would see it, too, soon enough. "We all want to feel alive, Sandra."

〜

THE WOODEN DOUBLE doors closed with a resounding thud. The sense of being inside a courtroom sprang to Special Agent Kate Reid's mind. But this was where Bureau disciplinary hearings were held. She now stood in the back of the room, eyeing the folding chairs that had been placed in rows. At the front lay a long table with five chairs behind it. Across from that, another, smaller table. Only two chairs behind it. One of them was meant for Senior Unit Agent Nick Scarborough and the other, his FBI union representative.

The room began to fill. She recognized Unit Chief Cole at the long table, talking to others she didn't know. He was one of the five. The heating hadn't yet been turned on and a chill climbed up Kate's arms beneath her suit jacket. It was December in D.C., and winter had come on with a vengeance.

She took a seat on the lightly padded wooden folding chair. A few other people entered. Some were Unit Two team members who had come to support their former senior unit agent. The one person she didn't see was Georgia Myers—a member of Nick's team. Kate had long ago dismissed that he would have ever fallen for Georgia's attempts at rekindling their relationship. Still, she didn't miss Georgia's presence.

Her marriage to Nick Scarborough had been tumultuous from the beginning. Both holding careers as federal agents in one of the most difficult and disturbing fields, Behavioral Sciences. They went after violent, brutal, horrific serial killers. But that was before Nick left for Unit Two, whose focus was mainly on cybercrimes. Then Nick was promoted to head up the joint task force, which had him oversee representatives from several top agencies. Their job was to ensure open communications between the letter agencies in all matters cyber-related. And things had been all right for a while. But when Nick wrecked his car after too many drinks, nearly killing himself, things went off the rails quickly. By the grace of God, no one else had been injured.

Nick was a recovering alcoholic. Everyone knew that. He'd battled it, successfully, until he didn't. Kate was in this room now, waiting for Nick's disciplinary hearing to begin, their marriage hanging by a thread.

At a time when she'd suffered the loss of a baby after returning from a disturbing case that saw so much death, Kate had reached the end of her rope. She had made the decision to leave Nick after learning about his accident. A decision derived from grief and anger, but one she'd stuck by, consequences be damned.

The two hadn't spoken in weeks. Nick had posted bond after the hospital and his DUI charges had eventually been dismissed. First-time offense, no other injuries, and having the Unit Chief vouch for you made a difference with the courts. He got lucky and they both knew it.

But none of that resolved the disciplinary issues with the Bureau. His actions had caused his dismissal from the task force, charges or not. Today's hearing would determine Nick's future. Kate hadn't told him she would be here today.

The rest of the panel was entering the room now. Kate captured Cole's gaze as he sat down. Both nodded in acknowledgment. He seemed a little surprised to see her. She was a little surprised herself.

Assistant FBI Director Bennett entered, taking his seat at the table. The other senior unit agents, including Cameron Fisher, were there now, too. Bennett clanked his water glass with a pen. "If the room will come to order, please. We can get started."

Kate looked around at the people who sat in the rows of chairs. About a dozen, give or take. All of whom were Nick's former colleagues and friends. The open hearing was unusual. But when it involved a senior unit agent with more than a decade at the Bureau, the rules were changed.

Once all were seated, Senior Unit Agent Nick Scarborough entered. Kate's husband. And the man who'd brought her into the Bureau all those years ago. A lifetime ago.

He'd had a noticeable hitch in his step as he approached the chair. A lingering consequence of his car accident, and one that could also play a factor in these proceedings.

Kate had been so angry with him that night. Risking his life for what? Because he couldn't handle making a decision that would've affected troops overseas? She didn't understand it. How he could've been so careless with his own life? And so, after sticking by his side for years while he battled his demons, she made the painful decision to leave.

Scarborough unbuttoned his suit jacket and took his seat, facing the panel. He looked a little thinner now. He'd always been slim, but broad-shouldered and fit. These past several weeks had taken their toll on him.

Bennett flipped through the spiral-bound report that had been placed on the table. Everyone on the panel had a copy. "Senior Unit Agent Nicholas Scarborough. You're here today to discuss disciplinary proceedings and possible dismissal from the Bureau for your actions on the night of November third. Capitol Police charged you with driving under the influence, which was the cause of the accident in which you were involved.

Bennett glared at him; deep lines etched between his eyes. A wide forehead, creased, and a gaze that reflected his disappointment. "SSA Scarborough, while your tenure at the Bureau has been long, you have not been without previous disciplinary action."

Kate recalled Nick's letter of censure years ago. It had been bullshit, just like hers had been.

"That's correct, Director," Scarborough replied.

Bennett looked over at Fisher, then to Unit Chief Cole. "You have allies here who've come today to signal their desire for you to maintain your current post. I've read their letters of support for you. I would be lying if I said they were nothing short of moving."

Kate listened as the hearing went on. Bennett threw back into Nick's face everything he'd ever done wrong. She considered how long that list might be had it been aimed at Bennett, himself.

When the time had come for Fisher to make his statement, he peered beyond Nick, directly at her. Absent his habitual toothpick between his lips, Fisher looked at her with resolve. His face was clean-shaven, eyes soft, their usual hardened former NYPD edginess, now gone.

She knew Fisher would do everything in his power to help Nick. This was despite his misgivings over Nick's heading up of their team long ago. A wound that had finally healed.

"I can say that my experience working under SSA Scarborough has made me a better agent," Fisher began. "He brought out the best in his entire team. He is an exceptional investigative force. And while no one, especially Agent Scarborough himself, condones his actions, it should not bring about the end to an otherwise stellar career." He paused, briefly shifting his gaze to Nick. "I understand the assistant director's reason for this hearing. However, protocol shouldn't be a factor in determining this man's ability to do his job. As I made clear in my written statement, his record stands head and shoulders above the rest. Including mine. Thank you."

Kate's emotions rose to the surface, knowing that Fisher had just put his credibility on the line. She was grateful. It was far more than she had done for Nick.

Then it came to Cole. The man who'd not only given Kate more opportunities than anyone else but who'd also given Nick a chance to find his place inside the Bureau when he'd stopped believing there had been one.

"I've known Agent Scarborough for more than a decade," Cole started. "He helped shape the current Unit Four team, implementing new and effective procedures, and building a cohesive unit until his move to Unit Two. He and his team there helped thwart a Russian cyber-attack."

"I'm aware of Agent Scarborough's accomplishments, Chief Cole," Bennett said.

"Of course, but they bear repeating." He glanced at Nick. "The decision to possibly take the life of anyone, let alone several US servicemen and women, should never be taken lightly. It was an unusual ask for our people. Too much to ask, if I may say so, sir. And Agent Scarborough's difficulty in making a recommendation from the task force culminated in a highly regrettable situation for him. One I am certain he would not make again."

Kate didn't have the same confidence as Cole just displayed. But listening to her mentor now, maybe he was right. Then again, he wasn't married to Nick. She was.

Soon, the hearing concluded. The panel's recommendation would be given to Bennett in the coming days, leaving Nick to swim in a purgatory of uncertainty.

And as the panel departed, Fisher offered a final glance and a nod at Kate as he left the room. That was when Nick turned around. They locked eyes. Kate felt her lips tremble but remained steadfast.

Nick's eyes softened. A hint of a smile curled his lips, but only for a moment. As he made his way to the exit, he looked back again. Kate dipped her head in an almost imperceptible nod. Then, he was gone.

Dr. Fuller stood at his window. Their session no\
eyed Sandra opening the door of her white Toyota \
climbing inside. The engine hummed to life, and she rev
of his driveway.

When she left his sight, he turned away from the \
walking back to his cherry wood desk that had seen bett\
His worn leather chair creaked under his weight as he sat
opening his laptop with a soft click. Her file was already
screen, and her life's secrets laid bare in digital ink.

Sandra... beautiful, young, naive Sandra. Her hazel eye\
an innocence that belied the turmoil within her. She was c\
up in a web of deceit, spun by her actions and decisions.
husband, a man she'd promised to honor and cherish, would n
forgive her for what she'd done. Fuller could almost see \
Dawes now – his face contorted with betrayal and hurt.

And then he wondered what Sandra would do to keep \
secret safe. Would she beg? Plead? As he added notes from toda\
session to her file, his mind spun with possibilities. Each keystrok\
was another thread in the intricate tapestry of Sandra's life – a lif\
teetering on the edge of destruction due to one irreversible
mistake. A mistake he now knew.

2

Tim Dawes returned to his desk, setting down his second cup of coffee and pulling up in his chair. He'd worked at DataSphere for more than ten years, right out of college, and not long before he'd married Sandra.

The IT company wasn't exactly cutting-edge, but they paid well and there weren't all that many software developers here in Camdenton, Missouri. The largest industry now seemed to be tourism. Still, he'd been happy enough, and only in his mid-thirties, he had time and room to grow here.

In the open workspace, a smattering of whispers began to sound around him. Normally, it was pretty quiet in here, except for keyboards clacking away. And now, he felt the eyes of his coworkers on him. They had little privacy with evenly spaced workstations around the room. No walls, not even the cubical kind. Tim opened his email, doing his best to ignore whatever was happening.

He had plenty of friends here, often going out for happy hour drinks with them, and traveling to industry conferences. He

considered himself well-liked, popular, even, with many of his female coworkers seeming to admire him from a distance. A safe distance he'd preferred to keep.

He scrolled through his inbox, landing on an email from a friend and coworker, which contained only two sentences. This friend sat a mere twenty feet away—Derek. But it was those two sentences that sent Tim's world crumbling around him.

His pulse raced. Sweat formed on his thick brow, and he clenched his square jaw to the point of aching. Was this real? Did Derek really send this email? He threw a suspicious glance at the man, who captured his gaze, but quickly turned away. This was why everyone around him was whispering, casting wary glances at him. Derek had sent this email to everyone. Every. Fucking. One.

A photo of his family, Sandra smiling with their two young daughters, stood on his desk. All he could do now was stare at it. At her. How could this be true? Sandra cheated? With the back of his hand, he knocked it over. The clanging of the metal frame drew more eyes, but this time, he didn't look back.

They had built a life together - a home, a family. And all of his coworkers—they're all going to know that Sandra cheated on him. A goddam one-night-stand with some rando. Anger heated his face, and humiliation churned in his gut.

Standing up, Tim's chair rolled hard against the desk behind him. He marched through the room, ignoring the looks, heading straight to Derek's desk. With his fists, he pounded on it. "What the hell did you do?"

Derek's eyes widened in confusion. "Whoa, calm down. Look, I don't know what the hell's just happened, but it wasn't me. I didn't send this, Tim, I swear to God."

"Oh, come on. It came from you, Derek. Is this some kind of sick joke?"

Derek looked at his computer. "Tim, I swear I didn't send this. I see my name on it, but I would never..."

"Save it," Tim spat. "I can't believe you would do this. Was it you? Did you fuck my wife?"

"You know me, bro. I didn't send this email. I definitely didn't sleep with your wife." Derek looked around at the others, who were now glued to the growing turmoil. "Look, maybe you should talk to Sandra, all right? This has gotta be some sort of misunderstanding."

"You're damn right it is." Tim stared at him a moment longer, his hands balling into fists. "I can't believe this." He spun around, marching back to his desk, hands shaking. The office rumor mill was already swirling all around him.

The mocking words of the email floated before his eyes, searing themselves into his mind. He felt them all staring at him. Judging him. Judging Sandra.

How could she do this to me? His thoughts raced as he struggled to rein in the tidal wave of humiliation that threatened to overwhelm him. Tim looked up from his desk to see his boss approaching. Son of a bitch. He knows. He'd read the email too, just like the rest of them. "For God's sake."

"Tim, uh, why don't you come on back to my office?" Michael Bradley, VP of Development, stood with his hands in his pockets. The look on his face...part embarrassment, part patronizing.

"Yeah, sure." Tim followed his boss, thinking he was going to get fired over this shit.

Michael ushered him inside, closing the door behind him. "Take a seat, Tim."

When he walked to the chairs, he glanced through the surrounding glass walls. All he saw was a sea of heads craning, rubber-necking like they'd just witnessed a ten-car pile-up. To be

honest, that was sort of how this felt right now. Like a ten-car pile-up, and he was on the bottom.

Michael returned to his desk, pressing a button on his phone. "Derek, would you come to my office, please?"

Tim clenched his jaw. "You know what he did to me?"

Michael raised a preemptive hand. "We'll get to the bottom of this right now."

Tim seethed, waiting for Derek, who he thought had been a friend. How the hell did he even know about Sandra? Was he making it up? And why send it to everyone in the office? None of this made sense.

The door opened and Derek entered. Tim was about to rise, no longer able to control his emotions.

"Sit down, Tim," Michael said firmly. "And you too, Derek. Take a seat."

Derek lowered onto the chair, launching into some sort of explanation. "Mike, I don't know anything about what's happening here. Come on. You know I'd never do something like this. How would I even know?" he looked at Tim. "Dude, you know me."

"I thought I did," he replied. "If you didn't send it, then who did, huh? What...did someone just break into your email and write it for you? Sending it to everyone here?"

"All right. All right." Michael took a breath. "There's clearly a serious issue here. Maybe even a security breach. Tim, why don't you take off the rest of the day, yeah? I'll get a team to look into this ASAP."

"Well, that's just great," he threw up his hands. "Everyone here thinks Sandra cheated on me and now, everyone out there is going to go through all my emails, all my files, to find out what we already know." Tim shot a glance at Derek again.

"Let me get to the bottom of what happened," Michael reiterated. "Go home. See your wife. The more likely scenario is that someone hacked Derek's email and sent the message. I don't know who or why, but I will find out."

"Fine." Tim got up, offering a final glare at Derek before walking out. His coworkers kept their eyes on him as he passed them by on his way back to his desk.

Now, he had no choice but to leave. Go home and tell Sandra what had happened. She would be humiliated, just as he was. He felt like he was in a bad dream, a nightmare, as he gathered his things and left the office.

The sun blinded him as he walked through the parking lot, fiddling with his keys. He stepped into his gray sedan and gripped the wheel a moment. Taking a breath, he glanced up, unable to see inside the reflective glass that covered the office building. Unable to see his coworkers eyeballing him, which he was certain they were doing right now.

He turned the engine, pulling out of the parking lot with reckless abandon. Could it be true? Could Sandra really have cheated on him? She had seemed distant lately, but he never imagined she would betray him like that. And with Derek? No. It just wasn't possible.

Within minutes, he'd arrived home. It was only late morning, and the girls would still be at school. Entering the house, he called out her name. "Sandra? You here?"

She appeared from the kitchen, concern on her face. "Tim? What are you doing home so early? Is everything all right?"

He studied her for a moment, searching for any sign of guilt. But all he saw was the woman he loved, the mother of his children. Still, he had to confront this head-on.

"I got an email at work today," he began, watching Sandra's brow furrow. "It was from Derek. He said..." Tim's heart pounded against his ribs as he struggled to say the words that made this all too real. "He said you'd slept with someone."

Sandra's mouth dropped open. "What? That's insane." Her gaze darted side to side. "Why-why would he say something like that?"

Tim eyed her with suspicion. "So, it's not true then? You didn't cheat on me?" She went quiet. Her face paled. Her eyes glistened. And that was when he knew. "Oh my God. You did." He felt the air leave his lungs as reality set in.

"How could Derek possibly have known?" she asked, her tone only a whisper.

He scoffed and threw down his laptop bag. Never mind the laptop inside. It belonged to the company. "That's your question? How in the world I found out? You should be asking yourself how you could do this to me. Do you have any idea the humiliation? Every one of my coworkers read the email, Sandra."

"I swear, I don't know how Derek found out," she replied.

"Oh, he denied it. The whole thing. Said he never even sent out the email, which was bullshit. It came from him." He raised his brow. "You want to see it?"

"No." Sandra turned away, regret masking her face.

He aimed his index finger toward the door. "Get out. Get the hell out of my house."

~

TIM STOOD outside their home as night descended, hands in the pockets of his dress pants, his breath, visible in the cold air. Heading down the driveway, Sandra hoisted the bag over her shoulder, ushering the girls into her SUV.

He'd considered insisting the girls stay with him, but even with her betrayal, he didn't have it in him to be that heartless. The girls were Sandra's whole world. Maybe that had been part of a problem he'd chosen to ignore.

They'd agreed to tell the girls Mommy's friend needed her to stay over for a while, and wouldn't it be great if they came along to play with the friend's children? Children they'd all known practically since birth.

Watching his family get into that car made him even angrier. Sandra had offered no explanation for her actions, only repeating how sorry she was, ad nauseam. The betrayal created a chasm between them that he doubted could ever be bridged. And now that the entire office knew about it, his personal life laid bare for all to see, how could he possibly return to his job? His entire world had imploded.

A nagging suspicion gnawed at him that it had been Derek, despite both party's denials. Sandra had refused to say who it was, making matters worse. If it was Derek, had he threatened to send this email if she didn't leave her marriage? Was this his revenge? But then, why deny it if all he'd wanted to do was blow up Tim's life? He'd grown tired of trying to make sense of it all.

When Sandra's car turned the corner, he walked inside, sinking onto his well-worn gray sofa as the streetlamps outside flickered on. The house felt chilled now after leaving open the front door.

Sandra's friend's house was twenty minutes away, which was where she was now headed. Estranged from her parents, they, too, lived nearby and had a large home nestled among the trees by the lake. But it had been years since they'd spoken. Tim couldn't recall the last time they'd seen the girls. They must've been babies or toddlers then. Now, they were in grade school. Ella, the oldest at nine. Marissa, seven.

Pushing off the sofa, Tim trudged into the kitchen and opened the fridge. Inside, he reached for a bottle of Peroni beer - a small luxury in their otherwise modest life. Popping off the top with a satisfying hiss, he chugged down half of it before wiping away the frothy residue from his lips.

Returning to the living room, he flicked on the television for some mindless distraction. But after finding nothing that offered as much, he tossed aside the remote and grabbed his phone from the coffee table. Scrolling through, he realized no one from work had reached out, not even Michael. Definitely not Derek. And when he opened his social media, it seemed many of his coworkers unfriended him. "Jesus," he scoffed.

Two beers down, he opted for a third and got up from the couch to head back into the kitchen. A buzz had kicked in, thanks to an empty stomach, and he didn't mind it so much. In fact, he wouldn't have minded another few beers to knock him out for the night. Anything to give him some peace.

As he shuffled toward the fridge, an unexpected knock echoed through the empty house. Was it Sandra? Had she come back to talk? Maybe tell him the name of the man who'd now torn them apart? That was the beer talking. Sandra had made her choice. It takes two to tango, as they say.

Tim spun around, walking back into the foyer and opening the door. His face pinched in confusion, squinting at the unfamiliar figure standing on his doorstep. "Yeah?"

Without warning, the man lunged forward, spinning Tim around with his hands behind his back, and clamping down a cloth over his mouth.

Panic surged as his eyes widened and he tried to speak. His fingers tried to pry away the intruder's hands, but Tim's world began to spin into a dizzying whirlpool of blurred shapes and muffled sounds. Then...blackness swallowed him whole.

～

It FELT a little like a slumber party—living with Eva Duncan these past few weeks. Maybe even reminded Kate of her college days back at UC San Diego. And of course, her dear friend, Sam, too. Back home in Rio Dell, the two would have sleepovers when they were young. The thought made her smile because it had been a long time since she thought about Sam. The pain of her loss, Kate still hadn't fully recovered from.

Eva Duncan lived in the same building as their other colleague, Levi Walsh. A strong and fit woman, she had her caramel hair pulled back in a ponytail, giving her a youthful appearance. Though she was only in her late thirties, which was still young by FBI standards. Her gaze drifted to Kate as they sat at her small breakfast table nestled in front of a window. She raised a glass of wine to her lips. "How long do you think it'll take for Bennett to decide?"

Kate pulled in a breath through her nose, crossing her arms. She turned to Walsh, who sat next to her. "I don't know. Levi, did you get any sense of timing from Cam?"

"He doesn't know when a decision is coming down," Walsh replied in his soft southern drawl that had faded a little since Kate had first met him. Built like a rock, the former Army intelligence officer, now BAU liaison with local authorities, had been like a brother to her. He was also loyal to Nick. "He was still waiting on Bennett to call another meeting with the entire panel. That could be days or weeks."

Kate ran her finger around the rim of her wine glass, pretending the answer to the question she was about to ask meant nothing to her. "Have you seen him?"

"I talk to him on most days, and yeah, I saw him last night. Made sure he was prepared for the hearing this morning," Walsh replied. "He's been clean, Kate. Since that night, he hasn't had a drop."

She raised her gaze at him, a half-smile on her face. "Did he ask you to tell me that?"

"No." Walsh snickered. "Figured I should, though."

Kate had no response. What more was there to say? She'd made her peace with her decision. No matter how much she loved Nick, it seemed there would always be times when he couldn't handle something. Couldn't decide on something. And he had the propensity to turn to the bottle.

She'd had plenty of reasons to do that, herself. In fact, it ran in her family. Her father, only barely clinging to sobriety as he'd aged. While his reasons for turning to booze were almost understandable, given Kate's history, she'd managed to keep her shit together. So why couldn't Nick?

"He didn't expect to see you there today," Walsh added. "He texted me afterward, asking if I knew."

"Yeah, well, it was a last-minute decision, I guess."

He nodded, seeming to know that wasn't true. It wasn't who Kate was. She didn't do things on the spur of the moment, not unless it involved catching a killer. "Well, he was happy to see you, nonetheless."

"So," Duncan cleared her throat in an attempt to change the subject. "Do you have any more interviews set up, Kate?"

She appreciated the change in topic. "I'm working on getting one lined up now. Hope to have a response soon. He's in Texas. Been on death row for almost twenty years. So, I imagine he'll be willing to open up."

Kate's decision to interview serial killers still in prison had come when she'd been at her wit's end. Feeling helpless to stop the killings before they happened. And being forced to wait until the killer left something behind or created some pattern of movement. Then, and only then, were they able to find their man, ultimately capturing him.

The lives lost were countless, and Kate had asked to interview these killers with the hope of learning more about them. It wasn't unprecedented. The agents who created the Behavioral Analysis Unit started off the same way. But times had changed. Humanity had become even more cynical, seeing other human beings as obstacles to be removed, in some cases.

"Are you taking Surrey with you?" Walsh asked.

"No. Just me, like always." Kate shrugged. "I prefer it that way. He knows that too." She checked the time on her phone. "I need to head out."

"Oh, you have an appointment tonight?" Duncan asked with a slightly mocking undertone, like maybe Kate was making this up to get out of any more talk of Nick.

"As a matter of fact, I do. But thanks for doing this. The pizza, a nice glass of wine, and mostly the talking. I needed it." She turned to Walsh. "It is nice having you so close. Now, if we can get the rest of the team in this building...anyway, I won't be late."

Kate walked back to her bedroom to grab her things. Staying here in Duncan's small apartment wasn't ideal, but she was grateful to have a place to hole up until whatever was going to happen, happened. She pulled on her coat and walked back down the hallway. "See you guys later. Night, Levi."

"Night, Kate."

She carried on through the corridor and down the elevator to the parking garage. Stepping inside her Ford Explorer, she quickly texted. *Leaving now. Be there in fifteen.* Kate exited the garage and drove toward the meeting spot.

Near the center of D.C., she reached the park, cast in the soft glow of streetlamps. It was cold tonight, and she pulled her coat tightly around her slim waist, raising the hood over her head as she got out of the car. Ahead of her, sitting on a bench, was the person she was scheduled to meet. Why this location, Kate could only surmise. A nice warm diner or cafe would've been preferable to this.

The figure ahead came into full view. Short red hair. Long legs, crossed. A gray peacoat, unbuttoned. Kate donned a hesitant grin on her approach. "Georgia, thanks for meeting me."

"Thank you for braving the cold." She gestured to the bench. "Have a seat, Kate. It's nice to see you again."

"You, too." She sat down beside her. Georgia Myers. A former profiler from whom Kate had learned a great deal. Their relationship had soured after Georgia and Nick split up. "How's the task force handling all this?"

"Nick has a lot of friends. A lot of support," Georgia replied. "I can't deny he was a good leader. Always has been."

Kate remained silent for a moment, waiting for her to continue. To give voice to the reason she was here now. They both knew, yet somehow, danced around it.

"I'm hearing he'll be given a shot at returning to the Washington Field Office," Georgia finally said.

Kate nodded. "I was aware that Dwight Jameson was in the process of transferring to Texas."

"You two were close, weren't you—you and Jameson?" Georgia asked.

"Yes." Kate smiled at the memory of her time at the WFO, and her time with Dwight. Seemed forever ago—those days. "In fact, I saw him a while back, but before he opted to transfer. My understanding is that he has family he wants to be closer to. Or his wife does, I can't recall. But that does leave an opening..."

"It does," Georgia cut in. "Though I thought Agent Vasquez might take over as SSA."

Kate nodded. "I assume Nick would be offered the assistant special agent-in-charge position, taking the baton from Campbell."

Georgia clasped her gloved hands in her lap. "Would he do it?

If offered, would Nick take the position? It'd be a step down for him. And he'd be completely out of BAU."

Kate looked out over the silhouettes of the trees with their bare branches. A light but bitter breeze shifted them. "I don't know, Georgia. I really don't. Nick's tired of the politics. The violence of the job. I think he's seen too much, which was part of the reason he'd accepted the spot on your task force."

"But he couldn't handle that either," she shot back.

"No." Kate looked down, gripping the seat of the bench. "Cole made a strong case for him today."

Georgia nodded. "Yes, he did. They all did. But I can tell you that I don't think he'll be offered anything else. And we both know, if left to his own devices, if left without purpose of work, Nick won't survive. At least, he won't be the same man he is today."

Kate scoffed. "If there's one thing I've learned in all these years with Nick, it's that he's always evolving. But you're right. This is his last shot. His last chance. Assuming Bennett agrees, and the deal goes through, it'll take some convincing for him to accept the position."

Georgia smiled, taking in Kate's expression. "Well, I think we both know if anyone has the ability to sway Nick Scarborough one way or the other, it's you, Kate. It's always been you."

3

_____

Shapes formed around Tim as his consciousness returned and his vision cleared. A tingling in his hands shifted his focus and now he realized they'd been tied behind his back. Wherever he was, it was dark. But he must've been inside a room, a building because he didn't feel cold, as though outside.

The smell was new but instantly recognizable. Water. "The lake." The earthy, mossy, slightly acrid scent he'd grown up around. Even in the winter, the odor prevailed. And in the winter, around here, people were scarce. He could scream and chances were fair that no one would hear him.

Was this a house? He was bound to a wooden chair. Shifting his weight, he quickly discovered it was sturdy, like the old dining chairs his grandmother used to have. Solid oak, the thing must've weighed forty pounds.

A throbbing in his skull forced him to squint. It localized to his right temple. "Hello?" he called out. "Is anyone here? I need help." A door opened and Tim turned away from the bright light that cut the room in half.

A man stood in the doorway, silhouetted against the glow. While Tim's vision still suffered, he could make out that the man was slender and gangly. Not someone who would otherwise pose a threat to him had he not been bound at the moment.

"How's that head of yours?" the man asked. "You've been out for a while. I was getting concerned. Thought I'd rattled your brain the second time around." He stepped into the room and shut the door behind him, plunging them back into darkness. "You came to pretty quickly the first time. Had to take you out again the old-fashioned way after that."

Footfalls sounded and then a click. Light spread out from a lamp on a desk in the corner of the room. It was a den, of sorts. Windowless. The desk, and an old black futon. A couple of shelves mounted on the wall and worn wood floors. And here he was, in the center of the room, tied to a weighty chair.

The gangly man grabbed another wooden chair and dragged it over, the noise sending goosebumps on Tim's arms.

He sat down, facing him. "Boy, I bet you got a lot of questions, don't you?"

Tim regarded the man, his features, his body language. Still groggy and disoriented, he had no clue to this man's identity. "Do I know you? What did you do to me?"

"Oh, you did this to yourself, Tim." The man stood again and pulled out a knife from his back pocket. He flicked it open, a sharp click echoing in the room. Then he leaned over, his mouth practically touching Tim's ear. "If you try anything right now, I'll kill you where you sit." He reached around to Tim's hands.

As the man cut away the rope, Tim launched from the chair, knocking it over with a resounding thud. But before he had a chance to move, a hand clamped hard onto his shoulder yanking his arm back.

Tim yelled out in pain. Someone else had been in the room,

kept out of view, and now, it was over. Whoever these people were. Whatever reason they'd chosen him for, he wasn't getting out.

"I told you not to try anything." The man eyed his partner. "Take him out front."

"Stop. No. Wait!" Tim pleaded. "What did I do? What do you want with me? Please, just let me go."

The man walked on, glancing over his shoulder. "Don't beg, Tim. It's beneath you." He led the way through the house. An old cabin, more like.

He struggled against the iron grip of the man guiding him, but it was no use. He was dragged through the neglected cabin and out the front door. The cold night air bit at his skin and the moonlight cast a menacing glow through the trees. The area around him was remote. No sign of other houses. No sign of life anywhere.

In front of the cabin lay a clearing surrounded by dense forest. Tim scanned the immediate area. A car was here, unfamiliar to him, just as these people were. He searched for any means of escape, but as various scenarios ran through his head, reality sank in when the men forced him down a dirt path, leading away from the cabin. They were heading toward the lake.

"After this, we're square, right?" the larger man asked his partner while he led Tim in front of him.

"Shut the fuck up and do what you're told," his partner replied. And when he stopped, only a few feet from the water, he turned to Tim. "On your knees, buddy."

This was it. He was going to die. Sandra, Ella, Marissa—their faces filled his mind. The rest of it, all but forgotten. "Please, I—I have some money. You don't need to do this."

"He said, on your knees." He motioned for the larger man to push Tim to the ground. And he did.

"Why are you doing this?" Tim choked out in desperation. "I don't even know you."

The man smiled through his scraggly hair that clung to his narrow cheeks, his large teeth, visible in the darkness. "Ah, but I know you."

His partner lugged a masonry block that seemed to appear from nowhere. He pulled it toward Tim and then tied a rope around it. Then, the rope around Tim's ankles. "Please. Stop. This is all a mistake. I've done nothing wrong."

The man squatted, looking him in the eye. Tim saw hatred. Bitter anger. Rage. Yet the reason for this remained unclear. "You've got the wrong man, I'm telling you."

"I don't think so, Timothy Dawes. Married to Sandra Dawes. Two beautiful daughters, Ella and Marissa."

Tim's skin crawled. "Don't you dare touch my children."

"You're in no position to make demands." He tilted his head. "What, no concern for your wife? Your loving wife who fucked another man?"

His face fell. "How did you know about that?"

"I know everything." He yanked the knife from his back pocket, flicked it open, and lay it against Tim's cheek. Sliding the cold steel along his skin, the blade left a trail of blood.

The sting forced Tim to clench his jaw, but he held firm. If this was how it was going to end, he wouldn't give this asshole the satisfaction of watching him react to the pain.

The gangly man returned to full height, eyeing his partner. "Ready?"

Tim didn't hear a response, but since he was yanked up, he assumed the partner had been ready. He thought about his children. The happiness he'd known with Sandra, no matter what she'd done. He loved her and their family. He regretted ignoring her. Dismissing her. Taking advantage of her kindness and support. He regretted all of it now. A little too late, it seemed.

The tip of the knife now pierced his back. As it was pushed deeper, the hot, searing pain worsened. When the large man ripped out his blade, Tim's legs went numb and wobbled. Shock from the force of it made him gasp. Warm blood spilled down his legs, soaking his pants. He grew weak, his knees buckling.

"Start walking," the voice behind him said.

Tim's breaths shallowed. It became harder and harder to suck the air into his lungs he was sure had been pierced. Pain, unlike anything he'd ever known, pulsated throughout his body. The numbness climbed up his legs, he could barely put one foot in front of the other. Tears spilled, but he remained silent.

The sound of water reached his ears. They were close to the lake now. Looking across the lake, he saw lights dotted through the trees, where a few full-time residents occupied their homes. The wind came off the water, sending shivers down his arms, but it did nothing to distract from his pain. His eyes fluttered as his stomach grew queasy.

Then, he felt the icy water surround him as he stepped in, deeper and deeper until the water reached his chest. A splash reverberated as the masonry block dropped next to him. His eyes open, he could barely see the rope in the murky water, but he felt its tug.

It began pulling him down into the depths of the lake. Tim opened his mouth in search of air, but it filled instead with water. His body convulsed; his eyes bulged. The water, tinged red with his blood, surrounded him, the block pulling him down into the blackness. The moonlight above him dimmed.

His last breath, he thought of her. *Sandra.*

~

THE COPPERY AIR of blood was the first thing Kate smelled; a scent so potent that it seeped into her very pores. She wasn't even inside the old, dilapidated house, yet the scent carried on the wind, a grim harbinger of what lay within. She was alone. Her team, Nick—no one else was around. Only the eerie silence of the night accompanied her.

Time sped up in a disorienting rush, and now, Kate stood inside the room. The kill room. The fetid odor triggered her gag reflex, a vile cocktail of decay and death that clung to the back of her throat. Blood dripped from the table, each droplet echoing loudly in the oppressive silence. An arm lay on the floor, sawn off from a body that lay somewhere else, a grotesque reminder of the monster she was hunting. "Where are you?" Kate held out her weapon, her voice steady despite the fear gnawing at her insides. "Come out. You won't get away."

She took cautious steps, trying not to slip on the blood that flowed everywhere like a macabre river. Each footfall seemed to echo in the deathly quiet room.

A man came into view, holding a butcher knife slick with fresh blood. His eyes held a chilling emptiness as he stared at her. "Stop, or I'll shoot!" she threatened, but her words seemed to bounce off him like harmless raindrops.

KATE BOLTED UPRIGHT WITH A GASP, heart pounding against her ribcage, hair drenched in sweat, clinging to her forehead. Darkness surrounded her. She scanned the unfamiliar room for any sign of danger. Breathless and disoriented, she clutched at her phone on the nightstand. "Where the hell am I? What time is it?"

The answer to only one of those questions was on the phone. The time displayed two thirty in the morning. As far as where she was? It took a few more moments but then she recalled that this was Duncan's apartment. This was the spare bedroom Kate had been staying in for weeks. Her pulse slowed and the panic subsided. She wiped her forehead, slowly regaining her bearings.

This wasn't the first time nightmares had plagued Kate's sleep. However, those days were long ago, and the nightmares happened for very different reasons. What she'd seen in Texas, in that kill room, still haunted her. The memories lurked in the dark corners of her mind, waiting for the quiet moments to strike.

Recent events—losing the baby, leaving Nick—they'd torn down the walls she'd so carefully constructed to keep out the horrors of her job. Horrors that eventually led Nick away from the Violent Crimes division of the BAU. Was it getting to her now, too? Did it get to all of them eventually? Maybe there was a ticking clock on sanity for everyone who dared to walk this path.

Kate took another steadying breath, her rhythm returning to normal. Tossing her phone onto the bed, she got up, standing in a long stretch. A stitch pulled at her lower abdomen. She winced at the mild pain that lingered from her hysterectomy.

Duncan had seen her through the first few days after the surgery, but it didn't take long for her to heal. Modern techniques, lasers and such, made recovery much faster than in years past.

Kate pulled on a pair of jeans and a sweater. Sleep would not return, so there wasn't much point in trying. Instead, a drive sounded nice, taking her mind off things for a while.

She slipped on tennis shoes and snatched her keys from the dresser, along with her phone and handbag. Tiptoeing through the quiet apartment, careful not to wake her roommate, Kate slipped out.

Frost hung in the air, on lampposts, benches, cars, and landscapes. Still, the roads were mostly dry. The sky was clear, and the moon shone brightly.

Kate drove through D.C., virtually empty at this time of night.

She headed north, already knowing her destination. And on her arrival, she stopped in front of the familiar building. Against the backdrop of the bay, it stood tall. Moonlight glistened off the water. The muffled sound of masts clanked in the light breeze. She stepped out, checking her surroundings out of habit. Not a bad one to have in this world.

Kate walked toward the entrance and entered the passcode at the main door. It still worked. She walked inside, heading straight for the elevators, riding up to her old floor. It felt as though no time had passed. Like she was coming home from work on any given day. But much had happened in a short span. Now, standing outside the door, Kate texted him. "I'm in the hall."

It took a few moments, but she heard the locks disengage, and the door opened. Nick stood before her, dressed in boxers and a white T-shirt.

"You didn't respond. I didn't think you were coming," he said.

Kate shrugged. "I was up."

He glanced down, a smile on his face. "Yeah, me, too. Come in. It's good to see you."

∾

THE SUN BEGAN to warm the frosty morning air as it shone down on the lake. Perfect conditions for a few hours of fishing. While the water was cold, plenty of fish hung out in the shallow parts of the deeper waters, still attracted to spinner bait and a finesse jig.

And with the summer people gone, the lake was quiet. A pleasant time for retired salesman, Al Hinkle, to take out his boat. He and his wife, Leanne, had saved their whole lives to buy a house out here on the lake, and then the boat. They owned one of the few remaining smaller, older homes that could still be found in the resort community, which otherwise had become a haven for the wealthy. Multimillion-dollar homes peeked through the now-bare trees.

But for Al, all he wanted to do was fish. Be out on the water, listening to the wind pushing through the trees. So that was what he'd set out to do.

Launching his boat, he pressed the ignition. A slight rumble and sputtering water splashed near the engine at the back. He drove out a ways. This lake was a hell of a lot bigger than most people realized, and Al knew damn near every inch of it. He had his favorite spot, which was where he headed now.

On his arrival, he cut the engine and threw the anchor. It was a little deep here, but still in the fast-moving current where the fish would swim. Al baited his line and cast it out. A soft plunk sounded as it landed in the water, sending ripples out in a small circle. He reeled in the line, nice and slow, making sure the fish got a good look at the spinner. Patience was required and Al had plenty of that nowadays.

A cup of coffee in a travel mug beside him, he took a sip and prepared to cast out again. Over and over, he cast his line, just waiting for a bite. The sun rose higher, and the air warmed a little, but he persisted.

An hour had passed. His coffee mug was now empty. Al cast out the line once again. And once again, he reeled it in nice and slow. But when the line resisted, Al's lips curled into a smile. "There we go. Come on now, little fishy. Take a good hard bite."

The end of his rod bent over as he tugged again, reeling in the line just a little more. "Hang on little guy. I got you." This little fishy wanted to challenge him, so Al creased his brow. "Well, shit. You can't be that big. Must be getting tangled up in something. That's not good."

He pulled harder, struggling to bring in the line. "Good Lord. Come on now." But when his gaze landed on what bobbed at the end, Al stumbled back. "Jesus H.... Oh, my Lord. What in the..."

He pulled it in as close as he could get it. Reaching for the net, he bent down and tried to scoop it out. And when an arm landed in his net, his gag reflex kicked in.

The net was stretched as Al carried it over, setting it down on the floor of the stern. An arm and a hand. Just that. Nothing else attached. Al grabbed his phone and dialed 911.

"What is your emergency?" the operator asked.

"Yeah, uh, my name's Al Hinkle. I'm out here on my boat. Dear God, I just reeled in an arm."

"Sorry, sir, can you repeat that?"

"An arm!" he shouted. "For God's sake, send the police. I'm on the lake."

"Sir, please give me your coordinates," she asked.

He looked at his GPS and read them off to her. "I—I don't know if the rest of him's down here or what, but you gotta send someone, like right now."

"Water Patrol's on their way, sir. Just stay where you are. Where is the body part now, sir?"

"In my boat. I'm looking right at it. Damn thing was caught on my fishing line, and I reeled it in thinking..." His voice faltered. "What do I do?"

"Just wait. It'll be a while before they can get to you, sir."

"All right." He peered out over the water. No other boats in sight. He looked down at the arm again and noticed a ring on the hand. "Uh, ma'am? I see a ring on this hand." Maybe the operator was in just as big a shock because she didn't answer back.

He spun around at the faint hum of an engine. "I think they're here. Yes, ma'am. I see them now in the distance." He ended the call, dropping the phone in his pocket. He laid on his horn, waving his hand in the air. "Over here, fellas!"

Another minute or two passed before the Water Patrol boat reached him. A man, who appeared to be the one in charge, moved toward the side of his vessel as they slowed next to him.

"Morning, sirs. I'm Al Hinkle."

"You made the call?" he asked.

"Yes, sir. That was me. You gotta come see this."

The boat pulled closer. A couple of fenders were placed between the two vessels as it slowed, coming to a stop. The Water Patrolman stepped over onto Al's boat. It didn't take him long to spot the severed arm.

"You see that?" Al aimed his index finger. "Pulled it right out the damn water. Lord knows where the rest of him is."

The patrolman squatted low for a better look when Al moved in. "I noticed that ring on the finger, there. Could help you figure out who this poor soul is."

"Yes, sir." He examined it more closely. "I'm pretty sure I know who it is."

"You do?" Al asked.

He stood up again. "I do." He looked over at the officers on his boat. "Hey, looks like we got ourselves that DEA agent over here."

"What's that?" the officer called out.

"That missing DEA agent. Better call this in."

4

After dropping off her kids at school, Sandra returned home. With her key in hand, she unlocked the front door, pushing it open. The house was quiet, the blinds, still drawn. Tim's car was still in the driveway. And as she closed the door, she called out. "Tim? It's me. Can we talk?"

Sandra made her way to the living room, pulling open the blinds, and allowing the morning light to spill inside. She headed into the kitchen, opening the curtains on the bay window behind the breakfast table.

Her gaze soon landed on the coffee maker. It wasn't on. "Tim?" She walked toward the stairs, climbing up to their bedroom. The door was open and on looking inside, her shoulders slumped. Their bed was still made. "Oh, no."

Returning downstairs, Sandra grabbed her phone from her purse and pressed Tim's contact. The line rang through the phone, but there was also a ringing somewhere in the house. Her brow creased as she followed the sound.

It was coming from the living room. Sandra stood in front of the TV, trying to pick up the exact location of the noise. "The sofa." There was no phone lying on the cushions, so she shoved her hands in between them as the muffled ringing continued. Her fingers wiggled around, soon touching the phone. She yanked it out, her call having gone to voicemail. "What in the world?" Sandra shot a glance at Tim's car through the living room window. "Something's wrong. Your phone's here. Your car's here. Where are you?"

Panic rose in her chest as she made another call. "Kevin, it's Sandra. Is Tim with you, by chance?"

"No. Why would he be? He should be at work."

Kevin was Tim's brother and the two were close. He lived only a few miles away. She didn't want to alarm him. After all, they'd had a fight last night. Maybe Tim was doing this on purpose. A payback, of sorts. "If you see him, could you have him call me?"

"I don't expect to see him," Kevin replied. "But I'll text him and let him know you're looking. You two have a fight last night or something?"

"Something like that. But there's no point in texting because, uh, he left his phone at home. Listen, I gotta go. Thanks, Kevin." She hung up, dropping onto the sofa, having no idea what to do next.

Tim's office seemed a logical place to check, but after what happened, he wouldn't have gone back there. Besides, his car was still here, so unless he started walking...

Leaping from the sofa, Sandra ran upstairs and into their bedroom again. "The closet." She ripped open the closet doors. Nothing was missing. And she would know because she bought all of his clothes. Rushing to the dresser, she opened the drawers. Fear caught in her throat. "You didn't pack anything. Oh my God. Where the hell are you?"

Various scenarios ran through her mind, trying to make sense of Tim's vanishing act. He would never just up and leave the girls. Even if he was angry with her, he was a good father. But in the back of her mind, the reality was that Tim's car was still there and so was his phone. If he left...it wasn't voluntary.

She returned downstairs and grabbed Tim's phone, entering the passcode because they didn't keep secrets. At least, not until she decided to have a one-night stand. Scrolling through his recent calls and messages, nothing seemed unusual. Then she opened his email. There it was. The email Derek had sent. Sandra's eyes filled with tears as she read it. "How did you know?"

But nothing else appeared suspicious. No calls she didn't recognize. No emails or texts threatening him. Nothing.

Sandra closed her eyes and steadied her breath. "I can't sit here and do nothing. I just can't." Grabbing her purse and keys, she headed out the front door. The only thing to do was to go to his office. Surely, his boss knew something. Maybe Derek too. Someone had to have seen or heard from him today.

As she navigated the familiar roads, Sandra strained to glimpse Tim's figure walking along the sidewalk or parked at a nearby coffee shop or storefront. But each mile revealed nothing. No sign of him anywhere.

The five-story glass building that was Tim's office appeared in the distance. Sandra's pulse quickened again, uncertain of what was to come. They'd all seen the email. Would they look at her, judging her? Of course they would. But what choice did she have?

Hurrying toward the entrance, Sandra opened the door to a blast of warm air. Her shoes clicked on the tiled floor as she made her way to the front desk. "Is Tim here, by any chance?"

The young woman regarded her with a look that spoke volumes. She clearly knew about the email. "Mrs. Dawes. I'm sorry, but Tim didn't come in today. We all figured it was because...you know."

Sandra closed her eyes, doing her best to stop the tears. "Then I need to see Derek. Please. I have to talk to him." She thought it best to hold off alerting Tim's boss, Michael because Derek set this off. He must know something.

The woman appeared to consider the request. She wasn't much older than Sandra. Maybe even had a family of her own. Would she understand any of this?

Within moments, the call was made. "Yeah, uh, Sandra Dawes is here. She's asking to see you...Okay, thanks." She ended the call. "He's coming up now."

Sandra offered a polite nod and walked toward the waiting area. Pacing, her arms folded, Derek appeared from around the corner, but he wasn't alone. Tim's boss, Michael walked alongside him.

"Sandra, you should've called first," Michael said.

She looked straight at Derek, ignoring Michael's gaze. "Why did you send it? How could you do that to him? He's your friend."

"I didn't," Derek cut in. "You have to believe me. My email was hacked." He glanced at his boss. "Right?"

"That's what we're trying to determine," Michael replied, his gaze still on her. "Sandra, please tell Tim that he still has a job here, okay? None of this changes anything."

Humiliation couldn't begin to describe how she felt right now, but she needed answers, and this was her fault to begin with. "I don't know where he is. Have you heard from him?"

The men traded glances.

"We figured he was at home," Michael replied. "You haven't seen him?"

Sandra's lips trembled. "No. I'm sorry, but I have to go."

⌇

THE SUN WAS DIRECTLY above the lake now. Amid blue skies, its radiant beams shimmered on the rippling waters. Several Missouri Water Patrol Division boats and a few Coast Guard vessels formed a semi-circle around the gruesome discovery made by Al Hinkle. He had reeled in a man's severed arm, an arm that authorities believed had belonged to a DEA agent, who had been reported missing almost a month ago.

The nearest DEA office was in St. Louis. It held jurisdiction over several counties including Camden, where the lake was located. Of course, the lake stretched across multiple counties. And now, DEA Special Agent-in-charge, Thomas Kleman, was aboard one of the Coast Guard vessels, observing the operation.

A rope line dotted with bright buoys marked off the search area. This part of the lake wasn't quite as deep as other areas, where depths reached an intimidating one hundred and thirty feet or more. But it was still a daunting task to scour the underwater terrain for any other remains of this missing agent. Divers stood ready on the edge of the deck.

Coast Guard Lieutenant Dean Crawford stood before them, his broad shoulders and thick trunk loomed over the divers. The stocky thirty-five-year-old raised his square chin. "As with any dive, remember to take caution in your surroundings. Underwater hazards will be prevalent. Keep in constant communication with us above board and down below with your team. If you find more remains, you have the means to bring them up carefully – taking every precaution to avoid further damage."

One by one, divers were aided with their gear – full oxygen tanks, masks adjusted to fit snugly, and radios checked for clear communication. As each of the four men plunged into the water, all that remained was left to do...was wait.

～

THE DIVERS DESCENDED into the murky depths, bubbles trailing behind them as their fins propelled them farther down. Diver One splintered off, the cold water enveloping him, muting the sounds of the boats above. He switched on his dive light, casting a hazy green glow into the abyss.

Visibility was poor, with sediment and debris churned up from the lake bottom as the other divers searched. He swept his light back and forth, hunting for any sign of the remains.

The cold pressed in on him as the light above faded, and soon, only the beam of his flashlight cut through the darkness. Sediment swirled up with each kick of his fins, reducing visibility to just a few feet in every direction.

The quiet of the underwater world was broken only by the sound of his breathing inside the mask. He thought back to the stories about this lake, where there had once been a thriving city. That was before the dam flooded it decades ago. He knew these depths hid secrets - a flooded town, an entire way of life lost beneath the surface. And now a killer's work too.

There. The light glinted off something pale half-buried in the mud. He steadied his breathing as he approached. It was a bone, human for sure; the flesh, all but decayed. He swam closer, fanning sediment away with his hands. A human ribcage came into view, picked clean by fish and time. Nearby lay a femur and pieces of a spinal column. This wasn't the missing agent. These bones had been here for some time. The diver checked his gear, then carefully scooped up the remains, placing them into a collection bag.

"Base, this is Diver One," he reported into the radio. "I've located additional remains inconsistent with our search. Beginning recovery."

THE MISSING AGENT'S PARTNER, FBI Agent Keith McDaniel had arrived, boarding the Coast Guard's vessel alongside DEA Special Agent-in-Charge Kleman. He'd worked with the missing Agent Andre Draker for the better part of a year on this joint task force investigation. And when he disappeared, McDaniel had done everything he could to find him. This was the last place he ever thought to look.

"Jesus." McDaniel set his hands on his narrow hips. "How many bodies are down there? They keep sending up more and more remains." He scratched his overgrown beard, eying the bones with brown eyes that were underlined by purple half-moons. A sign that he'd lost a lot of sleep recently.

Another diver emerged, holding a bag. "Sir?" he called out to Coast Guard Lieutenant Crawford. "Uh, you might want to see this one."

Crawford eyed the other federal officers before approaching the diver. "What'd you find?"

"The other arm—I think. It's, uh, still got most of the skin on it." He handed it over.

Crawford glanced at Kleman and McDaniel. "Hey, you two might want to come check this out."

A sinking feeling settled in McDaniel's gut like this was about to be confirmation that the arm they'd found did, in fact, belong to his partner.

He and Draker were after an organized crime operation trafficking drugs in the region. A particularly widespread problem here in the Ozarks.

Not long after a meeting with one of their informants, Draker had gone dark. McDaniel assumed it was for his own safety, but when he never resurfaced, he figured something had happened.

McDaniel had followed every lead to find Draker. Talked to

all their informants, including the one who'd seen Draker last, but he'd turned up zilch. "Show me what you found."

Crawford opened the bag and peered inside. "Oh, Christ." He turned away in disgust.

McDaniel looked inside. "It's the right arm. Can't say for sure it's him, though." He felt Kleman's hand on his shoulder and glanced back.

"Son, I know you want to stay positive, here, but the left arm... that's Draker's. That was his wedding ring. So, it's safe to say this one, here, belongs to him too. He was my agent. This one's on me."

McDaniel knew this was no longer just about finding his missing partner. The scope of this horror was much larger. "This goddam place is nothing more than a mass watery grave."

Kleman looked on. "We need a forensics team here immediately to process the area and identify the victims. Where's the nearest FBI field office?"

"Springfield, sir," McDaniel replied. "But given what we have here...Quantico has a specialized team for this kind of mission. Given the state of these remains, their forensics operators are our best hope. I can put in a request for an evidence response team."

Kleman nodded. "Do it."

As McDaniel stepped away to make the call, he stared out at the divers working in the lake. The number of body parts suggested multiple victims spanning a significant period of time.

He ran through possible scenarios. A serial killer dumped his victims in the lake. Someone using the watery depths to hide their kills. Drug deals gone bad. None of the options were good and all spelled a major operation involving multiple jurisdictions.

But why take Draker's life? A DEA agent? Had he gotten close to something? Was this connected to their original investigation?

"Yeah, uh, this is Special Agent Keith McDaniel. Springfield

field office. I need Forensic Pathology. Evidence response, ASAP. We've recovered what appears to be the remains of multiple victims, including a DEA agent."

"I'll transfer you now," the operator replied.

Within moments, McDaniel was on the phone with Dr. Olivia Bailey, lead pathologist at Quantico. He made the request and soon returned to ASAC Klemen and Coast Guard Lieutenant Crawford. "Quantico will take the remains and get to work on them immediately." He looked out over the lake. "We can't search this entire area. It would take—"

"I'm aware," Kleman cut in. "Do you think Draker got close to something?"

McDaniel pulled in a deep breath. "Last time we were in contact, he was scheduled to meet with an informant. Standard operating procedure and we'd done it every week. I, of course, already tracked down said informant. He claimed he and Draker parted ways, nothing unusual."

"And you believed him?" Kleman asked.

"Yes, sir. I did." McDaniel widened his stance, clasping his arms behind his back. "Until Quantico can look at this, I have no idea what we're up against."

∽

ALMOST A WEEK HAD GONE by and still no decision on the fate of Nick Scarborough and his position inside the FBI's Behavioral Analysis Unit.

Kate didn't tell Duncan where she'd gone last week, in the early morning hours. Duncan didn't ask either. Turned out, she made a pretty good roommate. Kept her distance. Didn't get too involved. Even though they were close friends, Duncan was the type to only offer advice if asked.

What happened that night lingered in Kate's mind. She and Nick had talked about the hearing, had talked about everything. And then she went home, back to Duncan's apartment. He didn't ask for her forgiveness, only offered comfort in light of having lost their unborn child, even if it had been early on in the pregnancy.

In hindsight, answering his text, and going to see him...it wasn't fair. Not to either of them. It only prolonged the anguish of their separation. This was much harder than she'd expected it to be.

Her talk with Georgia Myers had sunk in. She brought it up to Nick, who didn't answer when pressed as to whether he would accept the position at the WFO. Kate dropped it. It wasn't her decision, and it no longer affected her life.

The knock on her office door brought her back into the moment. "Come in."

Fisher stepped inside. "Hi, you have a second?"

"Of course. Take a seat."

Senior Unit Agent Cameron Fisher had led the team since Nick's departure. And he'd finally come into his own, leading them with confidence. Approaching fifty, Fisher's black hair was now streaked with gray, seeming to turn grayer with each case they took on. And of course, he wouldn't be Fisher without the toothpick hanging from his lips. Kate suspected he'd taken to chewing on that thing when he'd quit smoking, long before she knew him.

Fisher sat down and she already assumed why he'd come. "I take it, Bennett has reached a decision?" she asked.

He glanced down, folding his hands in his lap. Not a good sign. Kate swallowed her nerves before continuing, "Cam, what did Bennett decide? And does Nick already know?"

He raised his gaze to her again with a softness in his features she wasn't used to seeing. Fisher was exactly the type of man to have been a New York detective. And now, leading a team of highly trained agents who hunted down serial killers. So, this side of him was rarely seen.

"Chief Cole came into my office a few minutes ago and told me. And yes, he'd already talked to Nick," Fisher replied.

Kate closed her eyes for a moment, feeling her chest tighten, anticipating the worst.

"Bennett has decided, and the rest of the panel agreed—"

"Including you?" she cut in before he'd had a chance to get to the meat of the issue.

He nodded. "Including me. Because no one else was injured in the accident, and Nick was already in an AA program... It was decided that the dismissed DUI wasn't substantial enough to warrant a discharge from the Bureau. Especially considering Nick's tenure and the work he's done."

The boot lifted from her neck, and her breath returned.

"However...." Fisher continued.

Here it was. The other shoe.

"He will lose his top secret security clearance, meaning he will no longer run the joint task force. And he has a choice as to where his next assignment will be." Fisher removed his toothpick, licking his lips.

"Where, Cam? Where are they sending him?"

"It's up to him. The Washington Field Office, taking over for SAC Campbell, or Los Angeles, where he'll run their cyber crimes unit."

Kate's brow knitted. "L.A.?"

"That's what Cole said."

"And he'd already talked to Nick about this?" she asked. "Did he tell you what Nick's decision was?"

"Apparently, he's thinking about it." Fisher inhaled a deep breath. "Talk to him, Reid, okay? I know you two are separated, and all that, but come on, it's Nick." He got up, preparing to leave.

"Oh, and I've been called out for a meeting at the lab. Multiple human remains were found in the Lake of the Ozarks in Missouri about a week ago. They were all transferred here. One of them was a DEA agent, but the guys in Forensics think they have the partial remains of several people."

"Is this something we'll be stepping in on?" she asked.

Fisher shrugged. "Not sure, but I'll keep you posted."

5

Why the police hadn't felt the need to take Sandra seriously had puzzled her. But they were taking her seriously now. And she was fairly certain it was because of what they'd found in the lake. The story was all over the news. It frightened the hell out of her.

It had been a week and still nothing from Tim. She'd reached out to every one of Tim's friends. None had seen or heard from him. His family...nothing. And when Sandra had gone to the police after two days, they showed little concern.

But they were here now, and they wanted to search her home. Sandra sat outside in the Adirondack chair on her porch. Her daughters were at school, thank goodness. She'd told them their father was on a business trip. Lying to them wasn't ideal, but until more came to light, what could she say?

Inside, the officers collected fingerprints. Outside, they'd collected prints from Tim's car. They'd asked to take Tim's personal laptop, and she agreed, knowing his passcode. But she'd already looked at it and just like his phone, nothing seemed out of the ordinary.

"Ma'am?"

Sandra was pulled back into the moment and turned to the officer. "Yes?" She shot up from the chair, leaving it rocking in her wake.

"We're all finished here now," he said. "I have a tow truck scheduled for later today to pick up your husband's vehicle. It'll need to be further examined for evidence."

"Yes, I understand." She stood there a moment, studying the officer. "Do you think what they found at the lake...could that have also happened to my husband?"

He looked away, which told her all she needed. But then he looked back. "I don't know, ma'am, but we'll do our best to find out."

He called out to the other officers, and they began to leave. She stood near the porch railing, watching them enter their cars. It looked to be a sunny day ahead as the morning clouds parted. She noticed a few neighbors standing outside, curious as to why the cops were at her home. Sandra said nothing, only offering a small smile and a polite nod. A final glance around and she walked back inside, closing the door behind her.

Her appointment with Dr. Fuller couldn't have come at a better time. Sandra was at her wit's end. Terrified that her husband was dead, she needed to talk to someone because going to her parents wasn't an option. And her friends, well, they'd been there for her over these past several days, but they had their own problems. Their own families to deal with.

She had managed to pull herself together, showering and throwing on some fresh clothes. Appearances had once been important to her, but not right now. With a few hours before the girls needed to be picked up from school, Sandra drove on.

Dr. Fuller's home, with its separate office entrance, was just ahead. She parked along the curb and stepped out. The door was unlocked, as it usually was during his business hours, and Sandra walked inside. The waiting room was empty. Either he'd had someone in his office, or she'd caught him on a slow day.

Closing the door behind her, Sandra took a seat in one of the soft leather chairs that lined the back wall. A coffee table in front of her, she reached for one of the magazines. An old issue of People from several months ago. As she began to read, doing her best to keep her mind off her missing husband, Dr. Fuller emerged.

"Sandra. Hello," he began. "Come on back. I was just finishing up some paperwork."

She entered his office while he held the door for her. "Thank you." It was all she could do not to burst out in tears before she even sat down.

The doctor closed the door, taking his usual seat. He seemed to study her for a moment. His eyes lingered for an uncomfortable amount of time. "I can see something's bothering you, Sandra. Care to talk about it?"

She looked at him, her eyes stinging. "You heard what they found in the lake?"

He creased his brow, expectantly. "Yes."

"Tim's been missing for almost a week now." She swallowed her rising emotions. "I think whatever happened to those other people, might have happened to him."

"What?" he asked, pulling up in his chair. "Have you spoken to the police?"

"Of course I have. They were just at my house." Sandra retrieved a tissue from her purse and dabbed her eyes. "They didn't believe me when I first went to them. When I came home, he was gone. His car and phone were still at the house. It wasn't until the lake...that's when they seemed to believe me."

"Oh my goodness," he said. "Sandra, I'm so very sorry to hear this. I wish you'd come to me sooner. I had no idea. The last we talked—well, it was when you'd mentioned your regret. Clearly, this isn't something you should be dealing with alone." He leaned closer. "Have you spoken to your parents about this?"

She closed her eyes, shaking her head. "No. You know we aren't on good terms."

"Yes, but this? This is, well, you need support right now, Sandra. More than anything." He paused, letting out a long breath. "You say the police were there this morning. What do they plan to do?"

She pressed the tissue against her nose. "They're looking for him, but they have no idea if he's in another car. He doesn't have his phone...I told them about the email. They said their next stop was his work. So..."

"I'm sorry, what email?" Fuller asked.

"So much has happened since I was here last," Sandra replied. "Someone in Tim's office—I don't know how or why—but they sent out an email telling the entire office about what I'd done." At this, her tears fell. "I don't even know how they knew. It was just all...all a horrible—"

"You must be beside yourself with worry," he cut in. "And the girls? How are they holding up?"

She emitted a strange kind of snort. "I told them Tim was away on business. What else could I say? I don't know where he is, who he's with, or if he's even alive. What am I supposed to do?"

Fuller leaned back, tilting his head as he seemed to consider Sandra's situation. "This is obviously distressing, but I wouldn't jump to conclusions just yet. There may be a reasonable explanation for your husband's disappearance. Especially given what you told me during our last session. And the fact that he'd found out."

Sandra glanced up. "I still have no idea how his co-worker would've known, but the email...the argument...I get what you're saying, but it's not like him to just take off without a word. He loves his children too much to leave them."

"Even so, people sometimes need space after a heated disagreement," Fuller said, his tone calming. "And if he left his phone behind, he likely wanted to be off the grid for a while, to clear his head without distraction. I would give it a few more days before panicking that something is seriously wrong."

"How can I possibly do that after what's been all over the news, Doctor? My God, what if Tim is dead? Murdered?"

He raised his hands in a calming gesture. "All you can do is let the police do their job. Right now, you need to make sure you're taking care of yourself - eat well, get rest, lean on friends for support. You have to remain strong for your daughters. Worrying yourself sick won't bring Tim home any faster." He scribbled something on a prescription pad and handed it to Sandra. "This is a mild sedative to help you sleep."

She took the prescription, slightly annoyed that this was all he could offer. How could she take these when she had the girls to look after?

"Maybe the best thing you can do is to stay on top of them...the police. Be the squeaky wheel," Fuller said. "I know they're doing their job, but sometimes an extra push from a worried family member can keep a fire lit under them."

"Sure, maybe you're right," Sandra replied. "It's just hard to think clearly right now. My mind is going in a thousand directions."

Fuller nodded. "Of course it is."

"But what I just can't get my head around was how...how his coworker could've possibly known what I'd done."

"The infidelity," Fuller added.

"Yes, of course. And then to send off a company-wide email like that. My God. How could he?"

"No point in thinking about that right now, Sandra. Your focus should be on the girls, and helping the police find Tim. I, for one, feel as though he's simply taking time for himself. As selfish as that sounds, he must've felt the need to do that."

"And not taken his car?" she shot back.

"Well, I can't explain it all away for you, no matter how much I wish I could."

She sighed, regretting lashing out at him. "Yes, I know. I just want him to come home."

Fuller donned a warm smile. "That's all any of us would want."

❧

FISHER ARRIVED at the FBI's Laboratory Division, which housed their forensic anthropology team. In a sterile, white-walled room where high-tech microscopes lay atop several desks, the scent of chlorine filled his nostrils. Bones and other skeletal fragments lay in near-perfect alignment on the metal tables in the center of the vast space. Glass partitions separated the workspaces, and he'd noticed a group huddled around one of the tables.

On his approach, he was met by a heavily bearded man in a suit, who offered his hand.

"Good morning. You must be Senior Unit Agent Cameron Fisher with the BAU. Special Agent Keith McDaniel." He gestured to the other man in the suit. "This is SAC Kleman, DEA."

Kleman nodded. "Agent McDaniel was working a drug trafficking investigation with my operative, Agent Andre Draker. This is what's left of him." He aimed his gaze at the table.

Fisher eyed the various body parts. "I'm sorry to hear that. Losing one of your own is never easy." He looked at the woman in the lab coat. "Dr. Bailey."

"Yes, sir." She shook his hand. "I was the one who requested your attendance. You head up the violent crimes unit of the BAU, correct?"

"Yes, ma'am. I do. And I doubt you would've requested me if you didn't think these victims weren't somehow connected to Agent Draker."

"As a matter of fact, that's exactly what I think." She turned to the table. "A fisherman, who'd gone out on the Lake of the Ozarks, reeled in the agent's severed arm."

"That must've taken him by surprise," Fisher said, still peering at the table. "What is it you'd like my team to do for you here, Dr. Bailey, Agent McDaniel?"

She moved closer to the table where several bones lay. "I've discovered some consistent markings on many of the bones."

"How many people do they represent?" Fisher asked.

"From what I can see so far, at least ten. I'm also working on dating the remains. I imagine they span a good deal of time, given the condition they're in."

Fisher nodded. "Any rough estimates?"

"Five to seven years. With the exception of Agent Draker."

"That's right," McDaniel cut in. "He went missing about four weeks ago. Right in the middle of our investigation."

"No suspects?" Fisher asked him.

"None that I've identified."

"Going back to the markings," Bailey pressed. "These saw marks are of particular interest. The obvious reason being..."

"Intentional disposal of the remains," Fisher cut in.

"Of course," she said. "Saws can either be manual, requiring the physical push/pull, such as hand saws and hacksaws, or power-assisted, such as reciprocating and oscillating saws. Power-assisted saws have a variety of blade types, including circular blades, that increase the variation in the marks. The type of blade, movement of the saw, and the teeth's distance, size, shape, and arrangement all affect the characteristics of markings."

Fisher tightened his smile, shoving his hands into his pockets. "I appreciate your knowledge, Dr. Bailey, but if you could truncate this, I'd be grateful."

"I apologize. My job is to get into the weeds, and that's probably not going to be helpful to you right now. So, these characteristics can be used to help identify the type of saw used by taking a physical comparison between the cut of interest and marks created by known tools. It appears that in all cases, a reciprocating saw was used. Including on Agent Draker. That's where you come in, SSA Fisher."

McDaniel turned to him. "You and your team are experts in not only developing a comprehensive profile of the killer or killers who committed these crimes but also in helping to find where they might strike next. Or if there will be a next time."

"Well, we don't have a crystal ball," Fisher replied. "But we have plenty of experience in hunting down these types, yes. If you'd like our assistance, we can step in."

McDaniel nodded. "Good. I'll send you the files from our investigation, including a list of names of those informants I've already run backgrounds on. But if you or your team can take a look, maybe something else will pop out at you."

Kleman moved in as he examined the remains laid out on the table. "I understand this involves several people, but my only concern is for one." He turned back to Fisher. "Find the person who did this to my agent."

"I'll keep my eyes open for the files. Thank you." Fisher began to leave when he heard footsteps following him. He stopped to see McDaniel catching up.

"Agent Fisher." He glanced back at Kleman and the others. "Listen, this investigation Draker and I were working...it never pointed to the potential for murder. And now, as you've seen, there are several possible murders."

Fisher regarded him. "And?"

McDaniel licked his lips. "The people around there...they've run things a long time. I think Draker, when he spoke with our informant, may have discovered these other victims, or at least, had heard about them and maybe even knew where they were. And that's what got him killed."

Fisher glanced back at the rest of the group. "We're all on the same side here, so we'll do what we can and keep you in the loop on our findings."

"I appreciate that. I'll get those files over ASAP."

Fisher continued out of the lab. The killers he and the team have hunted almost always had a consistent M.O., rarely deviating from it. From where they find their prospective victims to where they keep them. So, how was it that DEA Agent Draker managed to get caught up with whoever had killed the others? And given what Bailey had said, those murders spanned years. So, could this be someone who's in the drug trafficking trade, or is this someone with a different agenda?

He returned to his unit and found Reid and Surrey in her office. Peering through her doorway, he continued, "Hey, can I run something by you two?"

Kate eyed him. "This about the meeting in the lab?"

Fisher strolled in. "It is." He glanced at Surrey, sitting across from her.

The newest member of the team, Surrey had transferred from Denver. He'd replaced the troublesome Noah Quinn, and Fisher was glad to have him here now. He and Kate complimented each other with their own individual strengths and weaknesses. Surrey was in his mid-thirties, divorced, with a couple of kids. The only one of them with children. A brave decision in this line of work.

Fisher pulled out a chair. "Looks like the Bureau was working with the DEA on a drug trafficking case in the Ozarks. A DEA agent went missing about a month ago after a meeting with an informant. They found his remains among several that had been dredged up from the bottom of the lake. The lab thinks they're connected, given specific markings on the bones. But here's the rub." He raised his index finger. "The murders spanned several years, possibly more, with the exception of the agent."

"Signature?" Kate asked.

"A reciprocating saw was used on every body part recovered, including the agent."

"How was he found?" Surrey asked.

"A fisherman. Dragged up the agent's arm, and called the police. Coast Guard and Missouri Water Patrol showed up from there." He could see Kate's mind spinning. "First impressions?"

She glanced at her desk, appearing to think about his question. Soon, her gaze returned to him. "It's pretty early to be throwing out theories just yet, but if the agent was the most recent kill, stands to reason his remains would've surfaced first."

"Yeah," Fisher replied, waiting for her to elaborate.

"And the other victims were dead for years," she continued. "Most logical conclusion—someone who's come out of hiding, or a copycat."

~

THE PRESCRIPTION BOTTLE in Sandra's hand read, *Take only when you have six or more uninterrupted hours. Do not drive.* Sandra had hesitated to even fill it, but the relentless grip of exhaustion had worn her down. The nights of fitful sleep and haunting dreams since all this started had taken their toll. And now, with the girls at a sleepover with friends, she had the time for herself. As the doctor said, she needed to look after her health.

It was only late afternoon with the sun casting long shadows across her living room floor. But she wanted nothing more than to surrender to sleep. To forget about the gnawing worry and constant fear that inundated her waking moments.

With a glass of tepid water in one hand, she held the small white pill in the other. Placing it on her tongue, Sandra swallowed it down with a gulp. In the peacefulness of her house, curtains drawn against prying eyes, she lay down on her sofa.

As Sandra drifted off, the medication quickly taking effect, she sank into an ocean of tranquility. Hours passed as she slept, dead to the world and oblivious to its worries.

When she finally awoke, disoriented and groggy, the living room was pitch black. Sandra blinked in confusion, momentarily disoriented by the oppressive darkness. She reached for the lamp on the end table and clicked it on. Pale yellow light flooded the living room.

As her eyes adjusted to this sudden illumination, it took a moment to see that the blanket she'd had over her was gone. She sat up with caution as her head was still fuzzy from the medication. Hadn't she left a lamp on? Where was her blanket? Not on the floor. Not kicked to the end of the couch. It was gone. Unease pricked the back of her neck.

A jolt of fear ran through her as she realized that things were not as she had left them. Not only was the blanket gone, but the pile of unopened mail on the coffee table had been shifted as if someone had rifled through it. Her purse, which she'd left on the recliner, was now on the floor.

"What the hell?" Her mind was still clouded, but now, her heart raced. Someone had been in here. While she slept, helpless and unaware, an intruder had come into her home. But who?

She jumped to her feet. "Tim?" Was he home? Was he the one who moved these things, and if so, why didn't he awaken her? "Tim, are you here?" Sandra stood still, waiting for a reply, but none came.

If not Tim, then who? Someone else had been in her home and watched her sleep. Was it the same person who took her husband?

With the effects of the medication waning, Sandra grabbed her phone and car keys. The time on the screen showed eight p.m. and on stepping outside, the sky was already black. Only the sharp cool white glow of streetlamps dotted the road. "Where am I going?"

She slipped behind the wheel of her white SUV. "Anywhere. Just away from here." Sandra turned the engine and backed out of the driveway. Overwhelmed by uncertainty, she fled her home in search of the impossible—her husband. Because it had to have been Tim who'd come. He'd seen her sleeping and left again. Yes. That was it. Now, she must find him again.

The roads were dark and quiet. The town had already gone home and curled up next to their fireplaces, curled up next to their loved ones. Meanwhile, Sandra drove on, out to the lake, not far from her parent's home.

She parked at a nearby boat launch and stepped out of her car, pulling her light jacket tightly around her. Walking down toward the sloped concrete ramp, she stood there, staring out over the water, where only a sliver of moonlight glistened. The bodies were found out there, somewhere. "Where are you?"

The cold air penetrated her light fleece. The soles of her ankle boots sank into the soft earth. Hot tears spilled down her cheeks. "Where are you? I miss you, please come home. I'm sorry. I'm so sorry."

Several minutes passed, allowing the medication to fully wear off. Her head cleared. The cold had become too much to bear, so she turned back. Walking to her car under a silent stillness, she felt the weight of it all on her shoulders.

Inside the car, the vents filled the cabin with warmth as Sandra drove back the way she came. To be honest, it was all she could do not to keep driving. Leaving all the pain and anguish behind. But she was still a mother, and her babies needed her. And in her mind, the words churned... *If you hadn't screwed that guy, Tim would still be here.*

As she drove on, the pharmacy ahead was still open. The relentless pounding in her skull, a side-effect of the sleeping pills, no doubt, demanded a cure. Sandra parked and walked inside.

The bright fluorescent lights sent searing pain through her eyes. She squinted, searching for the aisle with the headache medicine. Here. This one. Sandra carried on, grabbing the nearest box, and then made her way to the refrigerators, snatching a bottle of water. It seemed the only other person in here was the cashier. She walked to the checkout and set down her items.

A voice called out to her. Sandra turned, her eyes widening, anticipating the voice had come from Tim. That he'd found her, and he was safe. But disappointment crashed down on her at the unexpected sight. "Oh, Dr. Fuller."

"Sandra, how are you? I'm surprised to see you out and about without your girls."

"They're at a sleepover. I went out for a drive, got a headache, and ended up here."

He stared at her, creasing his brow. "Did you take one of the pills I gave you?"

She nodded. "I did. But that was several hours ago. In fact, I'd been able to sleep and then when I woke up, well, I felt like going out." Sandra left out the part about feeling as though someone had been inside her home while she slept. "What are you doing here, Doctor?"

He held up a box. "I ran out of cold medicine, and I seem to be coming down with something, so I figured it was best to nip it in the bud. I'm glad to hear you're taking my advice and trying to rest." He then wore mild disappointment. "Though I would have recommended you wait for a while longer before getting behind the wheel. Never mind." He waved his free hand. "I'm glad it did you some good."

"I think so, Doc. Thank you." She turned back to the counter while the cashier rang up her items and felt his lingering gaze. It seemed strange he would be at this pharmacy, knowing it was several miles away from his house.

"Ma'am?" the cashier asked. "That'll be ten, eighty-nine."

Sandra shook out of her trance and swiped her card. "Sorry." While the cashier bagged her items, she still felt his eyes on her.

"Here you are." The cashier handed over the receipt. "Have a good night."

"Thank you. You, too." Carrying on toward the exit, she glanced over her shoulder. Fuller still stared at her, wearing a strange smile and waving goodbye. She nodded politely and returned to her Toyota.

Slipping behind the wheel, Sandra peered through the building's windows where Fuller stood at the counter. Only moments later, he stepped outside and caught her gaze. He smiled, tilting his head, and then entered his car. As he drove away, she wondered. "What the hell are you doing here, Doc?"

6

The files had been sent over from the FBI field office. Agents McDaniel and Draker's investigation involved drug trafficking and money laundering. Then Draker was found with several other victims' remains. This case was lining up to be anything but typical.

Kate had returned to her temporary accommodation, Duncan's apartment, and changed into comfortable clothes, then carried the files into the living room.

Duncan held a glass of wine, setting her gaze on them. "Those are the files Cam mentioned?"

"Sure are. Interested in taking a look?"

"Always." Duncan held out her hand. "Let me see what you have."

Kate handed over several of the folders. "According to McDaniel, he'd already spoken to the informant Draker had met with before he disappeared. Most of this, here, details their trafficking investigation. I think he's hoping we'll see something he didn't."

"Not sure about that." Duncan curled up her leg on the side chair and began to review the information.

They sat in silence, each mulling over the fine details, hoping to spot a potential lead.

"So, we have the remains of several victims, estimated to have been in the water between five and seven years. Nothing recent, other than the DEA Agent," Kate began. "We're talking about a trafficking investigation here. And the informant who'd been last seen with Agent Draker is a long-time resident."

Duncan nodded. "He could've known where the bodies were, did the same thing to Draker figuring no one had found the remains up to that point, so it was probably a safe place to dispose of him."

"That then leaves us with two options. He's the killer—of all of them—or like you said, he knows where the bodies are, so he knows who killed them," Kate replied. "And then decided to make it look like Draker was murdered by the same guy."

"Have we searched their unsolved murders yet?" Duncan asked. "Because this is going to be hard to pin down until more details from the lab emerge."

Kate flipped through the files. "I don't see anything here relating to murders from five to seven years ago. But that's something we need to follow up on with local PD. What else do we know about the area?"

"It's haunted," Duncan shot back.

Kate eyed her with a half-smile. "What?"

"Oh yeah. I looked it up. Long story short, a dam was constructed in 1929, finished in 1931. It flooded a small town that had been evacuated. Anyway, a bunch of creepy shit's gone on since then."

"I did not know that." Kate opened her laptop, deciding to see for herself the history of the Ozarks. Reading on, she continued.

"Okay, you're not wrong. So, here's something else. Searching the local newspapers there, I typed in unsolved murders and this popped up..."

"I'm all ears," Duncan said.

Kate scanned the article on her laptop screen. "A local paper wrote a piece on a man named Everett Knapp. Back in 2018, he was arrested for the disappearances of several people, mostly tourists in the lake area."

"Hang on," Duncan said. "Let me log into the database and see what I can find on Knapp."

"No bodies were ever recovered," Kate continued. "Yet this guy was convicted of murder anyway."

"No bodies? Jesus, who the hell was his defense lawyer?" Duncan stopped a moment. "Here we go. Everette Knapp. His file's in the system." She pulled back, creasing her brow. "Convicted on DNA evidence in his vehicle belonging to a tourist who'd gone missing. Found guilty on five counts of first-degree murder for other missing tourists, presumed to have been his victims." She looked up at Kate. "Oh my God. Presumed?" Duncan continued to read. "Went to prison and then after serving only a few years...he died."

"How?" Kate pressed.

"Natural causes."

A look of uncertainty traded between them when Kate went on, "So, did this fisherman who caught the arm just find all these presumed victims' bodies? And if so, do we need to be looking at people connected to Everette Knapp? Since the guy's dead, I don't think he killed the DEA agent."

"No." Duncan turned away a moment. "First thing we need to do is get these remains identified. Start working our way back to the beginning."

"I agreed." Kate glanced at her phone when a text message arrived. She shifted her gaze to Duncan, who'd noticed the name.

"You're talking to him again?"

Kate shrugged. "With the hearing and everything...I mean, we are still married."

"I know," Duncan replied. "How's he doing?"

"Okay. Going to his AA meetings. The hearing was tough on him, but Cam says he's been made aware of his choices. I don't know what he's decided. I haven't talked to him since Bennett came to his decision."

"What are his choices?" Duncan pressed.

Kate closed her laptop. "I figured Cam would've said something to you."

"No. Maybe he was waiting to talk to you first."

"Yeah. Maybe." She sighed. "His options are the WFO or L.A."

"Wow." Duncan scratched her head. "That should be a no-brainer for him, don't you think? He worked at WFO for years."

"That is true," Kate replied. "It'd be a step down, but so would L.A."

"He must've expected that would happen. To be honest, Kate, he's lucky Bennett's keeping him."

"I think he knows that too."

Duncan eyed Kate's phone again. "You should answer his message. Maybe he's made a decision?"

"Yeah, okay. You're right." She picked up her phone and stood. "I'll be back in a minute."

"Take your time," Duncan said, going back to the file in her hands.

Kate retreated to her bedroom and read the message again. Nick had wanted to talk. Had Duncan been right? Was he ready to decide? It shouldn't matter to her what his decision was because they were no longer together. Still...She dialed his number, and he answered right away.

"Hi," Nick said.

Kate closed her bedroom door and sat on the edge of her bed. "Hi. Sorry for the delayed response. Eva and I were taking a look at some files for a potentially new case."

"Oh? Anything interesting?" he asked.

"Yes, but you didn't call to talk shop, did you? Cam told me you'd been given another shot and I think it's great, Nick."

"Did he tell you my options?"

"Yes." She went quiet.

"What do you think I should do?" he pressed.

Kate paused, gathering her thoughts. "It's not my decision, Nick. But I know you, and I know how much the BAU means to you. Leaving would be incredibly difficult."

Nick let out an audible sigh. "Yes, it would. The BAU is my life's work. But so are you, Kate. If taking a demotion at the WFO means we have a chance to reconnect and rebuild what we had, I'd choose it in a heartbeat."

Kate felt her heart swell at his words but remembered it was her decision to leave him. And she needed to stand firm.

"I know my addiction caused you a lot of pain," he continued. "Part of me thinks a fresh start could be good."

"I understand that," Kate said gently. "I think you need to search your heart and make the decision that feels right."

"I can't leave you here," he whispered.

A lump caught in her throat and her eyes reddened. She'd always been a strong woman. Making tough decisions going back to Spencer. God, that was a long time ago. And everything she and Nick had been through together...it was tough to walk away from. But if it happened again, if he fell off the wagon, as they say, her trust in him would vanish…forever. At least now, they could still be friends. She closed her eyes knowing that would be impossible.

"Doesn't anything we've been talking about this past week… doesn't any of it mean anything?" he asked.

Kate loved him. She always had. But so much had happened between them. Getting over him would prove the most difficult thing in her life. And that was saying something. She'd suffered too much loss in her lifetime and while Nick was still alive, she felt this loss just the same.

A life with him was all she'd wanted for so long, but how could she overlook a mistake that could've taken him away from her? It already cost his career, to a certain extent. And if it happened again as it had before? How many chances was she expected to offer?

"It does, Nick. It's just…I don't know if I can go through that again. I don't think I'm strong enough."

"I love you."

She swallowed the lump in her throat, trying not to break down. "Love has never been our problem. But sometimes it isn't enough."

"It could be with work," he argued. "I swear I won't fall again. I've seen the pain I've caused you. The pain I've caused myself. The choice I made that night, the previous day… was made out of fear. Plain and simple. Not for me, but for the soldiers whose fate I might have sealed."

"It was your job," she said, her voice breaking a little. "Look, I don't want to argue. I just want to tell you that whatever you decide, wherever you decide to go, I'll support your decision."

"Kate, please…please don't let this be the end."

Tears streamed down her cheeks. "I have to go."

~

DISCUSSING whether or not the team would take on this unusual investigation was the agenda of this morning's meeting. Inside the conference room, Kate sat at the table, reviewing the notes she'd taken last night on the files McDaniel had provided. Knapp was at the top of her list.

DEA Special Agent-in-Charge Kleman was there, so too was Agent McDaniel. This was a big deal. Not only had they lost one of their own, a federal law enforcement officer, but to have unearthed several body parts from their watery graves didn't happen every day.

When Fisher arrived, they were ready to begin. He stood at the head of the table. "First of all, I want to extend our condolences for the loss of Agent Draker. After my meeting with the forensic anthropologists in the lab yesterday, I came back to my team and asked them to take a look to see whether our unit could provide assistance." He gestured to Kate. "Our lead profiler, Supervisory Special Agent Kate Reid. Agent Reid, your thoughts?"

"In our brief overview, one name stood out that Agent Duncan and I found particularly interesting," she began. "The case of Everett Knapp, who, back in 2018, was convicted for the disappearances of several people from the area, mostly tourists. Given the time frame, his victims may be the ones you've uncovered."

"As for Agent Draker?" McDaniel asked.

"It would suggest his killer knew Knapp and that Knapp had mentioned where he buried the bodies." Kate paused, glancing around the room. "And after reading the notes on the interview with Agent McDaniel's informant—the last person to see Draker alive—I'd say the attention needs to turn its focus on the people who'd known Everett Knapp."

Surrey nodded. "That would be the best place to start, I agree. I also had a chance to review the files. I won't dismiss the relevance of the informants' statements, and it's still something I'd pursue. But at first blush...whoever disposed of Agent Draker, is someone who knew where the other remains were located. It's far too coincidental to suggest otherwise."

"Unfortunately, Everette Knapp died in prison a few years ago," Kate added.

"Let me make sure I understand this." ASAC Kleman aimed his finger at them. "You two are the profilers on this team, and both of you think this is some sort of copycat killing, rather than being connected to the trafficking case the agents were working on?"

"I'm saying, it's early and more legwork needs to be done," Kate replied. "But this is one possible theory."

"What do you propose, then, Agent Fisher?" McDaniel asked. "The Coast Guard and the Missouri Water Patrol are still scouring the lake for more remains. So far, they've turned up nothing more."

Walsh leaned in, resting his elbows on the table. "Can I just jump in here a second? How did Everette Knapp die?"

"Heart attack in prison." Kate raised her finger. "But he had a daughter. She could provide some insight." This would be a perfect opportunity for her to continue her research. The killer was dead, but his daughter could reveal a lot. The question was, would Fisher allow it? If they had a copycat on their hands, could time away be devoted to her other endeavors?

Fisher leaned back in his chair. "We'll take on this investigation. I'll have Reid and Surrey develop a profile, considering possible insight into Everett Knapp. Agent McDaniel, you'll coordinate with Agent Walsh on local jurisdictional authority. Agent Duncan will coordinate with our lab as the remains are identified."

"Thank you," Kleman said. "You'll have every available resource we can provide at your disposal."

~

A KNOCK FELL on Sandra's door, echoing throughout the house. Peering through the window, the morning sun in her eyes, she expected her friend to be standing on the porch with the girls in tow. Instead, two patrol cars were parked out front like ominous black crows, and two police officers stood at her door.

A sensation akin to falling from a tall building mixed with rising anxiety and created a nauseous swirl in her gut. This was about Tim. Was he hurt or was he dead? The questions hung in the air like specters, their answers waiting on the other side of that door. The only way to know was to force her legs to move. To walk to the door and open it, waiting for the words to fall from their mouths and reach her ears - words that could shatter her world or offer a reprieve.

When the knock came again, persistent and demanding, answering it became the only option. Sandra shuffled along as if protracting the event would somehow make it easier to bear. Each step felt like wading through quicksand, every movement heavy with dread.

Her hand clamped around the handle, and she turned, opening the door to reveal the officers' grim faces cast in the shadow of the overhanging porch. Their expressions were etched with compassion.

"Mrs. Dawes?" One of the officers removed his hat. "Mrs. Sandra Dawes?"

"Yes, that's me." Her voice was barely a whisper, caught in the tight confines of her throat.

"Ma'am," the other officer began, his tone just as grave. "Is your husband Timothy Dawes?"

Her heart pounded so fast and so hard that their words were

practically muffled. Each beat was a drumroll leading to an inevitable conclusion. "Yes, he is."

"Ma'am, I'm sorry to tell you this, but we believe we found your husband. He has passed. We'd like for you to come down to the hospital to identify him."

"How?" she whispered. "What happened to him?"

The officers traded uncomfortable glances when one of them continued, "It's best for you to talk to the doc..."

"What happened to him?" she demanded, cutting him off.

The officer cast down his gaze. "He was found floating in the lake. I'm very sorry for your loss."

7

As the boat drove out to the site where the remains had been found, a cold mist blew back on Kate's face. With the wintry air, she zipped her weatherproof jacket and pulled up her hood.

The clouded skies kept in the cold and as Agent Jonathan Surrey stood next to Kate, wrapped in his North Face coat and wool hat, she smiled. "You're from Colorado, it's colder there than here."

He glanced at her, his eyes, mere slits to keep out the spray. "I'm a summer kind of guy. What can I say?"

Kate nodded, her attention, back out over the water. She'd come to appreciate Surrey. More than she had expected. He'd seen her through these past few weeks, simply by being there. Not offering more than was asked, yet still there, supportive.

His style was different from her own. Surrey could separate himself from the hunt. From the killer. Allowing him to see outside of it, which was sometimes a better alternative than Kate's desire to get inside a killer's mind. But with both of them together, they built a complete picture.

Agent McDaniel and Lieutenant Crawford were with them. It was the Coast Guard who they'd hitched a ride with this morning. And now, ahead, was the scene. Cordoned off by thick rope and buoys, this was where the remains of the DEA agent had been recovered. He wasn't alone, but the other remains had yet to be identified.

The boat rocked back as the captain throttled down, slowing to a stop. Now, as it swayed in the rolling water, Kate surveyed the area. An unnerving feeling overcame her, as though their presence, *her* presence, disturbed the natural order of things. But there was nothing natural about what had been found.

The lieutenant walked over to her. "My team has been in this water every day, looking for more remains. Nothing else has turned up."

She looked outward toward the shore. Trees, though mostly barren now, still shrouded the world behind them. They were one of three vessels in the area. The other two were for the dive teams and any more findings they might come across. "How many homes are in this immediate vicinity?"

A local officer from the Missouri Water Patrol headed over. "Sorry to butt in, but I figured I might be able to best answer that question." He aimed his finger ahead. "That way is Porta Chima. You'll find a lot of multi-million dollar homes out there. And back that way, toward the North Shore, you'll find some older homes. Same with the West Side. Old homes, built in the fifties. Not many restaurants or tourist spots there."

"Are those full-time residents on the north and west sides?" Kate asked.

"Oh yeah." He waved his hand. "Well, not all of them, but a good portion. The expensive homes are mostly the part-time folks, who only spend their summers and spring breaks here. The rest of them been here probably most of their lives."

Kate turned back to Surrey. "The other remains, the ones still waiting to be identified. Forensics dated the deaths between five and seven years ago."

He tucked his hands into his coat pockets. "With Knapp having already been convicted, it's an easy assumption those found last week were the bodies of his victims. So, if you're wanting to talk to some of these folks out here, might be best to talk to the full-time residents. Those who might remember Knapp and all that went down."

"Exactly what I was thinking," she replied. The sound of another boat approaching caught her attention and she regarded the patrolman. "Who's that?"

The officer eyed the vessel. "That's one of mine. I don't know what's going on, but I'll find out."

Kate stepped aside with Surrey, heading to see Walsh and Duncan, who were huddled nearby. "I want to find out who in this neighborhood was here when Knapp was taken into custody."

"Should be able to get our hands on that information pretty easily," Duncan replied. "What's going to help us, though, is getting IDs on those remains."

"Absolutely," Surrey cut in. "But these guys must have a list of missing persons cases. That'd be where I'd start."

"We'll follow up when we leave here," Kate added.

The Water Patrol's vessel stopped beside theirs. The officer, who Kate had spoken to, now stood near the edge, talking to another officer. Appearing to get what he was looking for, he soon returned, arms folded, pursed lips. "Looks like a deceased male surfaced about half a mile down the shoreline just this morning."

"Accidental death?" Kate asked.

"Un, no, ma'am. I don't think so. A knife wound was visible in his back. Some other injuries were possibly sustained during an attack. And there were markings around the wrists and feet," he replied. "At least, that's what I've been told."

She turned around back to the team. "Definitely doesn't sound accidental."

"But off the bat, it doesn't sound connected to this case," Walsh said.

"Only one way to find out." Kate headed toward Lieutenant Crawford. "You heard?"

"Yes, ma'am, I did."

"We're not far. Can we make a run over there? Could be connected to this," she said.

"If that's what you want, yes, ma'am." He made his way to the wheelhouse, and within moments, the engines revved, churning up the water, and they were on their way.

Kate looked on, thinking this was a hell of a strange coincidence. A drowned body with a stab wound and markings like a rope had bound his hands and feet?

"Could've been a case where the victim fought back," Surrey said, stepping toward her.

"What's that?" she asked, unaware he'd approached.

"I can see your wheels spinning, Reid." He peered out over the water as the spray hit them. "Doesn't make sense that someone else was killed out here, but not in the same manner as Draker."

The corner of her lips ticked up. "You read my mind. The victim didn't go down easily. The killer couldn't finish the job. Injured him and left him to drown, rather than taking his time dismembering him."

"Exactly. Even so," he continued. "I don't like the direction this is headed. Draker's killer knows we found more victims along with the agent—"

"And yet, it hasn't served as a deterrent," Kate replied. "Assuming a connection."

Lieutenant Crawford walked toward the bow, where Kate and Surrey waited. "This is it, just ahead."

The vessel slowed as it neared the shoreline. Several patrol cars poked out from behind the trees. Silent. Lights flashing. Officers stood inside the yellow tape, stretched between several trees. A tarp lay in a heap near the edge of the shoreline, a body likely hidden beneath it.

"Where's the family?" Kate asked. "Have they been contacted?"

Crawford turned to the MHP Water Division officer. "Family's aware?"

"Yes, sir. My team has spoken to the wife, Sandra Dawes. She'd reported her husband, Tim, missing about a week ago. They're taking her to the station. Once the body's transported, she'll be escorted to the adjacent morgue for an official ID."

"That was right around the time Draker and the other remains were discovered." Kate looked back at her team. "About a four-week cooling off period from when the agent was murdered." There was always a sort of cooling off between kills, in Kate's experience. Downtime for the killer to find his next victim. But when that timeline starts to shorten, the real trouble begins.

The bow of the smaller vessel slid onto the sands of the shore. Kate and the team were helped off and she walked toward the blue tarp. "Can I take a look? FBI," she asked a nearby officer.

He gestured outward. "Yes, ma'am."

Kate pulled down the tarp. Beneath it lay the victim. A young man, looking to have been in his early thirties. "He has a contusion on his right temple. A laceration on his cheek."

"Yes, ma'am," the officer said. "When we pulled him out of the water, that's when we saw the stab wound in his back."

She didn't want to move the body more than it had already been. "I'll have to wait to take a look at that." While the team huddled around the victim, she continued, "I see the marks. He was bound, but no signs of strangulation."

"What do we know about this guy?" Walsh asked the officer.

"Family lives in Camdenton. Wife, two young daughters."

"Christ," he replied.

"Wife's been coming into the station looking for news since reporting him missing," the officer went on.

Kate eyed Agent McDaniel as he neared. "We'll need to talk to this man's wife."

$\approx$

THEY HEADED TOWARD CAMDENTON, abandoning the review of the watery burial grounds, so they could talk to the wife of the newly discovered dead man. It could've been completely unrelated to their current investigation. And the manner of death suggested the events were, in fact, not connected. But none of them believed this wasn't otherwise one hell of a strange coincidence.

The wife waited at the local police station, while the body of the man believed to be her husband was sent to the morgue at the back of the building. The only way they were certain? He'd still had a wallet in his back pocket—and an ID.

Inside the station, it was the officer from the boat who made a beeline for the front desk. Kate and the team stepped aside as he did. She noticed Crawford and McDaniel in hushed conversation, and it became clear they held their own suspicions about this. With this many agencies involved, the Coast Guard, the DEA, the FBI, and Missouri Police, it would be all too easy to get caught up in the bureaucracy. And with the Coast Guard's responsibilities, the existing investigation...it all meant this could easily devolve into a convoluted mess. Kate had been in this kind of situation before, and getting permission to talk to this wife might be tough.

Soon, however, the officer returned wearing an expression that suggested they'd received the okay. "Is Mrs. Dawes here?" Kate asked.

"Yes, ma'am. I've received confirmation she has arrived. I'm waiting for the captain's buy-off and they'll let you all talk to the woman."

"Great. Thank you," Kate replied.

"Please..." he gestured to the waiting area. "Have a seat and I'll be back in a moment."

When they headed toward the rows of chairs, Agent McDaniel approached Kate. "I think you and your people might be wasting your time with this."

"How so?" she asked, noticing Surrey's disapproving stare. He didn't like being told he was wasting time.

"Because you're here to find out who murdered Agent Draker," McDaniel replied. "This...this here is a side quest."

"Respectfully, Agent McDaniel, we don't think so," Kate replied, spying the return of the officer.

The officer thumbed back. "Captain says one of you can go back and talk to Mrs. Dawes."

McDaniel gestured outward. "You want to talk to her, be my guest."

"All right." Kate offered a glance at the team and followed the officer to an interview room down the hall. On their arrival, she turned to him. "You put her in here?"

"Got nowhere else to put her, ma'am," he replied before opening the door. "Mrs. Dawes?"

"Yes?" The strawberry blond-haired woman had puffy eyes and tear-stained cheeks. She looked frail and scared, and sitting at a table usually reserved for suspects; she must've begun to feel like one.

"FBI Agent Reid is here. She'd like to ask you a few questions."

"FBI?" Mrs. Dawes tabbed a tissue against her eyes. "All right."

The officer nodded to Kate before stepping outside, closing the door behind him.

She pulled out a chair and sat down. "I'm so sorry they put you in here, Mrs. Dawes."

"It doesn't matter," she whispered.

"And I'm very sorry for your loss," Kate continued. "I know this is an incredibly difficult time."

The woman blinked away her tears, holding a crumpled tissue. "Thank you. I just can't believe Tim is gone."

Kate rested her arms on the table and wore compassion in her gaze. "Mrs. Dawes, can you walk me through the last time you saw your husband?"

"It's been a little over a week. We'd had a horrible fight. I left with the girls to stay at a friend's house. I came back the next day to try to make amends." A fresh wave of grief seemed to rise to the surface. "And he was gone. I thought he'd eventually turn up, but not like this."

Talking to the victims' families was one of the most difficult parts of Kate's job. Not that she couldn't relate, because...she could. But she felt their grief, their pain, and sometimes, it overwhelmed her. Hiding that feeling was almost too hard, yet encroaching on their pain was unacceptable. "I don't know how much you're aware of the condition in which your husband was found."

Confusion masked her face.

"Mrs. Dawes, he has marks on his wrists and ankles, indicating he was restrained before entering the water."

"No, I—" Her eyes widened. "Restrained? As in, someone forced him into the water?"

Kate wondered if she was aware of the stab wound but felt it might be best not to elaborate. She'd know soon enough. "Well, it's very early to know for certain, but I've been at this a long time, and I know restraint marks when I see them. Mrs. Dawes, I'm here helping out FBI Agent McDaniel, the Coast Guard, and the local authorities on a seemingly unrelated case."

"The bodies found in the lake," she said.

Kate glanced down. "Yes, ma'am. Now, I'm not saying what happened to your husband is part of this, but it's something I'd like to rule out so that the local police can discover what exactly happened to him."

"What is it you think I can do for you then?" Mrs. Dawes asked.

"I was briefed on the way over and wanted to ask you about your husband's workplace. I guess something had happened that sparked a disagreement between the two of you."

"Yeah. Something happened all right," she said, her tone laced with anger. "The awful person who told everybody...Derek Earley," she replied. "I don't know him well. Met him a few times at company functions. He seemed nice enough. I thought."

"Told everyone what, ma'am?" Kate asked.

Mrs. Dawes withdrew, lowering her gaze. "The fight Tim and I had...it was because I'd had a one-night stand and, somehow, Derek found out. And then he'd sent this horrible email to the entire office. Tim was humiliated."

This was unexpected. Kate tilted her head. "And is there any way that Mr. Earley would've known such a private detail about your life?"

"Not unless he was there that night at the bar," she replied, her tone flat.

Kate leaned back, considering how best to approach this. "Mrs. Dawes, may I ask you about the man you...met...that night?"

She closed her eyes, tears spilling over. "I don't know who he is. I didn't get a name."

"So everyone in the office knew about this." Kate sighed.

"There's someone else I told, too, about my affair," Mrs. Dawes continued. "My therapist."

This was growing more complicated by the minute, but Kate was here to find out who murdered the DEA agent. "Look, Mrs. Dawes, this is all information you need to tell the detective working this case for you. Derek Earley, the fight, the man you met at the bar."

"Yes, of course."

The nagging feeling that this murder was somehow tied to Draker's wouldn't relent. But a connection just wasn't yet tangible. Kate narrowed her gaze. "And you're certain you can't recall the name of the man? Where he lived? Anything?"

"No, I'm sorry." Sandra looked away. "What you must think of me right now."

"Not at all." Kate placed her hand over the woman's. "I'm just looking for answers, Mrs. Dawes. We all are."

～

A RETICENT NICK Scarborough stood in the doorway of Fisher's office. Only days after his disciplinary hearing, he faced life-altering decisions, while still holding out hope his wife would forgive him.

It took a moment, but Fisher looked away from his computer, spying his former colleague. "Nick? Come in. Sorry, I didn't see you there." He pulled the toothpick from between his lips. "I wasn't expecting you. Everything all right?"

Nick meandered inside. "That's a loaded question."

Fisher let out a nervous chuckle. "Yeah, sorry. Have a seat. Uh, Reid's in the field along with the rest of the team."

"I heard. Walsh messaged me. He's pretty good at keeping me in the loop, even if he has no reason to." Nick sat down, crossing his legs and resting his arms on the chair. "He said you guys are working with FAP on several remains that arrived a few days ago."

"That's right. They're working on dating them now in the lab. Dr. Bailey has identified what was used to dismember the bodies... a reciprocating saw."

Nick closed his eyes a moment. Parts of that job he'd loved. Others? Not so much, like the gruesome, horrific things human beings did to one another. "So Kate and the others...they're working with local authorities to find the killer?"

"Surrey and Reid will develop a profile," Fisher replied. "Walsh is the coordinator for both the Coast Guard and the Missouri Highway Patrol's Water Division. And Eva, well, she'll piece together a timeline and help the FAP with identifying the remains."

"Right. Well, it sounds like you have everything covered."

Fisher narrowed his gaze. "What's going on, man? I can see you didn't come here to shoot the shit. This about the hearing?"

"No. But I did want to thank you for having my back."

"Always," Fisher said. "So, what is it?"

Nick leaned back, running his tongue along his lower lip. "I, uh, I don't know..." Fisher's phone rang, stopping him in his tracks.

"Sorry, man. I need to take this." He answered the call. "Fisher here."

Nick could only hear one side of the conversation, but based on Fisher's expression, something had happened.

"Got it. I'll come down now. Thanks." He ended the call.

"Bailey has some news. I need to get over to the lab and talk to her. Care to join me?"

Nick felt a spark of gratitude. "Why not? Wouldn't mind seeing what you have going on."

Fisher got up from his desk. "Then let's go."

They passed through multiple buildings, making their way to the forensics lab inside the massive Quantico compound. Nick hadn't been there in a long time. Running Unit Two didn't require a trip. And it felt pretty good if for no other reason than to take his mind off looming decisions and getting a chance to focus on work —someone else's work.

Inside the lab, three tables lay side-by-side. Each one with bones placed meticulously. Dr. Bailey, a petite woman with round cheeks and short blond hair approached them.

"Agent Fisher, thanks for coming down." She offered her hand.

"Of course." He gestured outward. "This is Senior Unit Agent Nick Scarborough. He and I were in a meeting, and I wanted him to come down. I hope that's all right."

"Of course." She smiled, offering her hand to him. "Pleased to meet you, Agent Scarborough. I'm Dr. Bailey, lead anthropologist for the FAP."

"Pleasure's mine," he replied. "And it's *former* Senior Unit Agent." He felt Fisher's glance.

"Right. Well, come on. We can get started." Dr. Bailey looked over the bones laid out on the tables in the same manner as they would've been found inside a body. "As we continue to approximate a date, we've been able to narrow down the timeline based on a few key factors." She aimed her pinky finger at one of the bones. "First, looking at the degree of decomposition, the relative lack of tissue, and the staining on the bones, it's clear these remains have been submerged in water for at least five to maybe even ten years."

"A little longer than you first thought," Fisher said.

"Possibly. We can also see evidence of animal and insect activity, which gives us a window into how long they were exposed to the elements before ending up in the lake."

She gestured to another set of bones. "Now, this one shows some damage to the ribs and sternum. You can see multiple fractured ribs on both sides, as well as a severed xiphoid process on the sternum. The nature of these injuries indicates that the cause of death was most likely blunt force trauma to the chest. And you can also see peri-mortem cutting marks here on the vertebrae and other bones, suggesting dismemberment."

Moving down the row, Dr. Bailey pointed to a third set of remains. "With this victim, we found a titanium rod that had been surgically implanted to replace a femur." She regarded Fisher. "We did find a serial number on the rod, though it's difficult to make out. We are working on that." She continued her evaluation. "In addition to the bone analysis, we ran radiocarbon dating tests on the organic tissue still clinging to some of the bones. Those results corroborate our other findings, suggesting this victim was killed sometime between 2015 and when the most recent victim, Agent Draker, was murdered only weeks ago."

It had been a long time since Nick had been involved in a case like this. While it remained a horrific crime, the details, the puzzle that needed to be pieced together, it spurred his thoughts, sharpened his mind. "Sounds like they're dealing with a killer who lives in the area. Someone who knew where the other victims had been disposed of." He eyed Fisher.

"This does point to a local resident," Fisher said. "Someone with knowledge of the lake's history. Of where the summer visitors go, and as you say, knew where the bodies were. And that brings me to another potential issue...it's a highly popular tourist destination. Are they the targets?"

"Identifying all the remains may be the only way to answer that question," Nick replied. "Short of pulling missing persons' files over the past five to ten years."

"I do find it interesting the killer would go after someone in law enforcement," Fisher said, still peering at the various remains.

"Could've been someone who got too close," Nick speculated. "Saw something he shouldn't have. It's something you and the team will need to keep an open mind about because this DEA agent might not be related to these other killings. Not directly. Careful you don't wear blinders thinking it has something to do with the trafficking investigation."

"How'd you know about that?" Fisher pressed.

He shrugged. "Kate might've mentioned it."

"I see." Fisher looked at Dr. Bailey. "Thank you for this. We'll add your report to the file, sending it over to the field agents as well. In the meantime, how much longer before you'll start to ID the rest of the victims?"

Bailey removed her gloves, tossing them into the nearby trash can. "Some of the skulls still have teeth. We've already begun a search there. The rest...it'll probably boil down to the missing persons' reports."

Fisher nodded. "Thanks again." He patted Nick on the back as both turned around to leave. "I almost forgot how good you were at this."

He grunted. "Guess it never really leaves you, does it?"

8

Sandra Dawes' interview gave Kate pause. Maybe it was the subtle tremor in her voice, a flicker of fear in her eyes—like she knew something more but was afraid to speak. Her mentioning of her therapist seemed unnecessary. Kate couldn't yet piece it together, but headed back to the team, letting the local authorities handle the distraught woman.

Her husband's murder seemed to have no connection to those whose remains had been discovered. Certainly no connection to the DEA agent either. So why wasn't Kate convinced that Sandra Dawes' role in this investigation wasn't yet finished? Why did a nagging feeling persist?

She returned to the bullpen, where her team waited along with Agent McDaniel and Lieutenant Crawford. "I didn't find any reason to think that the murder of Tim Dawes has a connection to our case."

Surrey leaned against one of the empty desks, crossing his arms. "So there are two killers in this town? That's a fairly high ratio."

"Yeah, well, just because I didn't find a reason, doesn't mean there isn't one," Kate added. "The timing is suspect, but for now, our focus should be on finding whoever murdered the DEA agent." She glanced at McDaniel, who had already stated this was their sole purpose for being here. "Maybe you were right, and this was a waste of time, but it had to be ruled out." Which Kate knew had yet to be done.

"Identifying the remains is the only way to put the issue to bed," Surrey added, his attention shifting to the rest of the team. "And our only shot at coming up with something actionable."

McDaniel walked to another desk and picked up a stack of files. He carried them to Surrey, his expression solemn. "Here are the missing persons cases dating back to twenty seventeen, Agent Surrey."

"Looks like at least fifty case files there," he replied.

"Are these all tourists?" Kate asked.

McDaniel regarded her. "I haven't gone through these yet. Just got my hands on them. But it happens all the time around here. This place gets tens of thousands of visitors every summer. Frankly, I'm surprised there are only this many. Then again..." He shot a glance at Lieutenant Crawford, a silent communication passing between them. "Coast Guard and MHP Water probably have a good deal more unsolved missing persons."

Crawford pressed his lips tightly. "Unfortunately. I can only imagine the sheer number of remains lying at the bottom of that lake." He eyed Kate. "So, Agent Reid, while I understand your conclusion—comparing missing persons to the remains that have been found—it's a drop in the bucket. And it's a mighty big bucket."

The reality check sunk in. These people, who knew the area and its history far better than she did, put it to her plainly. The task at hand wasn't an easy one. And maybe it wasn't the right one.

She could admit that this forced her to rethink her usual strategies. Because it now seemed that it just wasn't going to work this time.

It took another moment or two for Agent McDaniel to set down the files again. Kate studied the pile. "Then maybe the best thing to do is to wait for the lab to do their jobs and discover the identities of the victims recovered...so far." She glanced at Surrey, Walsh, and Duncan. "While they do their job, we'll do ours. And Agent McDaniel, that means you'll need to bring us up to speed on your informant...the last person to see Draker alive."

He nodded. "You want to talk to him, I can arrange it."

"Thank you." She hesitated a moment, words lingering on the tip of her tongue.

"What is it?" Surrey asked.

Feeling uncertain as to whether she should mention this, Kate relented. "Just thinking about Mrs. Dawes. The M.O.'s don't match, but I'd still like to learn more about what happened to her husband. The timing..."

"Strikes me as more than coincidental, too," Surrey replied. "I think it does for all of us."

~

THE POLICE ESCORTED Sandra Dawes to the room where they kept the bodies. At least, the ones whose families had yet to claim them. Now, it was her turn to claim the body of the man she loves —*loved*.

The officer stood at the table, hands on the sheet. "Are you ready, ma'am?"

All she could manage was a slight nod, otherwise frozen in heartache. Her palms dampened and her skin rose with a thousand goosebumps.

He pulled down the sheet with painstaking deliberateness, as though trying to prolong her agony. Tim's dark hair clung to his head, stiff and matted from the water. His face, a bluish hue, bore a long cut down his cheek. A few scrapes from confrontations with tree branches and stones as he'd settled on the lake floor.

"I was told he was also..." She swallowed hard. "Stabbed in the back?"

The officer nodded. 'Yes, ma'am. You want me to turn him over?"

Sandra swatted away the notion. "No."

A bloated figure, she looked away in pain for what he had become. The federal agent told her the markings on Tim's wrists and ankles suggested he'd been bound. But by whom? Who would want her husband dead?

"Stop." Sandra lost her breath, a wave of nausea swirling in her gut. "That's enough."

The officer looked at her, a compassionate gaze that only served to further rattle her emotions. "Is this your husband, Timothy Dawes?"

"Yes. It's him." She spun around, rushing to leave the room, desperate to go home and see her children. And tell them what?

Standing in the corridor, her back pressed against the wall, she closed her eyes, forcing the welling tears to spill. Footfalls approached from the other end. Sandra stopped and composed herself. Looking over, she saw a burly man in a dark uniform.

"Mrs. Dawes are you all right?" he asked. "I'm Lieutenant Crawford, US Coast Guard. I was called out the scene where your husband was..."

"I see." She wiped her cheeks. "They made me come here to identify him. I apologize if I'm not at my best at the moment."

"Of course. I understand." He lowered his gaze. "I'm so sorry for your loss."

Sandra drew in a cleansing breath, clearing the emotions from her throat. "Am I free to leave now?"

"Uh, I'm sure that will be fine. I'll speak to the investigating officer." He reached for a card in his suit jacket, handing it over to her. "Please feel free to contact me with any questions at all. I don't know if I'll be able to do much myself, but I'll know who to ask, if not."

"Thank you, Lieutenant." Sandra took the card and walked past him, through the station, passing by the federal agents who seemed uninterested in what had happened to Tim. The female agent told her something about other murders, but Sandra didn't care about other murders. She cared about her husband's murder.

Outside, Sandra took in the cold air as the skies turned gray. The air soothed her skin which had heated with emotion.

Stepping into her car, she drove away, the police station fading in the rearview mirror. She was alone for the first time in her life. Tim had always been there for her. Since college, as a matter of fact. She was still a young woman, but with two young girls to now raise on her own.

Dr. Fuller had tried to help alleviate her guilt over what she'd done. He'd offered sound advice to aid the police in their efforts to find out what happened. So much of this made no sense at all. And now she wondered, with all these other people here, the FBI, the Coast Guard, would anyone care about Tim?

A grocery store lay ahead and all she wanted right now was a goddam drink. She and Tim weren't big drinkers, but there was usually a bottle or two of wine at the house. Not anymore.

Sandra parked the car, pulling down the visor to check her reflection in the mirror. Red eyes, swollen from tears. Pale skin. "Never mind what you look like. Your husband is dead. Someone killed him."

Anger boiled in her gut as she shoved her shoulder against the driver's door and stepped outside. Her lips quivered and she did her best not to crumple onto the blacktop.

Taking a deep breath, she walked inside without her coat. God knows what people thought of her right now. She shouldn't even be driving, but there was no one else to turn to. No one else could help her.

A cashier smiled at her, with obvious hesitation behind it. No doubt because of Sandra's appearance. "Evening, ma'am. How are you tonight?"

"Fine. Thank you." Sandra walked through the store and down the booze aisle. She scanned the various labels, realizing it didn't make a damn bit of difference. So she grabbed a bottle. And then another. Heading back toward the checkout, a familiar voice sounded.

"Sandra, good evening."

She turned around. "Dr. Fuller?" Her brow knitted and she shook her head. "What—uh—what are you doing here?"

He glanced at the bottles in her hand. "Funny running into you again." He raised a loaf of bread in his hands. "I ran out."

No way was this another coincidence. Not a chance. Had he been there at her house too? The blanket, her purse, the mail. Jesus, what the hell was happening? "Well, I should get going." She walked by him. "Just ran in to pick up something on my way home."

"From the police station?" he asked.

Sandra stopped in her tracks and turned back to him. "How'd you know?"

He thumbed back as if someone behind him had the answer. "It's all over the news."

"Tim?" she asked, placing her hand on her chest.

"Uh, no. The whole FBI and everyone here for the lake."

"Right, of course. So, you don't know about Tim?" she pressed.

And when he didn't respond, she continued, "He's dead, Dr. Fuller. My husband is dead." Sandra pressed on, walking faster now. She set down the bottles of wine on the cashier's counter and walked out.

"Ma'am?" the cashier asked.

"Never mind." Sandra waived back and pushed through the exit. Outside, she looked left, then right. There it was, the doctor's car. "Were you following me?"

~

THE DRUG TRAFFICKING investigation McDaniel and Draker had been working seemed to have zero connection to the discovery of what Kate now believed were the bodies of Everett Knapp's victims. Yet she couldn't deny an underlying possibility.

Kate stood on the dock, overlooking the lakeside restaurants, hotels, and luxury homes. Lights began to flicker on as the sky had grown darker. Cloudy mist now clung to the treetops. This truly was a paradise, no matter the time of year. It was hard to imagine the atrocities that had taken place. "This was where he last contacted you?"

Agent McDaniel stood next to her, hands clasped behind his back and gazing out over the water. "Yep. He was set to meet with one of our informants. Sent me a text about thirty minutes prior to the meeting...that was the last I'd heard from him. This was where they were scheduled to meet."

She glanced at Surrey, who'd been meandering around the dock as if hoping to find some overlooked clue. "I'm sure your people have already scoured this area for evidence."

"We have," McDaniel replied.

Surrey approached them, his peacoat flapping in the breeze, revealing a charcoal gray suit beneath it. "Another set of eyes can't hurt. There are several homes surrounding this location. Someone might've seen something."

"Most of those homes are owned by the part-timers, and the meeting took place after dark," McDaniel said. "I know they met up here. Since Draker's phone hasn't been recovered...I have no idea where he went afterward. Phone records show no other calls sent or received after about ten p.m. that night. No texts, which means he was probably using an encrypted app to communicate. So, he could've vanished into thin air for all I know."

Kate wasn't a detective. She'd never worked undercover or had to deal with informants. But Marshall had, and she had worked for SDPD for a time. Protocol would've dictated some form of backup out there. Draker never should've been alone. "You said you talked to your informant, who'd had the meeting with your partner. What was his story?"

"I'd contacted him the day after the meeting when I'd realized Draker wasn't responding to my calls or texts," he replied. "The informant had arrived by boat, then left about half an hour later after the meeting."

"By boat?" Kate tilted her head. "Where is this boat now?"

McDaniel peered out over the water again, seemingly hesitating. "Couldn't tell you. I reached out to the informant several days later, and...he went dark."

"You don't know where he is now." Kate didn't know if that was a question or a statement, but this was an important detail McDaniel failed to disclose sooner. Why? "Seems to me that we should be looking for him, or the boat. Maybe both."

"Look, Agent Reid, I can see you think I don't know my ass from my elbow, but I promise you, I've done everything I can to find him...my partner and our informant. I've already had my people put drones in the air to search for the vessel," McDaniel added. "It's not in the water, but that doesn't mean it isn't in someone's boathouse."

He squared up to them, raising his chin in defiance. "The thing is, Agent Surrey, Agent Reid, is that I've been searching for Draker for weeks. It wasn't until his arm was pulled out of the lake that I knew for sure he was dead. Then all these other victims started popping up and we asked for Quantico's help. They sent us your team to profile the son of a bitch who killed him, and apparently, several others. So, how about you leave the investigative work to me and my people, while you focus your efforts on telling me the kind of killer we should be looking for?"

It was hard to argue his point. They weren't there to investigate, but as far as Kate was concerned, the only way to understand who killed the DEA agent was to understand how he died. To find a connection between him and his killer. "I appreciate your perspective, Agent McDaniel, and I do get where you're coming from."

She stepped across the weather-worn boards of the dock. Several boats swayed nearby in their slips and the cold wind brushed against her skin. "Someone who's as highly trained, as Agent Draker would've been, isn't generally going to go down without a fight. He was taken by surprise. He trusted someone. Maybe your informant."

"And your informant is gone, which doesn't put him in a good light," Surrey cut in.

"I appreciate the work you do," Kate continued. "So I ask that you respect our process." Her gaze drifted out over the water. "These people...the ones who prey on other's darkest fears, taking them in manners that can only be described as monstrous." Her mind flashed back to the kill room in Texas. The blood dripping from the table. The pictures of victims on the walls. She cleared her throat. "They mostly follow a pattern—an M.O. So when

Agent Draker crossed paths with his killer, it was because he stumbled onto that pattern, not because he was targeted. That much, I know for certain. So, our job is to find out why."

McDaniel pressed his lips together, returning a nod as he looked down. "You're right, Agent Reid. No disrespect intended."

Now that she'd cleared the air, Kate continued, "In the meantime, there is something else I'd like to do."

"Of course," he replied.

She offered a glance at Surrey before continuing, "I'd like to speak to the daughter of Everett Knapp."

"Why is that?" he asked.

"Because she probably knew her father better than most," Kate added. "And it's possible, she knew who he was talking to before he died. Whoever murdered Agent Draker knew where Knapp put the bodies. That's the connection we need to follow up on now."

9

The dinner invitation Fisher had extended was welcomed. Over these past few weeks, Nick had never felt more alone, more detached from the life he once knew. Whether Fisher had felt obligated, he couldn't be sure, but it was a kind gesture, just the same.

Now, the two sat at a restaurant not far from the Quantico compound. Nick sipped on a glass of water after finishing his meal. Things almost felt normal, even if they were anything but.

"I appreciate you letting me get a peek into what you and the team are working on," he said. "I never got much opportunity to work with FAP."

"Same here." Fisher set down his glass of Coke. "It's an interesting case. Possibly a copycat. Reid thinks so, anyway. A man who'd been convicted back in twenty-eighteen could be the one responsible for the recovered remains."

"But not the recent death of the agent." Scarborough wiped his mouth. "Well, you know Kate. She'll dive right in. I'm glad you have the rest of the team there, too. Word starts to spread quickly, and you'll need everyone to keep control over the narrative."

"Given that we're talking about the death of a DEA agent, especially in that manner, yeah, it's gonna be a circus soon enough." Fisher glanced at his phone as a call rang through. "Speaking of Reid...Hang on, would you?"

Nick grabbed his phone while Fisher took the call. He began scrolling through his email, wondering if Unit Chief Cole had contacted him. He hadn't yet made his decision, and he knew Cole wanted him to stay in D.C. Part of him hoped Kate would tell him to take the job at the WFO. Instead, she'd left it up to him, meaning, he was truly on his own now.

"No, that's good news," Fisher said. "We'll head back to the office now. See you in about thirty minutes." He ended the call, a hint of a grin on his lips.

"The lab?" Nick asked.

"Dr. Bailey wants me to come check out her findings. Thinks she got a hit on an identity." He licked his lips, hesitating only a moment. "Listen, I know it's getting a little late, but I wouldn't mind your thoughts on this...if you have the time."

Nick chuckled. "Cam, I got nothing but time right now."

Fisher raised his hand for the bill. Soon, the server arrived, and he paid the tab.

"You didn't have to buy me dinner."

"Sure I did," Fisher replied. "Besides, it's on the Bureau's dime." He smiled, slipping out of the booth.

Nick trailed him outside as night blanketed the city. The brisk air reminded him that he'd forgotten an overcoat. But then, he didn't think he'd be spending so much time with Fisher today. Not that he was complaining because it felt pretty damn good.

Since all this had happened, he'd wondered whether Fisher and the others, especially Walsh, would ever forgive him. Walsh had been there for Kate that night she lost the baby. The same night of his accident. And while it was still too much to think about, he would enjoy this moment, participating in his life once again.

They drove back to Quantico, heading straight for the Forensics Anthropology lab.

Inside, Dr. Bailey greeted them. "Thanks for coming back after hours." She shook Fisher's hand.

For a moment, Nick thought he saw something in Bailey's gaze, a spark of attraction for his former colleague. He looked at Fisher, but he seemed oblivious.

"Show us what you found." Fisher jerked his thumb at Nick. "You don't mind Agent Scarborough tagging along again."

He'd posed it more as a statement, rather than a question, which Nick appreciated.

"Fine by me," Bailey replied. "The more eyes, the better. Come on back." She waved them back.

Nick shot Fisher a sideways glance, catching him eyeing the doctor. Maybe Fisher had picked up on her signal after all. And then, for a moment, it was as though nothing had changed. That this was where he was supposed to be.

He missed all of them. They'd been through a lot together and he'd chosen to leave so that Kate could find her own success, knowing he had been a shadow over her shoulder. Yeah, Noah Quinn might've had something to do with it, too, but he would soak this in while it lasted.

Dr. Bailey approached one of the tables where bones still lay. "We just got back our composite reconstruction of the facial features on this skull." She held a tablet, and after tapping the screen a couple of times, aimed it at Fisher. "This young woman appears to have a twin, according to facial recognition data. DNA will, of course, confirm, but I'd say we found her family."

Nick hovered over Fisher's shoulder to see the screen. "Is the twin still alive?"

Bailey tapped on the screen again. "This is what we found."

"Sandra Dawes," Fisher said. "Last known address... Camdenton."

"Who is she?" Nick asked. "Any idea?"

Fisher took hold of the tablet, studying it closely. "No."

~

KATE FOLLOWED McDaniel and Surrey as they headed back toward the car. Her phone rang and she eyed the caller ID. Coming to a stop, she answered. "Reid, here."

It seemed Surrey noticed and dropped back, now standing beside her.

"Where are you?" Fisher asked.

"On the dock where Draker was last seen. We were just about to head back to the station."

"The lab identified one of the victims," he added. "They tracked down family based on facial recognition. Now, we have a name."

Kate shot a glance at Surrey. "Who is it? Who'd they ID?"

"A young woman who'd gone missing and was presumed to be one of those killed by Everett Knapp. Her name was Ashley Holland."

Kate searched her thoughts, trying to recall that name. "Ashley Holland. It doesn't ring a bell."

"What about the name Sandra Dawes? Formerly Holland," Fisher continued.

Her brow raised. "Sandra Dawes?"

At this, Surrey's interest appeared to grow. He snapped his

fingers to garner McDaniel's attention. The agent turned around and walked back to them.

"Married to Timothy Dawes. Her twin sister, Ashley—"

"Twin?" Kate asked. "Sandra Dawes lost her twin? Why didn't she mention this to me?"

"You talked to her?" Fisher pressed. "When?"

"Earlier today." A frightening revelation knotted Kate's gut. "Her husband was just found murdered, left to drown in the lake after being stabbed, hands and feet bound."

"Jesus," Fisher replied. "You'd better track her down because you're going to need to talk to her again."

"Yeah, I will. We'll get back in touch with you soon. Thanks, Cam. Bye." Stunned, Kate ended the call, pocketing her phone again.

"What's going on?" McDaniel asked, not privy to the other end of the conversation.

"Our lab identified a victim," she began. "A missing woman named Ashley Holland."

"Okay." He put his hands on his hips, appearing to anticipate more news.

"She has a twin and that twin's name is Sandra Dawes." Kate eyed him. "Mrs. Dawes never said a word of this to me. Why do you think that is?"

"She must not have believed it to be relevant to her husband's murder," Surrey replied. "Not sure how that's possible."

McDaniel narrowed his gaze. "You believe her husband's death is connected to her sister's?"

Kate raised a shoulder, trying to fit this new piece in the puzzle. "If it isn't, then it's one hell of a coincidence. And I think we've had enough of those now. Her sister's killed, then years later, her husband?" She marched back to the car. "We need to get in touch with her and give her the news. If their parents are still alive, then we need to talk to them, too." Kate stopped and turned back as she reached the car. Surrey and McDaniel trailed a few steps. "And you said talking to her was a waste of time."

McDaniel reached for his keys, unlocking the doors. "I stand corrected."

~

THE NOTION that the murder of DEA Agent Draker was committed by someone who must've known Knapp still played in Kate's mind. Knapp had been convicted of murder in the disappearance of several other victims, including Ashley Holland. And he'd been convicted without anyone ever having discovered a body. According to the files, DNA evidence from one of the missing had been found inside Knapp's truck.

A tenuous conviction to be sure, but the man admitted his crimes, so there was that. There now appear to be ties to this community that ran deeper than Kate had expected. And the only way to learn more was to speak with the killer's daughter, who had moved away after her father's sentencing.

On their return to the station, Kate pulled Surrey aside. McDaniel regarded them a moment and she raised her hand. "We'll be right behind you."

McDaniel shrugged and continued inside. When he fell out of earshot, Kate began, "I want to talk to the killer's daughter. She lives about an hour from here."

"When? Now?" Surrey asked. "After what we just learned about Dawes? We have to talk to her."

"We do, yes, but I feel like this has to be addressed before we go down this road with Dawes." Kate tossed a glance at the entrance. "I have some time. It's late now, but McDaniel is still going to have to get in contact with Holland's parents and Sandra

Dawes. He'll want files sent over from the lab before he does anything, wanting to see this for himself. I can go first thing in the morning and be back before all this gets out."

Surrey took a defensive step back. "I get you feel the need to do this, but identifying this woman is the best thing to happen for us since we arrived. We can't let this lead go cold."

"It won't." Frustration tightened her chest. "Look, one thing we know for certain, is that Draker was killed by someone with intimate knowledge of the original murders." She didn't want to pull rank, but if he didn't...

"You're right," he said. "You were right about a connection to Dawes' husband, and you're right about this." Surrey peered through the double glass doors. "It is late, and it will take time for McDaniel to put all this together. So, do what you have to do. Just...don't take too long. Come on, he's waiting for us."

She smiled. "I'll set it up for first thing in the morning."

⁓

KATE SAT IN THE CAR, peering at the hotel still shadowed by the early morning sun. An overwhelming desire to call Nick gripped her. It had become a habit that proved hard to break. They often bounced ideas off one another during an investigation. She missed that about him. She missed a lot of things about him.

The meeting had been set. A reluctant Jill Graves, daughter of Everette Knapp, had agreed to see Kate this morning after a call last night. She'd gotten a chilly response, which wasn't unexpected.

Kate knew first-hand how a past always seemed to creep into the present. To say nothing of the fact she had been hounded for years by reporters, publishers, all of the above, to talk about her experience with the serial killer, Joseph Hendrickson. Even her friend, Marc Aguilera, now a big-time news anchor, wanted to write her story. So, for the daughter of Everett Knapp, she understood the woman's reluctance.

Kate headed out for the hour-long drive amid a backdrop of sunshine and tall, barren trees that lined the highway. Would the daughter open up about her father? That depended on the type of relationship this woman had had with him.

Knapp was fifty-five at the time of his death. Relatively old for a serial killer, but not unheard-of. Meaning he would've been in his late forties at the time of the murders. And from what Kate had read, he'd owned one of the bait shops along the lake. Popular with tourists, no doubt.

She wondered what kind of person the daughter, Jill Graves, was and how she would react to Kate's questions about her father. As a profiler, Kate knew that the children of serial killers often struggled with complex emotions - love, shame, denial. She hoped that Jill would speak with her openly.

The Graves' home appeared ahead; the drive having passed by in a blur. It was a modest bungalow set back from the road. Shrubs lined the front of the house, some still green, some only bare branches. The grass was still green, though, and neatly trimmed.

Kate pulled onto the driveway, behind another car, and sat for a moment, preparing herself. Then she walked up to the front door and knocked. After a moment, Kate heard footsteps approach, and the door opened a crack. A petite woman with short brown hair peered out.

"Jill Graves?" Kate displayed her credentials. "We spoke on the phone last night. I'm Special Agent Kate Reid."

The woman hesitated, clearly conflicted, but then opened the door wider. "You might as well come in, then."

Kate followed her inside to a small, but neat and clean living room. Muted, earthy colors, contemporary and stylish. Jill perched on the edge of an armchair, standoffish, while she gestured for Kate to sit on the couch. No offers of water or coffee. No pleasantries of any kind were exchanged.

This wasn't going to be easy, so Kate took a deep breath and gathered her thoughts. "First of all, thank you for agreeing to meet with me on short notice. I'm not immune to the specifics of your situation, and I know bringing up the past is never easy." She shifted her weight. "As I mentioned on the phone, the remains of several bodies were pulled out of the Lake of the Ozarks over a week ago. No doubt, you heard about it on the news." Kate waited for a response, but none came. "Right now, it's believed they could be the victims of Everett Knapp...your father. But in addition to that, another, much more recent victim, was also discovered. A DEA agent...found in exactly the same location, murdered in the same manner as the others. So, I'd like to talk to you about your father's time in prison, and who he had been in contact with at the time."

Jill stared down at her hands, twisting a tissue between her fingers. She couldn't have been older than thirty, thirty-five maybe. No ring on her finger. No signs of children Kate could see. "I haven't spoken about him in years. After he was arrested, my mother and I moved away and tried to start over. New town, new names."

Kate nodded. "I understand—more than you know. As I said, I'm primarily interested in who might've visited him in prison. Or maybe even a cellmate. Because the thing is, the DEA agent? The similarities are too great to ignore. The killer seems to be copying details from your father's murders."

Jill raised her eyes to meet Kate's gaze, pain and uncertainty etched on her face. "You have to understand when I knew him, he was just my dad. He took me camping, taught me how to fish. I had no idea..." Her voice broke.

Kate leaned forward on the sofa. "I want you to know that I'm not here to judge you or your father. I simply need some information to help with an ongoing investigation."

Jill nodded, her eyes downcast, her narrow shoulders slumping. "Honestly, I don't know much. Dad never confessed anything to me directly. All I know is what came out at the trial." She lifted her eyes to Kate's. "But I can tell you this. My father was not a violent man. He never raised a hand to me or my mother. The man they say committed those murders...that wasn't the man I knew."

"But he confessed," Kate said.

She scoffed. "You want to know why he confessed, Agent Reid? That so-called DNA evidence they found in his truck? Let me tell you where that came from." Jill displayed a renewed conviction. "My dad owned a bait store on the lake, not far from one of the launch ramps. Do you have any idea how many idiot tourists bottomed out their vehicles at that ramp? Got them stuck or whatever bullshit it was that happened with their boats? They'd go inside the store and ask my dad for help."

Kate shook her head.

"A lot, and I mean a lot of people asked for his help," Jill continued. "My dad had to use his own truck more times than I can count to bail out those idiots. So, when you say DNA evidence was found inside it, it's because he helped so many people. They didn't say blood evidence, did they? No," she answered before Kate had a chance to respond. "It was hair, skin, whatever. But not blood."

"That doesn't explain why he would admit to killing anyone, though," Kate pressed.

Jill leaned back on the edge of that armchair, a smirk on her lips. "Because he didn't want it to affect us...me and my mom. The shop shuttered within weeks of the charges being filed. No one wanted to go near him. And the cops...they had to keep the lake safe for the tourists and their dollars, so they hounded him. Hounded all of us. And eventually, they broke him."

Kate had seen this before...a child in denial of the crimes a parent committed. Especially crimes as heinous as murder. And while Jill seemed entirely convinced of her father's innocence, the prosecutor likely had more evidence, outside of DNA, to help prove his case. And a jury did convict him. Still, this was a distraction from why she was really here.

Someone knew where those bodies were, adding Agent Draker to the pile. So was it someone who knew Knapp from prison? Or, if he was innocent, was it the true killer?

10

Everett Knapp's daughter had made a compelling argument but didn't provide the answers Kate needed. Not entirely. Now, her only option was to pull prison records and more background information on Knapp to learn who was in his circle. Or who else could have known where to dump Draker's body after cutting him up with the same type of saw used on the other victims.

She returned to the station, still early enough not to have missed much. More still awaited, now that a victim had been identified. This was a step in the right direction and one that might mean more than her Knapp side quest. Time will tell.

Inside, Walsh caught her attention, and she headed toward him. "Hey. What'd I miss?"

He regarded her. "Nothing yet. McDaniel and Lieutenant Crawford are in with Mr. and Mrs. Holland, Ashely's parents."

"He tracked them down, then," Kate replied, looking into the hall. "How long have they been back there?"

"Not long," Duncan said, making her way over. "It took a while to get the parents to come down."

"Why is that?" Kate asked.

"Guess they needed convincing that what McDaniel had to say was true," Walsh replied. "Their daughter has been missing for years, so their hesitation is understandable."

"I can't imagine how that news went over." Kate looked at the team, eyeing Surrey as he joined them. "I met with Jill Graves, Knapp's daughter."

"How'd that go?" Walsh asked.

"She talked, which was better than I could've hoped." Kate perched on the edge of a desk. "She doesn't believe her father killed anyone."

"Denial?" Surrey asked.

Kate knitted her brow with a gentle shake of her head. "Maybe. But she made a good argument. One I would've hoped Knapp's defense attorney had also made at the time. In the end, though, I feel like she had come to terms with his incarceration, even though she never believed he was guilty." She tilted her head. "Did McDaniel contact Sandra Dawes yet?"

"Not that I'm aware of," Walsh replied. "I think he was waiting to tell the parents first. My guess is, the parents will reach out to their other daughter."

"I can't imagine losing a sibling," Duncan began. "Let alone a twin." She walked over to her laptop bag and reached inside. "Before I forget, I wanted to get your take on this." She retrieved a file and carried it back, handing it to Kate.

"What is it?"

"While you were out, I had a chance to listen to some of the audio recordings of the interview these guys here had with Everett Knapp when he was first arrested." She aimed her finger at the file. "You might want to listen to them. The flash drive's inside."

Kate opened the manilla folder. "Can you give me the abridged version?"

"Let's just say that Knapp's daughter, Jill Graves..." Duncan shook her head. "She's wrong about her dad. This guy did it. And if you listen to the recordings, you'll hear it too."

"Thanks. I will." Kate turned around at the sound of voices behind them. McDaniel, Crawford, and an older couple emerged. "Looks like they're finished."

McDaniel led Mr. and Mrs. Holland out of the interview room, his arm gently guiding the mother, who appeared distraught and unsteady on her feet. Her husband had his arm around her shoulders, his face stoic but eyes red-rimmed behind his glasses.

"I hope this offers closure for you after all these years," McDaniel said.

Mrs. Holland sniffed, dabbing her eyes with a tissue. "I just can't believe it. Our baby girl, after all this time..." Her voice broke off in a sob.

"We're very grateful that her remains were finally found," Mr. Holland added, his voice thick with emotion. "At least now we can lay her to rest."

As they reached the bullpen, McDaniel made eye contact with Kate, giving her a subtle nod.

She offered a gentle, but tight-lipped smile in return.

After he led the parents outside, he said something to Crawford before the two parted ways. He then made his way back to the team. Pushing a hand through his thick brown hair, McDaniel sighed. "They took that about as well as could be expected."

"Did you tell them how we found the remains?" Surrey asked.

He shook his head. "Just that we had recovered them, and that the FBI was certain they belonged to Ashley. I figured we could spare them the grisly details for now."

"Have you notified Sandra Dawes yet?" Kate asked.

"They said they wanted to tell her, and I didn't fight them on it. I also made no mention of Tim Dawes. I wasn't sure their daughter said anything, and for now, it's being handled by the local guys."

Kate glanced through the window into the parking lot, where the couple had just stepped into their car. "They clearly didn't know about their son-in-law, then. If they had, they'd have told you."

McDaniel crossed his arms. "Apparently, they're estranged from Sandra. Said they hadn't spoken to her in years, not since their other daughter went missing, or shortly thereafter."

One of the local law enforcement officers must've overheard the conversation as he moved in. "Pardon the interruption, but those folks who just walked out of here?" He aimed his finger ahead. "They're drug traffickers. Running this area for the last few years. Fact is, everyone knows it, but no one's been able to prove it yet. I been here for years. Long before the Knapp killings. The Hollands were a good family once, but then it all went to shit after Ashley went missing. Figured that was what drove them to the dark side, you know? They spent all their time searching for the truth. Ran out of money. Lost their jobs. Guess this was their solution."

Kate turned a curious eye to McDaniel. "Did you know this? Or maybe Draker did?"

"Believe me, when we began this investigation, they were at the top of our list," he replied. "But it had since been put in the rearview. Draker and I kept our focus on a cartel connection we uncovered after a bust last year in Kansas City. That was how I got involved. And, needless to say, I didn't bring it up after telling them we found their daughter's remains."

Kate glanced at the officer, who still appeared interested in their conversation. He shrugged and pursed his lips. So who was she to believe? The local authorities or a trained federal agent and his DEA partner? "That could explain why Sandra doesn't speak to them," she said. "Maybe she believes they are drug dealers. Thank you for the information, Officer."

"Anytime." He walked back to his desk.

As he walked away, Kate set her sights on the team. "So, how long do we wait to talk to Sandra Dawes ourselves?"

∽

THE WEIGHT of it all bore down on Sandra. From the driver's seat, she peered out at the school her daughters attended. She still hadn't told them about their father, pretending nothing had happened and telling the children he'd simply been away on business.

They deserved better. She couldn't put it off any longer. And she would have to tell Tim's parents. Her own as well, though she hadn't spoken to them in years. After her twin sister, Ashley went missing, Sandra had pulled away from them. Then they became criminals. As far as she was concerned, Henry and Jean Holland no longer existed.

The bell rang. School was letting out. Her daughters were in first and third grades. Sandra loved them more than life. Now, she was about to break their hearts.

There they were, running down the sidewalk toward her Toyota, smiles as wide as can be. As the girls climbed inside, Sandra peered over her shoulder at them. "Everyone have a good day?"

"Yeah," they replied in unison.

"Good. Buckle up then." Sandra began to pull away from the pick-up curb when a woman approached, waving her hands. But this wasn't just any woman. "Oh my God."

"Mommy?" Marissa asked from the backseat. The seven-year-old stared through the window.

"It's okay, honey. Just hang on a second."

Ella was nine. A little older. A little wiser than her sister. She'd held her tongue.

The older woman moved in, reaching the driver's side. Sandra rolled down the window. "Mom, what are you doing here?"

Jean Holland was in her early sixties but appeared much older. Overweight. Almost completely gray on top. Sandra hardly recognized her, but she'd seen that look in her eyes before. And that was what really concerned her.

"I need to talk to you. It's about Ashley."

Sandra glanced back at the girls before pulling over into the nearby parking lot. "I need to step out a moment, okay? Just hang tight. I won't be long." She climbed out of the SUV, walking a few steps away from the vehicle, her mother catching up. "What about Ashley? And why didn't you call me first?" She thrust out her hand. "You just show up at my daughters' school unannounced? This isn't a good time."

Jean peered into the backseat of the SUV, noticing her grand-daughters. "They've grown so much."

"What do you want to say, Mom? I have to go home."

Jean turned back to her with reddened eyes. "The police called this morning. They found her remains. Pulled them out of the lake along with several others. You must've heard about all that on the news?" She seemed to wait for a response but soon went on. "Your father and I went down to the station and saw the renderings and the bones. I guess they're in Washington D.C. at some FBI lab. Anyway, the people there, they're sure it's Ashley."

Sandra felt her stomach churn. She took a deep breath to steady herself. "After all these years..."

Jean nodded, tears welling in her eyes. "I know. It's...it's almost too much to take in."

The two women stood in silence for a moment, the pain and grief over Ashley's death suddenly feeling, for Sandra, fresh and raw once again.

"The agent said they're still investigating what happened," Jean continued. "He wouldn't give us any real details. They do think they were Knapp's victims. Some kind of...burial site."

"Agent? As in the FBI?" Sandra shook her head. "We already believed it was Knapp. Does that mean they found all his victims? Jacob, too?"

"Like I said, the agent didn't tell us much else. But from what I gather, this discovery was prompted by the murder of some DEA agent," Jean replied.

Sandra crossed her arms, her expression darkening. "DEA? And you had no idea about any of that?"

"No. Of course not." Jean stepped back in disbelief. "This is the closure we needed, Sandy."

"Closure won't bring back my sister," she replied. "Nothing will." Was this the time to tell her about Tim? All of this seemed far too coincidental. It was all happening at once. And to see her mother again...it was too much to take.

"Listen, I have to go. I'm sorry." Sandra stepped back into her SUV and drove away. Glancing into the rearview mirror, her mother stood frozen, shock masking her face.

She couldn't tell her about Tim. She wasn't even sure her mother would care. Their strained relationship hadn't changed much since Ashley's disappearance. But with Tim gone now too, what family did she have left?

Sandra glanced at her daughters, busily playing games with each other in the backseat. They were close, much like she had been with her sister. Twins were always close, she supposed. And when Ashely disappeared, it felt like someone had cut her in half.

Ashley was young, both of them still in their twenties when it had happened. So much life left to live. They'd always talked about how when they got older and got married, they'd raise their kids together. Maybe even live next door to each other.

Overwhelmed by heartbreak after losing Tim and now this, Sandra needed to unload. And while her suspicions remained, Dr. Fuller would want to know about Ashley. Maybe she'd overreacted and their running into each other—twice—was just a coincidence.

With no one left to turn to, she picked up her phone. "Dr. Fuller, it's Sandra Dawes. I don't suppose you could fit me in today, could you? I'm really struggling. I got some news and I just...I need to talk."

"I'll clear my schedule. Can you come in now?" he asked.

A wave of relief swelled in her chest. "Yes, of course. Thank you so much." She glanced back at her girls. "Uh, can I bring the girls? I have no one to look after them right now."

"Of course. There's plenty for them to do in the waiting area while we talk. Come in now, Sandra. I'm here for you."

She ended the call, gripping the steering wheel with both hands. A glance into the rearview and she saw Ella, brow pulled tight.

"Are you okay, Mom?" she asked.

Her lips trembled, but she quickly swallowed her emotions. "Yeah, course I am. We just need to stop nearby where I have an appointment. You two can wait in the lobby while I go inside."

"Okay," Ella replied, appearing hesitant.

Sandra arrived at Fuller's home, the weight of grief and anxiety heavy on her shoulders. The once comforting familiarity of the hallway leading to his office now seemed to carry an undercurrent of unease. The walls, lined with diplomas and accolades, seemed to close in on her a little more than usual.

Dr. Fuller greeted her at the door with his usual warm smile. "Sandra, please come in and have a seat," he said, his voice steady as always.

Sandra looked back at the girls. "Why don't you both go over there? I see some coloring books and crayons on that table."

"Where are you going?" Ella asked while Marissa marched toward the table.

"I'm going to speak with Dr. Fuller." Sandra raised her brow. "Look after your sister?"

Ella nodded before walking to join Marissa.

Sandra walked on, entering Fuller's office, and taking a seat on the old leather sofa across from his chair. "Thank you for fitting me in," Sandra began, her words tumbling out in a rush. "I saw my mother today for the first time in years. She...she told me the police recovered my sister's remains from the lake." Sandra swallowed hard, trying to keep her emotions in check. "I just really needed to talk to you because I knew that you, of all people, would understand."

Dr. Fuller nodded, his expression neutral as he leaned back in his chair. "Of course. I'm glad you felt you could come to me." His tone was gentle but there was an edge to it that Sandra hadn't heard before, though she suspected the reason for it.

"You've had much to deal with lately. I can't imagine your state of mind at the moment," he continued. "Tell me what happened."

She relayed the events as they had unfolded, though Fuller seemed to wear a strange detachment. He looked through her as if his thoughts were elsewhere. "Dr. Fuller, the FBI, they talked to me, too—about Tim."

"I see." He jotted in his notepad. "Why is that? Seems to me a little outside their jurisdiction."

"They think...I guess they think it's all related to the remains they found in the lake. And it happened to include those of my sister." Sandra let her eyes roam over his shoulder to his desk, landing on the framed photograph that had always been there but was now turned around. She remembered it well—a snapshot of a happier time featuring Dr. Fuller's son.

"Jacob..." Her voice trailed off as she considered the implications. "What if they found his remains with Ashley's?" The question hung in the air between them like a dark cloud, casting a shadow over their conversation and adding another layer to an already complicated situation. "Since they were together that night," she went on. "Do you think it's possible?"

～

Jean Holland returned to the home she shared with her husband, Henry. A sturdy farmhouse nestled inside a three-acre ranch on the outskirts of Linn Creek. Married for forty long years, they had weathered countless storms together. But nothing, absolutely nothing, could have prepared them for the day they were told their daughter, Ashley, had disappeared into thin air. That day, their world had been upended in ways they never imagined possible.

Jean walked into the rustic ranch house, a cool draft whispering past her as she stepped inside. The familiar creak of the door echoed behind her as she closed it. "Henry, I'm back," she called out into the semi-darkness.

From the shadowy depths of their home, Henry emerged. He ambled across the red brick floor of the foyer, his heavy footsteps echoing against the walls. A robust man in his sixties with a full head of graying hair, he had a round face etched with deep lines. "You tell her?" he asked, his voice gruff with concern.

She nodded, her eyes reflecting a pool of unshed tears. "She didn't want to stick around and talk, so I guess we're back where we started."

He placed his hand on her shoulder. "Did you think she'd suddenly come round after hearing they found her?"

Jean hung her coat over the hook near the doorway and set down her car keys on the table. The metallic clink echoed through the silent house. "No," she admitted, "But I s'pose I thought she might want to know more about it. More about...the other remains they found."

"We don't know anything about what else they found," Henry said. "Except for that fed."

Jean walked toward their cozy kitchen with dark cabinetry and stone countertops. She opened one of the cabinets and retrieved a glass, placing it under the fridge's water dispenser. The sound filled the silence between them. "Which reminds me...we need to get rid of that phone."

"Whose?" Henry asked, feigning ignorance.

Jean shot him a look that was as familiar as the lines on his face. "Wayne's. Who else could I possibly be talking about?"

Henry nodded, creasing his brow. "You think they'll come looking for him next?"

"If they do." She took a sip of her water, its coolness doing nothing to quench the burning questions in her mind. "We best not have anything tying him to us."

11

The first two days in the Ozarks hadn't amounted to much. The team was divided on the best approach to the Dawes situation, not wanting to lose sight of their original purpose. Kate needed more to convince them it went hand in hand, as far as she was concerned.

She had no better idea than when they arrived who might've wanted the agent dead. And was willing to go through the lengths they had to send him where other bodies had also been found.

What Agent McDaniel wanted, though, was something she hadn't yet completed. It was too early to have compiled a thorough profile of the person he was after because too many things had failed to yet align. And the death of the DEA agent suggested he'd learned something he shouldn't have. He was not, as Kate believed, an intended target of the killer.

But that brought up another point. Everett Knapp. His daughter had defended him, but there was more to this and so Kate had to discover who'd been to see Knapp before his death. If nothing else, ruling out any of his connections was paramount to narrowing down an unsub's profile.

As the sun lowered in the sky, shadows filled the bullpen inside the stationhouse. Walsh stood up from one of the desks. "Might be best to clock out. Nothing more any of us can do tonight."

Kate turned away from the case board, the photographs and notes pinned to it still snaking through her mind. "Anyone seen McDaniel?"

Walsh tossed a nod. "Think he's with the Coast Guard lieutenant in the captain's office." He cocked his head. "You know, I was talking with the lieutenant. He was part of the original Knapp investigation."

Kate meandered toward him. "Really? Why didn't he mention it before?"

"He did...to me. You were out talking to Knapp's daughter. Anyway, I figure we ought to spend some time with him...away from McDaniel."

She peered at the rest of the team, who'd begun packing up for the night. "Why away from him?"

"Well, for one thing, Crawford lives here. He knows the history better than McDaniel." Walsh shrugged. "I don't know, but I think if we want the truth about this place. About the lake and the people around here...he's probably the one to go to."

She regarded him a moment, considering his plan. "Why do I have a feeling you think McDaniel might be keeping something from us?"

Walsh tossed a nod to Surrey and Duncan. "Because those two, over there? They see it too."

∽

DR. SHANE FULLER stepped out of his car, scanning his surroundings. Darkness had blanketed the quaint neighborhood in which he stood. Shadows crossed behind veiled windows in the homes of people who'd begun to settle in for the night. This was Sandra's neighborhood, and he assumed, she'd returned home to her daughters.

She'd left his office earlier today, consumed by grief about her husband and grappling with the knowledge about her sister's recovered remains. And her words to him... about his son...

He'd stopped thinking about Jacob long ago. Stopped trying to figure out what had happened and why. Yet he'd fed off Sandra's pain. Lived for it. And looking at her was just like looking at Ashley.

Amid the ambiance of the restaurant, glasses and silverware clattering, muffled voices drifting around, Shane Fuller drew the attention of his family. "I'd like to say how nice it is to have dinner with my son and his new girlfriend, Ashley." He raised his glass of wine. "Jacob, your mother and I can see how happy you are with her, and we couldn't be more grateful to have her with us here tonight. Cheers."

Jacob and Ashley exchanged a glance and a smile while Shane and Janice Fuller looked on with glasses raised.

"Thank you for inviting me, Dr. Fuller. Mrs. Fuller," Ashley replied. "It's wonderful to see where Jacob gets his personality from."

Fuller captured her gaze, and a spark ignited in him. She was beautiful. Strawberry-blond hair, hazel eyes. Freckles across the bridge of her nose. He was sure he saw the spark in her too. It was evident in her smile.

Jacob couldn't possibly know how to treat a woman like Ashley. He was just a boy, and she deserved a man. A successful doctor.

"You'll excuse me a moment?" Ashley pushed out her chair. "I need to use the restroom."

"Of course," Jacob replied.

He watched her leave, the elder Fuller, his eyes lingering on her slender figure and taut backside. "Come to think of it, I could use a pitstop." He excused himself and headed toward the back where the restrooms were located.

Entering the hall, he realized Ashley had already disappeared into the ladies' room. He waited outside, doing his best not to appear like a creepy lurker. A few minutes later, the door opened, and there she was.

"Oh, Dr. Fuller, hello," Ashley said, mild surprise on her face.

"Thought I'd take a break, myself," he replied. And then he grasped her shoulder, squeezing just a little. "It really is a pleasure having you join us tonight, Ashley. Jacob adores you."

"Thank you, sir. I feel the same," she replied, her cheeks turning slightly pink.

A man entered the hall and eyed Fuller. "Excuse me, sir." He slipped behind him, forcing Fuller a few steps closer to Ashley. His hand still clung to her arm. They stood just inches apart, and he felt heat rise in his groin.

"I-uh-I should probably get back," Ashley said, looking uncomfortable now.

"Yes, of course. I'll see you in a minute." He rubbed her arm, forcing her to hold his gaze until finally, she broke away.

THE RUMORS about the Hollands were nothing new. Everyone had suspected they'd made money from the drug trade after Ashley disappeared. An ever-expanding problem here where tourists, flush with cash, abounded. But Sandra never wanted to talk about them. Never wanted to talk about Ashley.

Fuller walked along the sidewalk, buttoning his coat to ward off the chilly air. Amber streetlights illuminated the tree-lined street. He'd parked two blocks away from Sandra's home, knowing that another coincidental sighting would set her on high alert.

To bump into her at the pharmacy and then at the grocery store was one thing. But to bump into her in her very own neighborhood was just asking for trouble. Still, he had to see her. He had to know what she was doing. She was alone now, just like him. Vulnerable. No one left to turn to.

As he approached Sandra's house, Fuller felt a rush of anticipation. Slipping into the shadows, he crept up to her living room window, the curtains, still partly open. Inside, Sandra sat curled up on the couch, clutching a blanket around herself. He could only see her from behind. Her beautiful, tousled strawberry-blond hair rested on her shoulders.

From where he stood, seeing the blanket pulled up to her neck, she appeared fragile. Pained. It nourished him. He imagined going inside, taking her in his arms, comforting her. The thought of having her so vulnerable and dependent on him felt exhilarating.

But he restrained himself. He had to be patient. She'd first come to see him six months ago. The strains of her marriage had been quite evident. Of course, she knew who he was, and that Jacob had dated Ashley, albeit briefly as their lives were cut short.

Not since the funerals, empty caskets and all, had Fuller seen Sandra, or her parents. That was years ago now. But he'd kept tabs on her. Knew where her daughters attended school. Watched as her husband worked long hours, leaving his family exposed, and unprotected. But Fuller had always protected Sandra, even now.

He'd suspected that Sandra's eventual decision to seek out help from him made her feel closer to her sister, keeping her memory alive. Though it had been years since her sister went missing, Sandra's outreach was unexpected and welcomed. Almost as if she'd felt a pull toward him. Much in the same way he was sure Ashley had too. He felt it in Ashley's gaze. Often lingering on him when Jacob wasn't looking.

Only in their early sessions had Sandra spoken of Ashley, steering clear of any mention of Jacob. It was the elephant in the room—that connection between them—and unavoidable. But as time went on, the truth about Sandra's marriage began to come to light. Tim Dawes was a good man, but distant, at least, as far as Sandra was concerned. It got especially difficult as their kids demanded more of her time. Sports, and other interests they'd had, becoming all too consuming.

In that time, he'd come to appreciate Sandra, maybe more so than Ashley. Now, he couldn't imagine life without her and wondered how things would change between them with her husband now gone. Her sister's remains, well, that was another issue altogether.

As he peered through the window, he saw Sandra's suffering as exquisite, but he wanted more. However, pieces still needed to be maneuvered into place. So, for now, he would have to be content with small violations, these furtive visits that allowed him to witness her pain.

Turning from the window, Fuller melted back into the shadows, walking the two blocks back to his car. Stepping inside, he quickly drove away from the neighborhood, soon returning home.

Upon entering his house—the silent, cold place it had become since losing his only son—he sat at his kitchen table. His wife, unable to cope with the loss, had left him too.

Fuller was completely alone, not unlike Sandra now. And all he needed to do was be there for her, taking care not to overstep his bounds regardless of his desire to do so.

With Ashley's remains finally discovered, maybe his son's would be next. And then, he and Sandra would be bonded forever.

~

Levi Walsh was a good judge of character. Maybe that was why he and Kate got along so well. He offset her sometimes rash judgments. So when he suggested pulling aside Lieutenant Crawford to talk to him, it was because he thought McDaniel had his own agenda. That the man seemed to be working hard to keep his ass out of a sling after his partner was killed.

Either way, Kate agreed. "All right, let's grab dinner with him tonight. See what he has to say about Knapp and this current investigation."

Crawford had emerged from the captain's office. McDaniel wasn't far behind. The two walked out in silence, barely acknowledging one another.

McDaniel made his way over to Kate and the others. "Listen, I'm heading out for the night. What's your plan?"

Surrey stepped forward. "Just heading back to the hotel. Reading up on more of the files."

"I'm holed up at the Holiday Inn. Bureau's stipend." McDaniel shrugged. "What can you do? Anyway, you know how to reach me."

"Sure thing," Kate replied.

McDaniel started away but stopped and turned back. "Have a good night." He pushed through the exit and fell out of view.

Crawford approached them, the broad-chested man, who walked with a slight swagger. "I know he seems a little curt, but the captain had his ASAC on the phone, gave him an ass-chewing. Can't blame the guy. DEA SAC Kleman is hounding him too, so there's that."

Kate studied him. "You don't seem on edge."

"Wasn't one of mine who went down, but I guess, you know, I've been around this a while," Crawford replied.

Walsh stepped in. "I mentioned to these guys you were on the original Knapp case."

"And we've been talking," Duncan chimed in as she approached. "Wouldn't mind sitting down with you over a bite to eat and picking your brain."

Crawford looked a little surprised. "Yeah, sure. I know a good place not too far from here."

Kate smiled. "All right. Let's go."

The team loaded up in a rented sedan and followed Crawford out of Camdenton and toward the lake. With Surrey behind the wheel, Kate looked out over the darkened parkway. "Why do you think we're here?"

"On this earth or this investigation?" Walsh asked with a chuckle.

Kate peered at him over her shoulder, a grin on her face. "The first one might take too long to answer. Why do you think we're here on this investigation? One where we're supposed to take at face value that the multiple remains found were victims of an already convicted killer."

"Who's dead, by the way," Duncan shot back.

"Exactly."

Surrey glanced at her. "What are you getting at, Reid?"

I don't know, I mean, McDaniel was supposedly on board with us stepping in to develop a profile, but it seems like he doesn't want us to even consider the remains found in the lake. And he's certain Tim Dawes' murder isn't connected."

"I think he just wants to know who took out his partner," Surrey replied. "And given that it happened in a similar manner, hell, maybe he's thinking they had the wrong guy initially, but doesn't want to say as much."

"But he had nothing to do with the Knapp case," Kate said. "Look, do I think there's a serial killer out there and he happened to cross paths with the DEA agent?" She shrugged. "Maybe. But I sure as hell won't be able to find out if I don't look into Knapp and the people he surrounded himself with."

Walsh pulled forward, grasping onto her seat. "Kate, you do what you need to do to get where you need to get, understand? It's how we do things. Don't let McDaniel, or the pressure he's under, sway you."

"As far as I'm concerned," Duncan jumped in. "Whoever murdered the agent, knew who murdered the other victims. All signs point to that, so that's where we need to go."

"Yeah," Kate nodded.

"We're here." Surrey turned into the parking lot behind Crawford.

The local spot they arrived at sat on the banks of the lake with a large deck jutting out into the water. Place was practically empty, and Kate figured it was probably one of only a handful of spots open this time of year.

Outdoor tables dotted around the expansive decking, offering a view that would probably be spectacular were it not pitch-black outside. A small stage in the corner of the deck suggested that they offered live music during the tourist season. It must've been hopping here in the summer.

They joined Crawford near the entrance.

He opened the door. "Hope this place is good with you folks. They have phenomenal ribs here."

"Sounds good to me," Walsh said, following him inside.

Kate took in the surroundings. Tables were scattered around. Pictures lined the walls depicting the history of the Lake of the Ozarks. The smell of burgers, fries, and barbeque infused the dining area.

They were seated at a large round table near the far end of the restaurant. It wasn't busy, but Kate imagined what it must've looked like during the summer months with all the visitors.

"So how long have you been with the Coast Guard?" she asked, wanting to ease into the conversation.

"About eight years, give or take," Crawford replied, taking a sip of his Coke as the server brought out everyone's drinks. "I grew up here, though, so I remember when this place was under different management. It was smaller. Not as good, if I'm being honest."

"Must've been difficult around a resort town like this when all those folks disappeared without a trace," Walsh noted.

Crawford unfurled his napkin and set it on his lap. "People around here still get spooked thinking about it. Thing is, Knapp was unassuming. Kept to himself. Took everyone by surprise, that's for sure."

He took a long sip from his glass of Coke. "When the first reports of the missing surfaced, people didn't want to believe it was murder. Boating accidents happen all the time around here. But when a third and a fourth person went missing, law enforcement started to think this wasn't boating. This wasn't tourists getting drunk and drowning in the lake."

He shook his head. "I was pretty green in those days. Not many people know the Coast Guard patrols these waters. We were overwhelmed, working around the clock trying to find leads. Working with the Missouri Water Patrol Division, too. But Knapp was meticulous, never left evidence behind, except that DNA in his truck. And he seemed to know the area better than any of us, all the hidden coves and inlets where he could take his victims, later dumping them at the spot where Draker was found."

Surrey leaned forward, seeming intrigued. "How did you eventually catch him?"

"Sheer luck, really," Crawford admitted. "Course, it was a joint effort. Knapp was seen with one of the victims. Then all eyes turned to him, and they searched his truck. Well, all kinds of DNA found its way there. That was all it took. Body or not."

Kate regarded him. "What can you tell us about Knapp that might not be in the official reports? Anything that could give us insight into his psychology or behavior?"

Crawford took a deep breath, glancing around before speaking as if to check for eavesdroppers. "There were things the public never knew, details we kept quiet to avoid panic. Like how he would stalk victims beforehand, learning their routines. The victims' families told us that they'd seen a man lurking around their campsites or hotels shortly before their loved-ones went missing."

Kate nodded. "Was Ashley Holland the only resident who went missing?"

"No, ma'am," Crawford replied. "Her boyfriend did too...Jacob Fuller."

"Knapp maintained his innocence," Crawford continued. "But everyone knew better. The man cleaned fish and sold bait for a living. Knew his way around sharp knives and other such things."

"How did you manage to get a conviction without bodies and only circumstantial DNA?" Surrey asked.

Crawford leaned back in his chair, looking out the window at the shimmering lake for a moment. "That was the hardest part. Not that I had a lick to do with it. As I said, I was a newbie in those days. So, the only forensic evidence tying him to any of it was some fibers found in his truck. Got a match to one of the missing and that was that. We always reckoned that he'd scout isolated areas of the lake, wait for someone vulnerable to be alone, then take them out in his boat. Never to be seen again."

"Did they ever search his boat?" Kate pressed.

"I don't know, but I'm sure they did. Our involvement ended

when they had their suspect. Turned it all over to the local authorities and Missouri Water Patrol to process."

Kate considered his story. It seemed a tenuous investigation, but she supposed she'd seen convictions based on less. "What did his daughter have to say? I assume she was interviewed."

Crawford looked at her. "Don't know. I wasn't privy to that. Like I said, we weren't involved for too long. But it's all in the files."

"Right, yeah, of course." Kate grinned. "I'll take another look."

~

THE DINNER, while it hadn't convinced Kate of anything, had been informative. It certainly seemed like McDaniel didn't want to dredge up the past, keeping focus on who killed his partner. But now, the two events seemed inextricably connected.

As she entered her hotel room, she kicked off her shoes and dropped onto the edge of the bed. It seemed, the more she learned about this investigation, the more convoluted it had become. Tim Dawes' murder still hung in the back of her mind. A coincidence like that seemed anything but.

It would help if the lab finished their job and offered up identities of the victims recovered from the lake. Though, they needed to know about Jacob Fuller, given who he was with when he went missing. Something about that situation still needed to be peeled back.

She checked the time on her phone. It was only ten o'clock, yet it felt so much later. The days were short and the nights long. She felt like there was more she should be doing.

Thoughts of Nick swirled in her mind. How could they not? He had been the biggest part of her life for several years. In all aspects. She wondered whether he'd decided where to go next.

D.C. or L.A. Seemed an obvious choice, but if he'd wanted to start over, L.A. was probably the place for that. And after spending most of her life in San Diego, she could understand the move.

The idea of him being gone, though...her eyes glistened. Yet she was the one who made this decision. Nick had made his choices that night, and she had made hers. But what was left was an emptiness she hadn't felt since losing Marshall.

A part of her wondered why it was that lasting happiness had been so evasive. Either her stubbornness got in the way, or someone else's bullet had. But it was her choice, stepping away from her marriage, and now she had to live with it.

Kate walked into the bathroom to wash her face and prepare for bed. From inside the bathroom, she heard her phone. "Damn it." Her eye squinted at the mirror, her face still covered in cleanser.

She wiped it away with a hand towel and returned to grab her phone from the bedside table. The caller ID was unfamiliar, a string of numbers without a name. A part of her felt mild disappointment it hadn't been Nick, but she swiftly pushed that aside and answered the call. "Agent Reid here."

"Agent Reid, this is Sandra Dawes. We spoke before about my husband?" The voice on the other end was shaky, fear edging into every word.

"Yes, of course." Recognition dawned on Kate as she sat down on the edge of her bed, her mind shifting gears to focus on the conversation. "What can I do for you, Mrs. Dawes?"

"Look, I...I know how this will probably sound," Sandra began. "But I think someone was looking in my house earlier. I'm here alone with my girls and I'm...I'm scared."

"Forgive me, Mrs. Dawes, but have you contacted your local police?"

"No. Uh, I wanted to call you first," she replied.

"Why is that, ma'am?" Kate pressed, knowing there had to be more to this.

"Because I think it could be the person who murdered Tim," Sandra admitted in a hushed whisper. "I think he could be coming for me."

At those words, Kate straightened, pulling back her shoulders in resolve. "Text me your home address. I'll leave now."

12

Kate was never a stickler when it came to protocol, occasionally bending the rules to suit her needs. However, if one was to ask any member of her team, they might suggest she deviated more often than she'd like to admit.

This time, however, gaining the trust of Sandra Dawes was in the best interest of her current investigation. Coming to her aid was part of that.

Kate arrived at the home, a modest two-story in a middle-class neighborhood. Lights shone through every window, as though Sandra was trying to ward off this suspected lurker.

Walking toward the front door, Kate aimed her flashlight at the hedgerow and the trees that bordered her neighbors. If someone had been here, it was likely they were now long gone.

Standing under the porch light, she rang the bell. After a few moments, the locks turned, and the door opened a crack. A sliver of Sandra's face peered out cautiously. Kate offered a reassuring nod and Sandra opened the door fully, relief masking her face.

"Thank you for coming so quickly, Agent Reid. Please, come in." Sandra stepped aside while Kate entered. "I hope I didn't take you away from something important."

"This is important, Mrs. Dawes. I'm glad you called me," Kate said, scanning the home. "If you don't mind, I'd like to have a look around. Where are your daughters?"

"Upstairs asleep. I haven't told them anything, I didn't want to scare them." Sandra twisted her hands. "Please, do what you need to."

Kate began a more thorough sweep of the perimeter, leaving nothing to chance. Bushes, trees, shadows. Nothing appeared to have been disturbed or seemed out of place. No obvious signs of footprints near windows. If someone had been here, he was careful to erase any evidence of it.

Returning inside, she holstered her weapon. "If someone was here before, Mrs. Dawes, they aren't now. Can you tell me exactly what happened earlier? What you saw?"

Sandra dropped onto the living room sofa. "After cleaning up from dinner, I went into the living room and sat down a moment. You know that feeling you get? Like you just know someone's looking at you?"

"I know it well," Kate replied, recalling a similar feeling when Hendrickson had been on the loose.

"That's what this felt like." Sandra's lips parted. It seemed to take a moment for her to find the words when she finally continued, "And I know you probably think this is all because of what happened with Tim and now they found my sister's remains..."

"Why didn't you tell me about her?" Kate interrupted. "Your twin. Why didn't you mention she'd gone missing, a presumed victim of Everett Knapp?"

"It's not that easy to talk about, Agent Reid." Her eyes

reddened. "And to be honest, I didn't think it was relevant to my husband's murder."

"Well, it seems a lot of terrible things have happened to your family, I'm sorry to say. I'd heard her boyfriend also went missing. What can you tell me about that?"

"Jacob? Yeah, they were together," Sandra replied. "Both disappeared into thin air. No one knew what had happened, and of course, everyone had assumed it was Everett Knapp who killed them."

Kate studied the home, glancing up the staircase. "I don't want to jump the gun, here, but it's too soon to say if the events are related. Regardless, I won't discount it."

"Agent Reid, I—I feel like maybe I should go away. I mean, take the girls and leave town for a while."

"I don't think anyone would blame you, Mrs. Dawes," Kate replied. "When you called, you said you thought that whoever was out there, watching you, was the person who killed your husband. Do you have any idea who that could be? Was it this man who you met in the bar?"

"No, no, that's just not possible." Sandra closed her eyes, pinching her lips before setting her gaze on Kate. "There've been a couple times...I've bumped into my therapist. At the grocery store, at the pharmacy. And this was all after Tim disappeared. It was so strange because in all this time that I've been seeing him, I've never run into him before." She looked at her hands, spinning a piece of tissue tightly between them. "I think my therapist might have a crush on me or something. And I think maybe he confronted my husband, and it ended in his death."

"Confronted?" Kate asked. "Do you know for sure they'd had a confrontation?"

"No, I don't," Sandra replied. "I just know that all this started after I told him...the problems in my marriage."

"Of course. Because he's your therapist." Kate considered whether this therapist had any connection to Draker or possibly, Knapp. "Can you tell his name?"

"Dr. Shane Fuller."

Jacob Fuller's name popped into Kate's head. "Sorry, you said Fuller? Any relation to Jacob Fuller?"

Sandra nodded. "Yes, ma'am. Jacob was his son."

～

KATE RETURNED TO THE HOTEL, but instead of retreating to her room, she knocked on Surrey's door.

He opened it, rubbing his eyes as though he'd been sleeping, yet he still wore his white dress shirt and black suit pants. "What's going on? Did something happen?"

Kate stepped inside without awaiting an invitation. "I got a call from Sandra Dawes a little while ago. She asked me to come and see her."

"What for?" Surrey closed the door behind her.

"She believed someone was lurking around her house and didn't want to call local police. She insisted I needed to check it out."

Surrey ran his hand through his only slightly disheveled black hair. "You?"

"Yep." Kate shrugged. "Maybe she doesn't trust the police. Anyway, I just got back. She thinks her therapist, Dr. Shane Fuller, is stalking her, and that he was there at her home. And get this, you remember when Crawford said Ashley Holland wasn't the only resident who'd gone missing?"

"Yeah. He said some other guy...uh...Jacob Fuller." Surrey stopped cold, fixing his gaze on Kate. "Holy shit. Relation?"

"Jacob's father," she replied.

"Okay. What are we supposed to do with that?" he asked. "How is this related to the hunt for Draker's killer?"

Kate took a seat in a nearby side chair. She considered his question, still uncertain of any link, herself. But something still poked at the back of her brain. "There seems to be a lot to unpack here involving the sister. But given Sandra's current state of mind, I didn't push her. So, is there a connection?" She shrugged. "There must be. We just have to find it."

"All right," he said, meandering toward the bed and perching on the corner of it. "You want to talk to this Dr. Fuller then?"

"We should be armed with a background check on him first, and then, yeah, I think we should talk to him," she replied. "The sooner, the better. Too many things are happening here, Jonathan, and I feel like we're clutching at quicksand."

"I agree." He drew in a breath. "McDaniel's still waiting on us to give him some sort of magic bullet."

"Our profile," she said. "I'm aware. But this is instrumental to completing one. Don't you think?"

"Not unless this therapist has a connection to Everett Knapp."

"The background might reveal something," Kate continued. "I wonder how long Fuller has been a therapist."

Surrey looked at her with uncertainty. "Not sure I follow."

"There was something else in the way Sandra Dawes spoke about him. Like she knew more and there was a legitimate reason she'd suspected him. Not just the couple of coincidental run-ins she'd had." Kate raised her index finger. "And if there's a connection between Fuller and Knapp? We might actually start to punch through this wall."

Surrey checked the time on his phone. "It's late. We'll hit this up early and see where it takes us. And, if we find what we want, we can tell McDaniel who he to look for."

"Yeah, okay." Kate got to her feet. "Good night. Thanks for hearing me out."

He opened the door. "We'll forget the fact that you told none of us where you were going tonight."

She grinned, sheepishly. "If I thought there was any danger—"

He raised his hand. "Save it. I'm used to it by now, Reid." As she stepped into the hall he continued, "One day, though, you might be wrong."

~

ELLA'S BEDROOM, a sanctuary of soft pink hues, was now consumed by the blackness of night. She could only make out a thin sliver of moonlight that managed to sneak in around her drawn shades as she lay in bed. Earlier, the muffled lullaby of her mother's conversation with another woman had drifted up from downstairs, their words swallowed by the thick walls and plush carpeted floor.

Her mom... something about her had shifted these past couple of days. It frightened Ella, this change. With her dad away on an urgent business trip, she felt an unfamiliar vulnerability creep in. Her dad was always there to shield her and her sister, Marissa - their protector against all things big and small.

At nine years old, Ella had picked up more about the world than what was shared in her third-grade classroom. Schoolyard whispers filled in the blanks that maybe her mom wouldn't approve of. They talked about her grandparents - a concept foreign to Ella until today. She had seen pictures of a smiling woman she knew to be her grandma and recognized her as the lady who had spoken with her mom at school earlier.

Her mom wanted to tell her something; Ella could see it in her eyes. This silent struggle scared Ella even more. Marissa had sensed it too, though by now she was likely fast asleep in her room down the hall.

Soon, she felt a heaviness in her limbs, like sleep was finally coming. Ella was exhausted from worry. She wanted her dad and knew her mom did too. But now, her lids closed, and that sinking sensation grew stronger.

A faint scraping sound at her bedroom window jolted her awake again. Was it real or had she begun to dream already? She strained to hear. There were no more voices from downstairs. The house was quiet.

Then sound came again, unmistakable this time. Her gaze was drawn to her window as it began to slide open, some unseen force behind it, cast in shadow. Panic seized her, every muscle in her small body tensed. She squeezed her eyes shut, praying it was all a cruel trick of her mind. "Go away," she whispered.

Paralyzed by fear, Ella huddled under her covers. "Go away. Go away." Her pulse roared in her ears like a rushing river. "Mommy," she said, her voice only a whisper.

A soft thud echoed in the room - shoes meeting carpet. She was no longer alone. Someone had come for her, but she refused to look, keeping her head buried as though the blanket offered protection.

The blanket was ripped from her hands. A shadow loomed over her. Before she could muster a scream, a hand clamped over her mouth - rough and forceful, smothering her terrified cries. She writhed against the intruder, tears streaming down her face, but his strength dwarfed hers.

"Shhhh," he said. "Don't make a sound."

THE LAST SPLINTER of light seeped out of the basement as the door closed. Ella cowered in the corner, the cold, damp concrete pressing against her back. The air was thick, saturated with the musty of smell old, forgotten things. She drew her knees up to her chest, wrapping her thin arms around them.

The basement was sparse, furnished only with an old bed on one side and a small wooden chair next to it. The thin mattress on the bed was torn, covered in tattered blankets. But she refused to lay on it. She wasn't going to be here for long. Her mother would come for her soon, she knew it.

Ella remembered the harsh grip of hands, a cloth over her mouth, and then darkness. Now, time had passed, though she had no idea how much. The initial terror had settled into a persistent dread. Each creak of the house seemed to her a sign of worse things to come.

A single bulb hung from the basement ceiling, its light extinguished, leaving her in darkness. Occasionally, she would hear the footsteps above her head—footsteps that made her heart race and her breath catch in her throat.

Ella leaned her head back against the wall and closed her eyes, trying to imagine she was somewhere else—anywhere else. She pictured her bedroom, with its soft pink walls. She saw her mother, humming softly as she folded laundry, her smile, warm and comforting. Her father, still away on business, coming home and running into his open arms.

A sudden noise broke her trance—a thud from somewhere to the left. Her eyes snapped open, darting toward the sound. "Is someone there?"

∽

THE ALARM on Sandra's phone blared incessantly. Morning light filtered around her curtains, spilling into her bedroom. She looked next to her, forgetting for a moment that Tim was gone. And then the wave of grief washed over her once again. That was how it happened—in waves.

She pulled herself up, perching on the edge of her bed. A chill raced up her arms. The house was cold. Too cold.

Getting out of bed, Sandra pulled on her robe and walked into the hall. It was even colder out here. "Where is that draft coming from?" Her feet were cushioned against the soft pile carpeting as she walked down the hall to check on the girls. They had school today and it was time for them to start getting ready.

She arrived at Marissa's door first, pushing it open. Inside, there she was. A slight thing with dark brown hair, looking an awful lot like her father. Same nose. Same little sound from her mouth as she slept.

"Marissa? Honey, it's time to get up and get ready for school." She approached her daughter, gently pulling down the covers. "Come on, now. I want to make sure you have time to eat breakfast." Looking at the girl's face, sweet and innocent, guilt weighed on her. She had to tell the girls about Tim. This secret was eating away at her. She couldn't allow herself to fully grieve yet because they'd wonder why.

"Okay. I'm awake," Marissa replied, rubbing her eyes.

"All right. Come downstairs when you're ready." Sandra walked out, her lips quivering. Tonight. She'd tell them tonight. They deserved to know.

Carrying on toward Ella's room, Sandra stopped as she reached the door that was open just a crack. A terrible draft pushed through. "Ella?" She stepped inside. "Is your window open, honey?" Her eyes were drawn to the shade that had been raised. The window was half open. And then she turned to Ella's bed. Only a lump of covers remained.

Sandra's heart dropped into her stomach. She rushed to the bed and threw back the covers, revealing only rumpled sheets where her daughter should have been sleeping.

"Ella!" Sandra shouted in a panic. She ran from the room calling her daughter's name, checking every corner. The bathrooms, the kitchen, even the attic yielded no sign of the girl. Sandra trembled as the terrifying reality sank in - Ella was gone.

How could this be happening? Just yesterday they had all been together, a family. Now Tim was gone and Ella...

Oh, God. My baby.

Sandra forced herself to take a deep breath. She had to pull it together for Ella and for Marissa, who had appeared in the hallway with a look of confusion on her face.

"Mommy, what's going on?" Marissa asked.

"Did your sister say anything to you last night?" Sandra asked, her voice cracking with desperation. "I need you to tell me the truth, okay?"

"No. She didn't say anything. Why? Where is she, Mommy? Where's Ella?"

Sandra took hold of Marissa's arms. "I don't know, baby. But I will find her."

13

A familiar buzz surrounded the team as they arrived at the Camdenton police station this morning. Scattered conversations, officers on phone calls. All the energy Kate had seen before, pointing to an ominous conclusion.

As she glanced at the others, who walked alongside her, their expressions confirmed what she had suspected: something major had gone down.

Surrey was the first to put words to their collective impression. "Looks like we have a problem here. Do we know if McDaniel is in yet? Has anyone heard from him this morning?"

Kate waited for an answer, and when none came, she jumped in. "Then let me find out what the hell happened and where he is." She walked to the front desk, where a young officer was busy on his computer. "Good morning. Special Agent Kate Reid. Can you tell me if Agent McDaniel is here?"

"Yes, ma'am." He aimed a finger straight ahead. "Down the hall, speaking with the captain."

Kate glanced into the corridor. "Thank you." She returned to the team, casting a serious eye to Surrey. "He's with the captain."

No sooner had the words left her mouth did McDaniel emerge from the captain's office, heading straight for them.

"Speak of the devil." Kate took a step forward. "Agent McDaniel, what's going on? I feel like we slept through something."

He peered down for a moment, as if attempting to find the words. Then he set his gaze on Kate. "Sandra Dawes. Her oldest daughter was taken in the night."

The news set her nerves on end as a wave of anger soared in her chest. And for a moment, Kate was transported back to her own abduction as a child. The memories— a torrent that threatened to drown her. The blindfold Hendrickson had forced her to wear. The dank smell of the basement where he'd held her captive. Putting her hands on him, and his on hers. Kate had barely escaped with her own life.

Though Hendrickson was long dead, the scars still lingered. Kate felt her chest tighten. Why this was hitting so hard, she didn't know. And when Surrey put a steadying hand on her arm, his forehead creased in concern.

"Hey, you all right?"

"Yeah. Fine." Kate pulled in a sharp breath and cleared her throat. Finally, she set her attention on McDaniel. "Are there units at the Dawes' house yet? Are they searching for the girl?"

"Of course. But given what happened to her husband, we may want to step in and provide assistance." McDaniel seemed changed now. No longer resistant to their ideas. He seemed to realize things had gone from bad to worse. "Agent Reid was right. Timothy Dawes' murder, I now believe, must be connected to our investigation. I don't know how, but with Sandra Dawes' daughter going missing...something else is at play."

Kate considered her conversation with Mrs. Dawes only last night. "She mentioned to me that she believed someone had been stalking her. That someone was her therapist. A Dr. Shane Fuller."

McDaniel set his hand on his hip. "She said this to you last night? When exactly?"

"I got a call from her sometime around eight or eight thirty," Kate replied. "I'd given her my card after speaking to her about her husband." McDaniel was clearly annoyed by this. "Look, I suggested she contact local police, but for whatever reason, she connected with me on a different level, and pleaded for me to come. So I did." Kate glanced at her team in search of confirmation she'd made the right call. Their faces seemed to suggest otherwise. "I had every intention of informing local authorities if I'd seen anything suspicious. She mentioned Fuller, and how the two had managed to bump into each other at odd times. He also knew about her affair, which could have been a motive to kill her husband." She left out the part about Jacob and Ashley, certain it would only muddy the waters at this point. Surrey knew, of course, but said nothing.

"I believed that whoever was handling Tim Dawes' murder investigation was well aware of all this. And at no time did I believe Mrs. Dawes, or her daughters, were in imminent danger last night," she added.

McDaniel fixed his gaze on her, his anger obvious to everyone now. "Looks like you were wrong."

"Hey, you're out of line, pal," Walsh said, stepping forward.

Kate pressed her hand against his thick chest to stop him. She shook her head as McDaniel walked away. "Leave it. He's getting it from all sides."

"I don't care what bug he's got up his ass, he doesn't get to disrespect you or any member of this team," Walsh shot back. "We're here to help him."

"Which we haven't exactly done yet," she added.

"So how do you want to tackle this?" Duncan stepped in. "Unless you want to help with the search for this girl, we should keep moving forward with a plan to find out who's responsible for murdering the DEA agent." She looked over at McDaniel as he stood near the front desk, speaking to another officer. "I do agree this isn't a coincidence. Sandra Dawes and her family are targets. I just don't know how the trafficking case they were working when Draker was killed ties to it."

Kate nodded. "I think we all know we can't sit here and do nothing while this girl is missing. If Sandra Dawes feared Dr. Fuller, there's a reason for it. So, I suggest Jonathan and I run him down, have a talk with him." She hesitated a moment.

"What is it?" Walsh asked. "I recognize that look, Kate. You know something else."

She pinched her lips and nodded. "When I interviewed Mrs. Dawes about her husband, she mentioned the two had had a fight the night he went missing. Apparently, he'd discovered she'd had a one-night-stand, and it had gotten out at work."

"With who?" Duncan asked. "Seems like that's the guy we need to be talking to right now."

"Agreed, but here's the thing," Kate continued. "Sandra doesn't know his name or didn't remember it. But it might be worthwhile to talk to the man who sent out the email telling the entire office about it—Derek Earley."

Duncan glanced out over the bullpen. "Do we know if the detective here has talked to him already?"

"I don't know. I'd find out, but if not, that might be a good place for you two to start." Kate raised her finger. "That's not all... Sandra told her therapist about the affair."

Surrey folded his arms. "Okay. So the therapist knows. Why kill the husband if the wife had the affair? I don't see a motive here."

"Unless Fuller is tied to Everett Knapp," Kate replied. "That's the only way this thing starts to make any sense."

~

THE SILENCE as Kate and Surrey drove out to talk to Dr. Shane Fuller suggested to her that he was holding back. He'd wanted to say something about her initial reaction to learning that Ella Dawes had been taken. Now, she felt the weight of his hesitation.

Surrey knew a little about what had happened with Hendrickson, something she had shared with him not so long ago. Some of the more disturbing details, though, had remained unspoken.

In fact, it was only her husband who knew the whole sorry tale. After all, he'd been there when Hendrickson had returned to finish what he'd started. Almost lost his life and would have, if Marshall Avery hadn't been there.

It all flooded back. Memories of things she'd tried so hard to push away, tucked into the darkest recesses of her mind. It sometimes tainted her perspective, and Surrey had taken issue with such things in the past. Would he still? Would he still, if he knew everything?

"You're quiet," he said as if on cue. "What are you thinking about?"

She glanced at him, knowing full well the meaning behind his question. "Wondering what I might see in Fuller. If he might reveal something to me."

"This girl—Reid," he said. "You're going to have to work hard at keeping perspective. I have a feeling your thoughts are elsewhere."

"Not elsewhere," Kate replied. "Just searching for the connection. His son went missing. The same son who happened to be dating Sandra's sister at the time. If there is a connection between him and Everett Knapp, what does that mean?" She felt his eyes on her still, but he said nothing more. Possibly, he'd learned from the last time she'd drawn upon her knowledge of monsters that it was best to let her think.

"This is his office address," Kate said. "Looks like he works out of his house."

"He's not expecting us," Surrey added. "And with Mrs. Dawes being a patient, he won't legally be able to say anything about her."

Kate pulled up to the curb and shifted into park. "I'm not worried about what he has to say about Sandra Dawes. I'm worried about what he doesn't say." She opened her door, stepping out into a blustery day. Cold and windy, dark, and gloomy. That was a little how she felt in this moment as her thoughts turned to the taken girl. What was the girl thinking right now? Probably wondering if anyone was coming to help.

Kate pulled her coat around her, zipping it halfway, and joined Surrey on the sidewalk fronting the home.

"We have no warrant. No reason at all to be talking to this man, except that Sandra Dawes is his patient, and she had a feeling about him," Surrey began.

"We both know that's not the only link between the two. And I think we'll know pretty quickly whether he intends to help us or protect himself." Kate started on toward the front door, noticing a second entrance near the garage. "That must be where his clients enter. We should probably go there instead."

Surrey nodded, gesturing for her to proceed while he fell in line behind her.

Kate reached the door and knocked. Both waited only a

moment when the handle turned, and the door opened. "Dr. Fuller?" She retrieved her FBI credentials.

"Yes?" It didn't take long for him to notice their IDs. "What can I do for you both? What's this about?"

"May we come in?" Surrey asked. "We'd like to talk to you about one of your clients—Sandra Dawes."

He hesitated, licking his lips, darting his gaze between them. For a moment, Kate felt like he might run, all but admitting his guilt. But it wouldn't be that easy. It never was.

"Mrs. Dawes is a patient of mine, so I can't exactly tell you much about her. You must know that. However, I'm sure she'd be willing to talk to you."

"We've spoken to her, Dr. Fuller," Kate replied. "Which is why we're here. Her daughter, Ella, was kidnapped last night."

"Oh my God." Fuller lay his hand on his chest. "I'm so sorry. I had no idea. How can I help?"

It wasn't lost on either of them, it seemed, the fact he still hadn't allowed them inside. Kate studied Fuller a moment, trying to get a read on him. His initial surprise about Ella seemed genuine, but there was something else in his demeanor that put her on edge. A nervous energy behind his polite exterior.

"May we come in and speak with you?" she asked again, more firmly this time.

Fuller hesitated, then stepped back. "Absolutely, yes."

They followed him inside to a small office off the main hallway. Degrees and awards lined the walls. But no personal photos. No family or friends.

She and Surrey took the chairs opposite his desk, while he settled in behind it. He was in the power position, trying to gain control over the narrative already.

"Dr. Fuller," Kate began, "When was the last time you treated Mrs. Dawes?"

"She comes in once a week. But after what happened to her husband, she had asked to come in yesterday, ahead of her usual appointment."

"You saw her yesterday?" Kate studied him. "Did she give you any indication that she felt threatened or afraid?"

Fuller shook his head. "No, nothing like that. She'd seen her estranged mother and after the tragic loss of her husband, it left her even more unsettled."

Surrey rested his elbows on the chair. "Are you aware that the remains of her twin sister had recently been recovered?"

He glanced away. "Yes, sir. I am. I'm afraid I can't offer you any greater detail than that."

Kate studied his expression and couldn't quite pinpoint whether he appeared saddened by the news, or fearful of it. "I assume you heard on the news that several remains, thought to be the victims of Everett Knapp, were recently recovered. Sandra's twin, among them."

"Oh yes," he said. "We're all painfully aware of all that. I'm just glad those families, including Sandra's, will soon get the closure they need."

Those families? As if his son wasn't among the suspected victims? "Do you have family, Dr. Fuller? Children?" Kate asked.

"A had a son, and a wife." A mournful grin tugged at his lips. "They're both gone now."

Kate had to remember why they were here—to get a sense if this man before her took Ella Dawes. Right now, he wasn't doing himself any favors—keeping secret the truth about his son. "I understand Everett Knapp had lived here a long time," she pressed. "Did you know him at all?"

He leaned back, furrowing his brow. "That seems an odd question, Agent Reid. But to answer it, no, I didn't know him."

"Dr. Fuller," Surrey cut in. "With Ella Dawes currently missing, I think it's best I get straight to the point."

"Then by all means, Agent Surrey." He gestured for him to continue.

"Mrs. Dawes indicated to Agent Reid that she believed you'd been following her in recent days. And that, as of last night, she no longer felt safe as your patient. Even suggesting you may have had something to do with her husband's murder. And wouldn't you know it, the very next morning, her child has gone missing."

Fuller's eyes widened. "My God. I would never harm a patient or her family. Or anyone, for that matter." He took a breath. "However, patient confidentiality prevents me from sharing details, as I'm sure you understand."

"A young girl's life hangs in the balance," Kate cut in. "If you know anything that could help us find Ella, you have a moral obligation to share it."

Fuller appeared to waver, conflicting emotions playing across his face. Surrey went on. "Think carefully, Doctor. Withholding information in an active investigation makes you complicit if anything happens to that girl."

He cleared his throat. "Off the record...I have to say that Sandra's behavior since learning of her husband's death, as you might imagine, has been erratic. She feels responsible. Then learning about her sister...well, it's been a lot."

"And her affair," Kate pressed. "Any other details you're at liberty to share?"

"Well, I assume Sandra would've shared anything relevant, and no, I'm not at liberty. I apologize," he replied.

Frustration tightened her chest because this was getting them nowhere. "Where were you last night, Doctor?"

His lips parted slightly, and he shifted in the chair. There it was. A split-second hesitation that revealed everything.

"At home, of course. Where else would I be?"

~

Walsh pulled to a stop inside the parking lot Tim Dawes' office. He gazed up at the glass structure. "So, we go in, talk to Derek Earley, and see if we can get more from him than the detective was told." He turned to Duncan, who sat in the passenger seat.

"Yeah, well, I'm not going to hold my breath. Still, we know more now than the detective did when he interviewed the guy, so..." Duncan shrugged. "Maybe we'll see if Earley's hiding anything."

"Since he'd claimed a hacker sent the email," Walsh continued. "They should have proof of that somewhere by now, right? Because whoever sent that email either knows who Sandra Dawes slept with or could be the man, himself. And if that's the case, then he's suspect number one."

Duncan nodded. "And as Kate said, how else could he have known the wife's personal details? Still, how the hell does any of this tie to Draker's murder? Or the other remains?"

He opened the car door. "Seems to me, everyone here has a secret. Like the whole goddam town was built on them. All I know is that there's a shit ton of dead folks piling up on us and we have no idea who's responsible."

As they stepped out, making their way to the entrance, Duncan continued, "This threw Kate for a loop—the girl being taken."

"Oh, yeah. I saw it in her face."

They entered the modern office building surrounded by glass. White, marble-look tiled floors and a sleek interior painted a picture of a successful business.

The two approached at the front desk and Walsh displayed his credentials. "Good morning. We're here to talk to Derek Earley."

The young woman behind the counter looked like she might ask a question but seemed to decide against it and reached for the phone. "I'll see if he's at his desk. One moment please."

The receptionist made the call and quickly returned her attention to them. "Yes, he'll be right down, along with Mr. Bradley. He's Derek's boss."

"Fine. Thank you." Walsh stepped away, eying Duncan. "Two for one."

"Sounds like CYA to me," she replied, glancing over at the elevator as the doors parted. "Looks like our people."

Walsh quickly spotted a nervous looking man and another, more poised and older gentleman beside him. The tension seemed to radiate off both of them.

"Good morning." Walsh offered his hand. "I'm Special Agent Levi Walsh. This is Special Agent Eva Duncan. You must be Derek Earley?"

"Yes." He thumbed back. "This is Michael Bradley. He's my boss."

"VP of Operations." Michael shook their hands. "Hope you don't mind my tagging along. We're all pretty shaken up about what happened to Tim. I assume that's what this is all about."

"In part, yes," Walsh replied, glancing around. "Could we have a sit-down somewhere in private?"

"Yeah, uh, sure. There's a conference room just down this hall. Follow me." Michael led the way to a large room with an oval table inside, surrounded by black executive chairs. "Right through here."

"Thanks." Walsh took his seat, gesturing for Duncan to do the same. And when the gentlemen got seated, he wasted no time. "Mr. Earley, do you know Sandra Dawes well?"

He hesitated, offering his boss a brief glance. "I know her husband well. *Knew* her husband, Tim. We were coworkers, and friends, I thought."

Bradley rested his elbows onto the table. "Tim and Derek had a falling out just prior to Tim's...death. In fact, the detective on the investigation had spoken to him about this already. Afterward, I'd asked Derek to take some time off, deal with all of it, but he insisted..."

"I do better when I'm working," Derek cut in. "Look, there was this whole thing about an email."

"The company-wide email you sent regarding Mrs. Dawes' transgression," Duncan shot back. "We're aware. That's the main reason we're here. To be honest, Mr. Earley, Sandra Dawes has been through the wringer these past few days. And this morning..." Duncan paused a moment. "Well, it turns out, her daughter was taken."

"Taken?" Derek asked.

"Yes, sir, as in abducted, right from her own bed," Duncan added. "Don't suppose you know anything about that?"

"Jesus, no, of course not. Why would I?" he asked.

"What is it you need to know, Agent Duncan?" Michael cut in. "Obviously, Derek has no idea what you're talking about and neither do I. But I think you already knew that. So what's really the question here?"

"All right, Mr. Earley," Walsh stepped in. "You told the detective your email had been hacked, and that someone else was responsible for broadcasting the private details of the Dawes' marriage." He leaned in. "Here's the thing, that email caused Tim Dawes to go home early that day. He kicked out his wife and children. Then that night, he goes missing, only to be found a week later floating in the lake. Stabbed in the back, hands tied, left to drown. So, if there's more you want to say on the matter, Mr. Earley, we're all ears."

14

Each step inside the Dawes' home felt like walking deeper into a dark pit of despair. Sandra Dawes was consumed by her anguish, her sobs echoing off the walls and suffocating the air. The Camdenton PD evidence team was scouring every inch in their search for a clue that could lead them to where young Ella had been taken.

And now, the BAU team, there to provide insight as to who butchered a DEA agent, arriving at the Dawes home, with far more questions than answers.

"They're here." Kate nudged Surrey as Walsh and Duncan entered the home. The look on Walsh's face confirmed they, too, had made little progress. "I take it, the interview with Derek Earley didn't yield much?"

"He says he never sent out that email, and of course denies he had anything to do with Tim's murder, or the girl's disappearance," Walsh replied. "His boss was there and let us take a look at what their IT guys found."

"Earley was telling the truth," Duncan jumped in. "They

couldn't trace the origin of the sender, but apparently someone else had accessed his email account."

"Convenient." Kate set her hands on her hips. "Is it worth getting our computer forensics involved?"

"Depends on whether you two turned up anything," Walsh replied.

"Not really, no." She looked at Surrey for agreement. "Fuller claims he was home when the girl was taken. Says he never stalked Sandra and that any meeting between them outside of therapy was coincidental. He went quiet after that. Patient confidentiality." Kate sighed. "I'm still not convinced he doesn't have an unhealthy attraction to his client, but we can't put him in jail for that."

It was then that Agent McDaniel approached them. Hands in his pockets, gaze downcast. "They've pulled prints from the girl's bedroom. Of course, it'll have to be compared to the family's prints before we're able to isolate any unknowns." He regarded them. "Where do things stand with you all?"

"The more we look for a connection between the murder of Draker and the that of Tim Dawes, the less certain I am there is one," Kate replied. "Except it just seems a hell of a lot of bad things are happening to the Dawes family right now. And that's on top of your partner's murder. And the worst part is that a girl is missing." She glanced at Sandra Dawes, a new theory beginning to take shape. "What if she's lying?"

Surrey peered back at the woman, narrowing his gaze. "About?"

"About not knowing the name of the man she had the affair with."

"You think she's protecting him?" Duncan asked.

"Could be," Kate replied. "Her husband is killed shortly after her brief tryst. Maybe Sandra had cut off all communication with this man. He didn't like it, so..."

"He comes after the family," Walsh cut in. "Kate, she seems to trust you. The connection we're all looking for could be this unknown man. What if he's tied to the trafficking case? Maybe he killed Draker."

Kate nodded. "I'll talk to her again right now. See what I can get." She headed toward Sandra, who stood in front of her fireplace, alone and afraid. "Hi Sandra, do you have a moment?"

She nodded, her face pale, as Kate ushered her into the hallway where they could speak in private.

"I can't imagine what you're going through right now, but I need you to be honest with me," Kate began. "For Ella's sake. My team and I...we've been going round in circles trying to get to the bottom of not only the DEA agent's death, but the remains that were recovered, including your sister's. We all agree that the timing of your husband's death is more than a coincidence. And now, of course, this..." Kate gestured out over the unfolding scene.

"I also understand your concerns about Dr. Fuller," she continued. "After talking to him...I'd be lying if I said there wasn't something off about his behavior. There's a lot you're not saying either, like the fact his son, who dated your sister, also went missing. Fuller failed to mention that, which..." Kate stopped and glanced at the team, remembering to keep her focus on the missing girl. "That said, we need more, Sandra. We need to know the name of the man you met in the bar. I don't know if you're protecting him or what, but we've reached a critical point. Believe me when I say this could mean your daughter's life."

Sandra's eyes filled with tears as she leaned closer, her voice, only a whisper. "It was just once, I swear it. Just a stupid mistake."

Kate raised her hands. "I'm not judging you, Sandra."

After a few moments, she relented. "His name is Wayne Clevenger. The girls were away. Tim was at work. I went out a bar." She scoffed. "Which is something I never do alone. And especially not here, given everyone knows who my parents are. Anyway, I met him there. We, uh..." She swallowed hard. "We went to his car and, you know...that was it."

"And your husband found out because of this email?" Kate asked.

Sandra nodded. "I don't know how Derek could've possibly known. And then you say he denies it?" She looked away, sighing. "I'm not surprised. From what I understand, Derek was a brown-noser anyway. So, if he wanted to make Tim look bad, I guess he succeeded."

"As I said, Mr. Earley denies sending it, and their IT department confirmed his account had been hacked. So, it's entirely possible the person who sent it was either this man or someone this man hired," Kate said. "Do you have any way of contacting Mr. Clevenger?"

"No. I never reached out or heard from him again. I wasn't looking to blow up my life." Sandra inhaled deeply. "Looks like it happened anyway. And now, one of my girls is missing."

"The entire police force, the FBI...everyone is doing everything in their power to find your daughter," Kate said. "But in the meantime, if you know anything more about Wayne Clevenger..." She waited, sensing Sandra still held something back. And when it seemed the woman had nothing more to say, she continued. "Okay. Thank you, Sandra."

Returning to the team, Kate began, "Wayne Clevenger. He was her one-night-stand. Though she says they never exchanged details. I have no idea why she'd consider protecting this person."

McDaniel's face darkened. "Oh, I think I have a pretty damn good idea."

"What do you mean?" Surrey asked.

The agent donned a derisive smirk. "Son of a bitch is one of our informants. He went dark around the same time as the informant who'd last met with Draker. I thought he was fucking dead."

Kate rocked back on her heels. "Wait, I thought you said you talked to your informant?"

"I did. But Clevenger...we had him too, or so I thought," McDaniel replied. "That's how this works, Agent Reid. You gather what you can from whoever wants to talk. And Clevenger vanished shortly after Draker went missing, right along with our other C.I."

"Jesus, you didn't put two and two together?" Walsh shot back.

McDaniel glared at him. "Well, since I knew he hadn't talked to Draker, and we had half a dozen other informants out there...no. There wasn't anything to put together, Agent Walsh."

Surrey stepped in between them, his hands out, keeping this from escalating. "Look, this isn't the time or place for this, all right? We know the guy's name. And clearly, Agent McDaniel, you know how to get hold of him. So that's what we do next."

"That's the connection, isn't it?" Kate said, a renewed vigor in her tone. "Between the Dawes family and the murder of Draker. Wayne Clevenger."

"Clevenger is a low-level drug runner," McDaniel said. "We used him to get names of higher-ups. Got one or two before all this happened to Draker." He tilted his head. "When did this one-nighter happen?"

Kate glanced over at Sandra, who'd been staring out her kitchen window. "About a month ago."

∽

SILENCE PERSISTED between Chief Cole and Fisher amid the hum of his office ventilation system. Fisher sat opposite him, legs crossed, rolling a toothpick between his fingers. The faint scent of coffee lingered in the air.

"Walk me through it," Cole said, his words clipped. "The Ozarks case—where do we stand?"

Fisher straightened, a hand instinctively smoothing his tie. "Still waiting for the rest of the remains to be identified. I was just informed that a child has been kidnapped, and from what Reid said, it's likely connected. It appears the investigation is splintering in multiple directions. It'll be up to the team to pull it together and help the local field office determine who murdered the DEA agent." He sighed. "Agent McDaniel is getting frustrated with a lack of progress."

"He should know that's the nature of the game," Cole replied. "And Scarborough...has he, by chance, confided in you his decision? I haven't yet heard from him."

Fisher shifted in his seat, uncomfortable about undermining whatever Nick had in mind to discuss with Cole himself. "We haven't discussed his decision, sir. He came in yesterday. Went down to the lab with me." He shrugged. "I could see in his face he felt—useful. Offered helpful information, too."

"A positive sign," Cole replied. "And Reid? What's her take? Do you know if Scarborough has asked for her input? They are married."

"I'm aware, but as far as I know, she's buried in this case, as is her style. And, honestly, we can't afford the distraction." Fisher replied, rising from his chair. "If that's all, I should be getting back."

"Actually, no." Cole laced his fingers together over his chest. "You should know I'm considering bringing Scarborough back into the fold—here—in your unit. You just said yourself, he offered useful advice."

"Offering advice and returning to his former position are two very different things, sir. I thought his options were the WFO or Los Angeles." Fisher's brow furrowed, and he crossed his arms, appearing defiant. "Chief, you've said nothing up to this point about bringing Scarborough back to our team. *My* team. With respect, sir, I think that's a misstep. It could throw Reid off her game, not to mention the rest of the team."

"How so? Scarborough is one of the best. My position on that has never wavered." Cole countered, dismissing the objection with a wave of his hand. "I'm not suggesting he take on a leadership role. I admire and respect the work you've done with the team. I'm simply suggesting, Scarborough might think he's finished here, but I don't."

"I won't argue his talent," Fisher conceded. "But the distraction factor—"

"Reid's a professional," Cole interrupted, his eyes narrowing. "She'll handle it. Besides, this isn't about her. It's about our ability as a cohesive unit to assist other field offices. And Scarborough...he gets results."

"Results aren't the only metric, here," Fisher replied with a pointed look. "Cohesion, focus; they're just as critical. And you know as well as I do, personal dynamics play a large part in it. Chief, bringing Scarborough back could fracture this unit. You've seen it before—personal entanglements clouding judgment, eroding the team's efficiency."

"You and Duncan managed," Cole shot back. "Look, you're still the senior unit agent. I'm not trying to undermine you or what you've done for the team. I'm asking you to consider the possibility. Hell, I have no idea whether Scarborough would even consider the move. He left the unit for a reason. And it would be an uphill battle with the director to get him back. So, let's put a pin in this until the team wraps up this Ozarks situation." Cole's attention diverted to the doorway, his expression, slightly surprised. "SSA Scarborough. I wasn't expecting to see you today."

Fisher turned around, just as surprised. "Oh, hi. Come on in. We were just talking about you."

An uncomfortable smile formed on Nick's face. "Sorry to interrupt. I was actually in Unit Two, tying off a few loose ends, and I figured I'd stop by and say hello."

"Well," Cole began. "I've got a meeting, so I'll let you two catch up."

Fisher placed his hand on Nick's shoulder. "Let's head back to my office."

~

IN THE HALLWAY, Nick realized he'd walked in on something he wasn't supposed to. And as he entered Fisher's office, he began, "I'm sorry, man. I didn't know you were with Cole."

"It's fine. Don't worry about it." Fisher took a seat, plunking a toothpick between his lips. "He wants to see you back here, you know—Cole."

Nick sat down. "Where?"

Fisher pointed his index finger downward. "Here. As in back in this unit, with us."

"What?" he asked, his mouth practically on the floor. "First of all, that wasn't one of the options I was presented with after the hearing. And then...the whole idea of..."

"Yeah, I know," Fisher cut in. "I think Cole's looking to drum up support for it."

Nick glanced down, nodding before regarding his old colleague and friend. "And what do you think about that?"

"What I think doesn't matter, Nick. We both know it comes down to what your wife thinks. So if Cole gets the support he needs from the higher-ups, it's something for you and Kate to discuss."

~

McDaniel led the team into the conference room back at the station and pulled out a file labeled "Clevenger." Inside were documents detailing Clevenger's history as a Bureau informant. "He initially led us to the Hollands, having worked for them in the past."

"Sandra's parents," Kate replied. "Who you later dismissed as not germane to your investigation."

"Because we'd had enough intel on other bosses, it became less and less likely the Hollands did anything more than push some weed every now and again," McDaniel replied.

Walsh hooked his thumbs into his belt loops. "Now their son-in-law's been murdered. Their granddaughter, kidnapped...I'm starting to think they got enough clout that someone else might want to take it."

"Is it possible Draker knew, or at least suspected someone might come for the Hollands and their extended family?" Kate asked. "His murder would start to make more sense, all things considered. But do we really think Clevenger would take the girl? His bosses' granddaughter?"

"Depends on his level of desperation," Surrey replied. "He could've been obsessed with Sandra Dawes. Hell, he could've had an ax to grind with the Hollands. Hard to say right now."

"Operation Wrangler," McDaniel said, handing Kate the folder. "I get you think I dropped the ball here, but Draker and me... We were trying to take down a new player bringing fentanyl into the area. Clevenger gave us a name. That was the extent of his involvement."

Kate flipped through the file. She knew as well as any of them that mistakes happened. Hunches sometimes went off the rails. It was the nature of the job. And so she'd begun to regret the animosity that had built up between her team and McDaniel. After all, the man just lost his partner. "We have to know when Clevenger was at that bar with Sandra Dawes. It's possible Draker was there, or somehow, Clevenger knew where he was going that night. Assuming we're all on the same page that we think this guy could be the one."

"Agreed," Surrey replied. "And what are the odds Clevenger, who'd worked for Sandra's parents, didn't know about her? He'd probably already met Sandra at some point?"

"I sensed she had more to say when I'd asked her about him, and this must've been it. She knew him and he knew her." Kate felt her phone buzz in her pocket. "It's Fisher." She answered. "Reid, here."

"We got an ID on another victim," Fisher began. "Just got the call from the lab."

"Hang on, I'm putting you on speaker." Kate pressed the button and waved everyone closer. "Go ahead. Who did they identify?"

"Jacob Fuller," he said. "Ring any bells?"

Kate eyed Surrey, creasing her brow. "Jacob Fuller," she repeated, already knowing full well who he was.

"That's right. Son to Shane and Janice Fuller. He was twenty-four at the time of his death."

"Oh my God." Kate ran her hand over her brunette hair, pulled back in a ponytail.

"I take it, you got some bells ringing," Fisher continued.

"We expected the lab might figure him out soon, but maybe not this soon," Surrey added.

"I'm not sure I get where you're going with this," Fisher replied.

Surrey hesitated a moment, appearing to regret they hadn't prioritized their information on Jacob. "We'd been informed by Coast Guard Lieutenant Crawford that a couple of locals were among those presumed to have been murdered by Everett Knapp. Ashley Holland, and her boyfriend Jacob Fuller."

"Boyfriend," Fisher said. "Interesting."

"We met with Dr. Fuller earlier," Kate added. "He treats Sandra Dawes, and, uh, he mentioned he'd had a wife and son, but that they were both gone now. He failed to mention Jacob's name or that he was with Ashley when he disappeared."

"Something tells me I just threw a wrench into your investigation," Fisher interjected.

"Something like that." Kate regarded the others. "We'll get back to you once we've had a chance to wrap our heads around this. Thanks, Cam." She ended the call, shaking her head. "Well, I guess we expected this."

Walsh scratched his head and sucked his teeth. "We should've put this together—Crawford's mentioning of Jacob Fuller." He eyed Kate. "But I suspect you knew this already. It's something you should've shared with the team." He shifted his weight. "Anything else you're not telling us?"

Guilt weighed on her shoulders because he was right. "I wasn't sure it was relevant until we'd gotten a chance to speak to Shane Fuller. When he left out the part about his son and Sandra's sister, we figured something was off about him." Her gaze vacillated between Walsh and Duncan. "I wasn't trying to keep anything from you two. I was trying to maintain focus on finding the person who murdered Agent Draker."

Walsh patted her shoulder and turned to walk out of the room. "We don't keep shit from each other, Kate. Didn't think I had to tell you that."

Duncan moved in. "He's not wrong, Kate, but I also don't think any of that helps us with Draker, or finding this girl." She eyed the door as it closed again. "He'll get over it."

15

Despite Walsh's disappointment, Kate's thoughts turned back to the Knapp murders...Why hadn't Dr. Fuller mentioned that his son had been murdered, or gone missing or anything of that nature? Instead he'd implied his son wife had simply left town. He kept it hidden for a reason, one which Kate had to now uncover.

With Ella Dawes still missing, Kate felt like this case had zig zagged in too many directions. It felt like... "Distraction."

"What's that?" Surrey looked at her as they remained inside the conference room.

They were now on the hunt for Clevenger's last known location, and Kate couldn't shake the idea..."We're being pulled in multiple directions. It feels...intentional." She dropped onto a chair. "We came here to help the field office and Agent McDaniel profile the killer of Agent Draker. Instead, we're looking for a kidnapped child."

Surrey nodded. "Agreed. But we can't dismiss the fact that

Sandra Dawes is a target. Her family are targets. First her husband, now her daughter? And Clevenger went dark?"

Kate sighed. "Yeah, I get all that. But it does nothing to further our progress in profiling a killer who dismembered a DEA agent, mimicking crimes committed by a man who'd already been jailed for them."

"And who's also dead, don't forget," Walsh said, walking toward them.

Kate returned a sheepish smile. "Right....listen, Levi—"

"It's okay," he cut in. "Grand scheme? We're here for the agent. This other stuff is backstory. It is a distraction. Right now, we have to find Clevenger. If he has the girl, problem solved. If he killed Draker, we'll figure that out pretty damn quickly too."

He perched on the edge of the conference table, his stocky frame slanting it a little. "Tim Dawes, who was stabbed, bound with rope, and left to drown in the lake, wasn't sliced and diced like the others who've surfaced, and the more recent agent. And then a kidnapping?" He shook his head. "Someone's begging for us to look in another direction. And I think that direction might be the Hollands."

"What do you propose?" Kate asked.

"The girl, Ella Dawes," he continued. "She has to be found, and soon. But I think we should be leaving that up to the local authorities and McDaniel if he wants to work with them on it. As for us? As much as I want to help find this girl, we have three recovered victims. Andre Draker, Ashley Holland, and Jacob Fuller"

"And?" Duncan cut in. "What do we do to find the person who killed Draker?"

Walsh raised his chin. "We have the file on Everett Knapp. According to Lieutenant Crawford, they had hardly any physical evidence to tie Knapp to the disappearances. Just some fibers found in his truck belonging to a missing person. No one even knew where the bodies were dumped until Draker's arm was caught in a fisherman's line. Years ago, Knapp had confessed to the crimes, but somehow decided to leave out the location of his victims? Seems strange, especially if he'd wanted to cut a deal."

Kate leaned back, the corner of her lip raising into a half-smile. "This isn't a copycat. Knapp wasn't the killer."

Walsh aimed a finger gun at her. "Bingo."

"He obviously didn't murder Draker," Surrey added. "But it doesn't clear Knapp of anything."

"It doesn't clear him...yet." Kate reached for her phone. "We'll call Fisher back and ask him to get in front of Dr. Bailey. Have her walk us through her findings on Draker. Maybe this will make more sense after we hear from her."

Surrey shrugged, glancing at the others. "Fair enough."

Kate pressed the speed dial for Fisher. He picked up on the second ring.

"Reid, what's going on?"

"Yeah, hey, we're all trying to piece this thing together and we could use some help from Dr. Bailey..." Kate quickly summarized their theories about Knapp's possible innocence. "Think you can go talk to her?"

"Let me head down to the lab and put you on speaker with her. She can walk you through the forensics. I'll call you back in a minute when I get there."

The line clicked. Kate stared at her phone, waiting for it to ring. Finally, his name popped up on the Caller ID. "Okay, here we go." She answered. "We're here. Go ahead."

Fisher's voice came back on. "I've got you on speaker here with Dr. Bailey."

Kate introduced herself and then went on, "Dr. Bailey, we're investigating the murder of a DEA agent, the one who was found recently in the lake where Everett Knapp's victims were also dumped. Can you summarize your autopsy findings compared to the older victims' remains?"

"Certainly," she replied. "The wounds on Agent Draker were inflicted by the same or a very similar weapon to the wounds found on the earlier victims. Those had serrated marks consistent with a serrated saw blade. The force and angle of the cuts were also similar on each of the victims, including Draker, suggesting the killer or killers were right-handed."

"Covers most of the population," Walsh cut in.

Kate grinned. "That it does. Go on, Doctor."

"It was evident that the remains indicated post-mortem dismemberment. However, given the length of time they were submerged in water, it's impossible to know the extent. And no soft tissue was found on any of the victims, except for Agent Draker."

Kate wasn't hearing much in the way of supporting the theory that Knapp might've been innocent. And even if he was, then who killed all those people years ago? What about Knapp might set him apart? What might be enough to rule him out as the killer in order to help point them in another direction?

She had recalled Jill talking about her father and his bait shop. And on reading his case file, she'd seen pictures of him. Kate's expression fell as she grabbed the file once again, flipping it open. "His fingers."

"Sorry?" Dr. Bailey said.

Kate pulled out a couple of photos of him. "Right here. Oh my God."

Walsh leaned over to see. "He's missing two fingers on his right hand." A smile spread on his face. "There it is."

"Holy shit," Duncan exclaimed. "He couldn't have dismembered the bodies with his right hand because it would've been too difficult to the hold the saw steady. He would've needed to use his left hand, going against what Dr. Bailey just said."

Surrey appeared confused. "Why didn't the prosecutor bring this up at trial?"

"Because no bodies had been recovered at the time," Kate replied. *It's the minutia,* Marshall used to say. "Sorry, Dr. Bailey, as you were saying, the angle of the cuts...the killer would've had to use his right hand."

"That's correct," she replied. "But I have to agree that missing two fingers would hamper the ability to operate a reciprocating saw. He would've had to use his left hand to hold it, possibly using his right to guide it. The angles would've been different, either way."

"Then what about Agent Draker? The same thing?" Kate asked.

"His markings are consistent with the other victims."

Duncan leaned toward Kate's phone. "Hey, Cam, can you take us off speaker a moment?"

"Sure." The sound of voices in the distance were now muffled as it seemed' he'd brought the phone to his ear. "Done."

"After what you just heard," Duncan continued. "What are your thoughts?"

He seemed to hesitate a moment, a long sigh coming through the line. "Seems to me you guys might've just exonerated Everett Knapp. But this tells us nothing about who killed those people and more importantly, who killed Agent Draker."

"No, but it tells us we're not dealing with a copycat." Kate looked around at the team. "And we might have a suspect in mind."

In the oppressive silence of the basement, darkness loomed over everything. The only company for Ella Dawes was the necklace around her neck, which she clutched onto for dear life.

She strained her ears against the quiet, desperate for any signs of her captor's presence. But all she heard was a metronome of dripping of water through the old pipes above her. And then, a door opened. Light spilled in, stinging Ella's eyes. A shadowy figure stepped into it. Tears spilled as she quietly sobbed. "Please let me go home."

He said nothing and stood silhouetted in the light.

Each passing moment tightened the grip of fear in her chest, like a snake choking its pray. She felt his stare and could almost see him. His eyes gleaming as he watched from the obscurity of the shadows.

"I want my mom," she cried out, her body trembling. She wanted to scream, to plead for mercy, but she was already hoarse, her earlier screams going unanswered. She squeezed her eyes shut, attempting to block out the shadowy man and all his terrors. But even behind closed lids, she still sensed his presence, looming just beyond her reach. "Please go away. Leave me alone. You're scaring me."

She heard footsteps. He was walking closer. Ella kept her eyes closed, afraid to look at him, unsure whether he was human or a monster.

"If I hear any more screams from you, I'll have to hurt you," he whispered. "And I don't want to hurt you, Ella."

He walked away again, and the door closed. Ella was plunged into darkness. She opened her eyes, sobbing harder now. "Mommy? Mommy, where are you? Please come get me. You have to come get me."

～

THE SPRAWLING Holland estate had been on the local authorities' radar for years. Henry and Jean Holland had raised their two daughters here, overlooking a sizable stretch of land.

Sandra had had virtually no contact with them after Ashley went missing. Their chosen way of life, she said, had left her ashamed regardless of the fact it was the only way for them to stay afloat. To keep from losing everything after dumping money into the search for Ashley. The authorities stopped looking after only weeks. Henry and Jean never did.

The shock of finding Ashley's remains hadn't worn off and was still being felt by Jean Holland now as she sat at her kitchen table, overlooking the grounds. When her cell phone rang, the screen revealed an unexpected caller. Jean answered the line. "Sandy?"

The line was quiet for a moment. Maybe she was ready to talk now. Jean could admit, going to the girls' school wasn't the best way to handle things.

"Mom," Sandra replied, her tone barely audible through the sobs.

Jean sat up, pulling back her shoulders, sensing something was wrong. "What is it, Sandy? What's wrong?" In that moment, she was transported back to the call she'd gotten from Sandy telling her about Ashley. Now, she felt the color drain from her face.

"Mom, Ella's been taken," Sandra replied.

"What?" Jean lost her breath a moment. Already full-figured, she was also pre-diabetic and didn't do a great job of taking care of herself. Her afflictions made her heart beat faster than it should. "What do you mean, taken? Taken where?"

"Gone," Sandra cried out. "She's gone, Mom. Taken from her bedroom last night while we slept. Was this because of you?"

"What are you talking about? You think I took her?"

"No. Was it because of what you and Dad do? Did you piss off someone, and they wanted to get back at you?"

"No. No, sweetheart, I have no idea what you're talking about. If Ella's gone...I mean, are you sure? Did you call the police?"

"Of course I did. They were already here, searched the house for fingerprints and everything. Now, they're about to start a search around the lake. But I swear to God, if you know where my baby is..."

"I don't. You know I would never hurt those babies of yours. They're my grandchildren, for Pete's sake," Jean replied.

"Then it has to be someone you know. Someone who wants something from you. Mom, they killed Tim. And now Ella's been taken right from her own bed. This is because of you and Dad."

"They did what?" Jean stood from the table, pacing the kitchen, until finally walking toward the foyer and out the door. The air was cold even with the midday sun shining down, having cleared from heavy clouds earlier this morning. "Lord in Heaven, Tim's dead?"

"Don't pretend you didn't know," Sandra shot back.

"I don't know what happened, Sandy. And as I stand here breathing; you have to believe that I had no idea about any of this. But I promise you, I will find your little girl. And I will bring her home." She ended the call, pocketing her phone and walking farther out onto the porch. "Henry! Henry, come quick!"

Henry Holland marched up the gravel driveway toward the porch. The older man, slightly rotund, and out of shape, was also out of breath. "What is it? What's going on?"

"It's Ella. Sandy says she's been taken. Right from her very own bedroom in the night. She blames us. And all this right after someone murdered Tim? She thinks it's cause of us and the people we know."

"Wait just a damn minute." He held out his hands. "What's this about Tim? What the hell you mean, he's dead?"

"I know. I can't believe it either," Jean replied.

"Lord in Heaven." He looked out over the grounds. "None of our people would have dared do such a thing. Certainly not friend, nor enemy would cross us like this."

She placed her hand on her husband's shoulder. "What are we gonna do, Henry? I'm beside myself with worry for that little girl. Now, I know Sandy wants nothing to do with us and I've made my peace with it, but her baby? No. Uh-uh. I can't do nothing about my son-in-law, God rest his soul, but someone's gonna pay for taking my grandbaby. I'll make damn sure of that."

∽

WALSH WALKED AROUND to the board they'd set up to lay out the case. "If we really think Clevenger could have killed Draker, then murdered Tim Dawes, it makes sense he might've taken the girl as some sort of retribution." He looked at Kate. "Who knows this guy the best?"

Kate considered who he worked for. "Our first connection to Sandra Dawes is her parents Henry and Jean Holland. According to McDaniel, Clevenger worked for them as an entry-level player." Her phone rang and she answered. "Reid, here."

"Agent Reid, it's McDaniel. I need you and your team."

"Why?" She peered at Surrey. "What happened?"

"We found the boat, the one I told you we'd been looking for. A drone the local authorities sent out to search for Ella Dawes picked it up."

He stopped for a moment and all Kate heard was the sound of his deep breaths. "Agent McDaniel, are you all right?"

"Fine, yeah. I've just never seen anything like this. You have to come out here. Now. Before we lose the light."

A ball formed in the pit of her stomach as dread settled in. "Send me your location. We're on our way." She pocketed the phone and eyed the team. "McDaniel...they found the boat his informant was on when he met with Agent Draker. He says we need to get out there and take a look."

Surrey got up and grabbed his keys. "That's it? That's all he said?"

"No." Kate checked her weapon and pulled on her jacket. "He said he's never seen anything like it."

"Shit." Walsh closed his laptop. "Let's get out there and find out what the hell's going on."

As they hurried to leave, walking out into the late afternoon sun, Duncan caught up to Kate. "I thought they were searching for the girl?"

"Sounds like they were," Kate replied. "A drone picked it up."

"Thank God for small miracles," Duncan said. "This could still lead us to her."

"I hope so."

They hurried into the parking lot and jumped into the rented sedan. With Walsh behind the wheel, they sped off toward the lake; the location, sent by McDaniel. As they drove, the sky darkened with heavy clouds, like the heavens might open at any moment.

"Rain is the last thing we need right now," Walsh said. "It'll wash away everything."

Kate looked on, praying they would find something on that boat that would lead them to Wayne Clevenger. If he had that little girl...

"GPS says it's up ahead, about half a mile," Duncan said.

"Got it." Walsh continued to drive, making the final turn toward the lake.

In the distance, a small cabin cruiser, partially submerged, appeared to have grounded near the tall reeds at the shoreline.

McDaniel and two local officers were waiting on the muddy banks.

"Here we go." Walsh killed the engine and stepped out.

Kate trailed him a few steps with Duncan and Surrey close behind. She caught sight of McDaniel, who nodded grimly as the team approached.

"It's not good," he said. "There's blood everywhere inside the cabin. The hull is riddled with bullet holes. Looks like a goddam scene out of Scarface."

Kate felt her stomach lurch. "Any sign of Ella Dawes?"

McDaniel shook his head. "No, and I think we should be grateful given what you're about to see. But there's something else..." He gestured for them to follow him onto the boat.

It wasn't just inside the cabin, apparently. The stern was covered in blood, dried now, at least until this rain comes. Kate followed McDaniel inside, where the air was thick with that familiar coppery scent. Blood was splattered over every surface - the seats, the floor, even the ceiling.

She steeled herself. The metallic tang hit her like a punch to the gut. "This is where Draker was murdered."

Surrey shone his flashlight around in the dimming light, taking in the carnage. "Yeah, there's no way anyone survived this."

Kate crouched down, examining the blood splatters. "If we're to assume it was Draker, then he was shot multiple times at close range, by the look of things."

McDaniel approached her. "When they brought up the rest of him, only two bullet wounds were identified."

Kate took in the bloody scene, considering his point. "Maybe Draker and the shooter weren't the only ones aboard. Which starts to jibe with the notion that your C.I., who'd had this meeting scheduled, told Clevenger about it. So, it was likely the three of them aboard. Has Draker's sidearm been recovered?"

"No," McDaniel replied. "But these random rounds everywhere weren't fired off by him. Forensics will determine the caliber, but he was a DEA Agent. He was trained, and if he did have his gun on him, he would've killed the shooter. But I don't think that's what happened here."

"I wouldn't be too sure," Duncan cut in. "Draker could've been firing off whatever shots he could in hopes of survival. Especially if he was already injured."

"If Clevenger was on this boat too, could some of this be his blood?" Kate looked at McDaniel. "We should be reaching out to the hospitals to see if they've treated any GSWs over the past month. Could provide us with information on his current whereabouts."

"Yeah, if he was hurt," McDaniel began. "It's all the more reason to think he's laying low somewhere. But if that's the case, do we really think he could've murdered Tim Dawes and taken the girl?"

16

The hunt for Ella Dawes was on. The crisp afternoon air took on an earthy scent near the lake. And, standing in the clearing, near the entrance to the wooded grounds, Sandra Dawes stayed back. Her youngest, Marissa was at her side.

Her nerves were shot. So much had transpired in the span of a few days that it was all she could do to disguise her anguish and grief from Marissa. The youngest daughter knew nothing of her father's murder but was keenly aware that her sister had gone missing.

The notion that Sandra's parents were somehow responsible for these tragic events lingered in the back of her mind. The rumors about them were true, but despite their estrangement, she hadn't had the heart to go to the police and turn them in. Nor had she had any proof, but it wouldn't be that hard for her to get.

This was no coincidence—Ella being taken. Not a chance. But right now, she had to keep her focus on finding her daughter. The rest—Ashley's remains and Tim's murder—would have to wait.

The sound of tires on the gravelly turnout for the lake drew her attention. Sandra looked over, the sun glaring in her eyes. She raised her hand to shield her view and saw the car stop, and a man step out. Recognizing him in an instant, her mouth fell ajar. "What are you doing here?"

"Mommy?" Marissa asked. "Did you say something?"

She looked down, clasping a hand on Marissa's shoulder. "No, baby. It's fine. Listen, why don't you walk over to the table there, where that lady is? Ask for a couple bottles of water, would you, sweetheart?"

"I'm not thirsty," she replied.

"For me, then? Would you get one for me?"

Marissa dropped her shoulders and shuffled to the table, where a volunteer had set up a snack and drink station. Volunteers had come out in droves, reminding Sandra that not everyone in this town was like her parents.

She planted her feet firmly on the soft earth, resting her hands on her hips. The man made his approach. "Dr. Fuller, what are you doing here?"

"Sandra, how are you holding up?" He placed his hand on her shoulder. "I heard about what happened. Is there anything I can do to help?"

"We're all still looking for her, Dr. Fuller. There's about half a dozen officers and at least double that in volunteers searching the woods up to the lake."

"They think she's all the way out here?" he asked, peering out into the distance. "That's quite a ways from your home."

She returned a sideways glance. "Yes, it is. But they searched around our area already, and since Tim had been found some-where out here..."

"They think there could be a connection to his murder?" Fuller pressed.

"It's a theory."

"My God. This is just awful." His gaze shifted out over the water. "Although, I understand what you're going through."

She looked at him, suddenly feeling guilty for her earlier reaction. "Of course. Jacob."

"And your sister." He nodded, still keeping his gaze ahead. "Those first few days...when no one knew anything."

"Days that turned into years," she added.

"That's right." Fuller turned to her, resting his hand on her shoulder. "Oh, Sandra, your family has been through so much. Would you like to sit down with me today or whenever you feel like it? Just to be able to unload some of the burden. I'm here for you. You know that."

Still unnerved by Dr. Fuller's sudden appearance, Sandra glanced over at Marissa, who was sipping a bottle of water as she chatted with the volunteer. She lowered her voice. "I appreciate you coming by, but I'd really rather not get into this right now. As I'm sure you can understand, my focus is entirely on finding Ella."

He nodded while his gaze remained fixed on her. She felt exposed under his steady eye as if he could see right through her poised exterior to the mess of fear and panic that lay beneath.

"Of course, of course," he replied. "I just wanted to offer my support during this difficult time. Please know that I'm here if you need anything at all."

Sandra managed a tight smile. "Thank you. I'll keep that in mind." She peered over at Marissa again. "Now if you'll excuse me, I should get back to my daughter."

As she turned away, Fuller's hand slid down her shoulder and gripped her arm; gentle, but noticeably firm. She stiffened.

"Sandra," he whispered. "Don't lose hope."

She paused, Dr. Fuller's words echoing in her mind. *Don't lose hope.* She knew he was trying to be kind, but instead, it felt intrusive. With each passing hour of Ella still missing, hope slipped further from her grasp. Sandra turned back to face him, nodding. "I'm trying."

It was another moment before he let her go. A long, unsettling moment that made clear his reluctance to leave. "Please let me know if there's anything I can do," he said.

"I will, thank you."

As Fuller retreated to his car, Sandra let out a shaky breath. She watched as he drove away, gravel crunching under his tires.

"Mommy, who was that man?" Marissa asked as she returned to Sandra's side.

"That was Dr. Fuller, remember? You went to his office with me the other day." Sandra smoothed her daughter's hair, pushing away her lingering fear of him. "It's not important."

~

THE TEAM WAS STILL EXAMINING the beached vessel that had been the very one Draker was last seen with an informant. Both the informant and the boat had been missing for a month. Only one was now found.

Kate took caution as she walked to the back of the boat's cabin, her flashlight casting erratic shadows in the dim light. The single window above the bench seat was smudged with grime and blood spatters. "Is there anything in here worth bagging as evidence?"

Walsh aimed his gaze at the floor. "Footprints in the blood. We should document these."

"On it." McDaniel opened his phone and began taking photographs.

Kate took in the scene. "If Agent Draker was murdered here, then he was dismembered here too. The blood patterns on the walls are consistent with the splattering of severed arteries. The pooling on the floor is spillage from the shower, where it looks like the parts were left to drain. But we won't get answers as to whose blood this is until it's analyzed, and we can get the DNA back. Only then will we know for sure this is where Draker was killed."

As McDaniel continued to document the scene, he replied, "Ella Dawes won't live long enough to wait for blood analysis. If it's Wayne Clevenger we want to find; to pin all this carnage on, then we'd better start looking. Rule it out one way or another."

"Duncan and I can make calls to the local hospitals in the area, like you said earlier," Walsh replied. "Find out if he'd been treated."

"It's a start," Kate replied, setting her gaze on McDaniel again. "Have you heard any news from the search team out looking for Ella?"

McDaniel picked up his phone. "I'll find out right now." He was about to climb topside to make the call but stopped short, standing on the ladder. "Hang on. Looks like we got ourselves some phone records."

Kate drew near. "Clevenger's?"

"Yep." He continued up the ladder and the others followed. Better light and fresher air up there. He opened the email as the team huddled around him. "I put in the request for his records when Draker went missing. No surprise, he'd used a burner to contact us. But I've been waiting on any additional records they could trace back to him. And it looks like they found some."

What do you show?" Kate pressed.

"Let me take a look." He scrolled through the records. "Last call from this number was placed November tenth. Eleven p.m. My partner was last seen three days prior."

"So the call was placed after you'd spoken to him in search of Agent Draker?" Kate asked.

"That's right. And I don't see on here that'd he been in contact with Medina."

"Sorry, who is that?" Kate asked.

"The informant who met with Draker. The guy who's gone dark on us. Clevenger must've contacted him with his burner as well because I don't see Medina's number on here."

"He could've been using multiple numbers as well," Kate said. "Who was this last call to, then?"

McDaniel narrowed his gaze as he studied the screen. "I have no idea. I don't recognize it."

"Let's think back to what Sandra Dawes mentioned...about the bar." Kate grabbed her phone and scrolled through her recent calls, knowing the woman had contacted her only yesterday. "Does this number show up on those records?"

McDaniel eyed the information and then searched the calls. "Holy shit. Yes, it does. It's the last number he dialed."

Kate regarded the team, feeling like they were about to break through this stalemate. "So, the last call Clevenger made was to Sandra Dawes."

"Unless he's using yet another burner. And she did admit to sleeping with him," Surrey added as if attempting to tamp down her expectations.

"Yes, she did," Kate replied. "But she also claimed the two never exchanged numbers or any information. We need to confirm that the date of this call is the date she went to that bar and then the timing... Did this call happen before they met up, or after? And we need to nail down how this call relates to the disappearance of Agent Draker."

Duncan stepped in. "Agent McDaniel, you said Clevenger had worked for Sandra's parents. Sandra would have known that I assume."

"They're estranged, so maybe not," he replied. "But that

doesn't mean Clevenger didn't get her number from them if he had access to their home."

"So he could've reached out to her and scheduled the meet-up, sensing Sandra's vulnerability," Kate said. "Then the Hollands must know where he lives, who his friends are...you don't just let someone into your operation if you don't know everything about them. This is our best shot at finding Clevenger, assuming he's still alive."

~

THE BRIGHT AFTERNOON sun reflected off the waters of the bay as Nick stood outside on the balcony of his condo. The briny scent, carried by the cold breeze, enveloped him. He'd had the night to sleep on the idea that Cole had wanted him back on the team. It had never occurred to him to go back there. Fisher hadn't seemed thrilled by the prospect, and he understood why. They'd butted heads many times, both vying for the leadership position, even though it was technically Nick's. Fisher had deserved it, being the most senior.

Chief Cole was a good man and always had Nick's back, but this? He looked down, taking in a deep breath. Kate would never go for it, and it reeked of desperation on his part. He wanted her back but forcing her to work with him again...that wasn't how to go about it. Not to mention how it would screw with the dynamics. No, it could never be a consideration for him. But what was? Los Angeles or the D.C. field office? The WFO held a lot of memories for him. Some good, some bad.

Still, a choice had to be made. The Bureau wouldn't keep his options on the table for long. But it was Kate who consumed his thoughts right now. What she would want. What he could do for her. If only he could go back and fix the mistakes. But that wasn't how life worked.

The memories of that night flooded back to him in a torrent. The mistakes he'd made. It was never more evident than in this moment how a single choice had the capacity to upend one's entire life. But here he was.

Nick appreciated the hell out of Cole's recommendation to bring him back into the fold on Fisher's team. But even if Fisher had agreed, which Nick doubted would happen, Kate wouldn't. She would leave, and her career would be cut off at the knees.

Besides, going back to that life...a life of monsters, demons, and everything in between...it wasn't for him anymore. Even if part of him kind of missed it after accompanying Fisher to the lab yesterday. Unfortunately, the job required a great deal more than analyzing forensic evidence. It required the talent to hunt down the monsters. An ability he once possessed, but no more. No, that was Kate's expertise now.

How he admired what she'd done. And continued to do. Meeting with the killers in prison to learn more about them. Behind it all, of course, was her desire to learn why Hendrickson had done what he'd done to her. His actions, always in the back of her mind, influencing her decisions.

Nick took a sip of his Coke as the cold breeze brushed against his cheeks. Confusion and uncertainty swirled in his mind as he swallowed down the drink.

Resigned, he returned inside, dropping onto the gray sofa sectional. Thoughts of his visit to the lab yesterday ran through his mind. The bones on the table, the forensic analysis of the manner of death. And in a moment of swift recollection, he drew back his shoulders, his lips parting just a little. "Where have I seen that before?"

He jumped off the couch and walked to his bedroom,

returning with his laptop. "I've seen this. Where? Where did I see it?" Nick began to search through his old case files, going back to the Washington Field Office.

When that yielded nothing, he went back farther, scouring his notes from his training days at the FBI Academy in Quantico because he had seen this before, but where and when?

An hour later, he still had found nothing, but the idea gnawed at him. "Come on. I know this...where do I know this from?"

He remembered being in the classroom, his professor, now retired, had been the lead profiler then. He'd pushed the students to search for a killer's motivation, predicting his next moves. It seemed that not much had changed in their field. And that was when he saw it...notes from an old case study dating back to the late 1980s, before DNA evidence became the norm, before the widespread use of the ViCAP database...all of it. His professor used the case to help the new agent trainees, or NATs, build their profiles without the aid of modern technology, sharpening their skills.

The investigation had involved a man who had murdered several people, cutting them up and dumping their body parts into the Lake of the Ozarks. He had been nicknamed the Pied Piper, luring his victims, mostly male, with promises of money and drugs. "My God, how could I have forgotten this?"

Nick's credentials were still valid, so he retrieved the archived file from the FBI database. There it was – the Pied Piper—Jason Belgrave. He'd been captured and sent to prison where he proceeded to commit suicide only a few years later.

As he reviewed the forensics, he noted the jagged, uneven cuts on the bones made by the serrated edge of the saw. The killer had used an aggressive back-and-forth motion, only differing from this current case in the type of saw used. The Pied Piper did his cutting manually, which required significant strength and patience. This current case? A reciprocating saw was used.

Still, maybe the type of weapon doesn't matter as much as the end result. So what was the connection? Is this new case another copycat? Because he'd heard from Fisher that Everett Knapp was convicted without any bodies having been recovered—until now, that is. He didn't know enough about the current investigation to be able to put two and two together, but Fisher did. He had to see him. Right now.

Nick picked up his phone and made the call. "Cam, hey, where are you?"

"At the office, why?" he asked.

"I'm coming down there. See you in thirty." He ended the call and snatched his keys from the entry table. Walking out into the hall, he locked the door and marched toward the elevators, heading down into the parking garage.

Nick jumped into his Lexus SUV and peeled away. The traffic heading toward the compound stymied his progress, but he pushed through. And as he approached Quantico, he reached into his wallet to retrieve his credentials, stopping at the entry gate.

"Morning, Sergeant." Nick held out his badge. "I'm here to see BAU Senior Unit Agent Cameron Fisher. He's expecting me."

The sergeant either didn't recognize Nick or didn't care. "One moment, sir." He turned back into the guard shack and made a call. Nick wondered whether he'd be allowed in. Soon, however, the sergeant returned with Nick's ID.

"Here you are, sir. Have a good day." He pressed the button and raised the gate.

Nick breathed a sigh of relief, driving along the winding road that led to the massive military compound, which housed the BAU as well as the FBI's Academy. As he arrived, taking the elevator up to see Fisher, the doors parted, and he stepped out. Here only yesterday, this felt different. No longer meandering around in search of a purpose, he'd just found it.

Down the hall was Fisher's office, so Nick pressed on, finally arriving. "Hey, I didn't catch you at a bad time, did I?"

"Not at all." Fisher removed the toothpick from his mouth. "Miss me already, did you?"

Nick walked inside, taking a seat. "Maybe a little. Listen, I found something I think you should see."

17

The Hollands must've had answers. They'd employed Wayne Clevenger, but did they know he was McDaniel and Draker's informant? And if they did, did they have him killed? With no sign of the man, the team's options were few. The Holland's granddaughter was still missing as well, and coincidences like that just didn't happen.

Daylight was fading, replaced by an orange and red glow that spread out across the sky as darkness edged its way in. Kate knew that the young girl's odds of survival diminished with each passing moment but felt more and more certain Clevenger was behind it all. The Hollands seemed to be at the heart of this entire situation. Now, it was time to confront them.

"Turn left here." Surrey aimed his finger ahead. He peered over his shoulder at McDaniel in the back seat. "When was the last time you talked to these people?"

"Not since early on in the investigation," McDaniel said. "As I said, we'd had bigger fish to fry, and Wayne Clevenger was hardly a blip on the radar."

"Well, let's hope their desire to find their granddaughter prompts some cooperation," Kate replied, making the left turn. "Is it that place, there?"

Ahead was a sprawling piece of land, yellowed grass with bare trees, and a log-pole entrance with the Hollands' name scrawled in iron at the top. Kate drove through.

A few lights burned under the covered porch and emanated through the front windows as dusk settled over the home. A car and a truck were parked next to each other on the pea gravel driveway. Nondescript. Nothing fancy like one might expect drug traffickers to own. They were smart not to flaunt their wealth.

It seemed surprising that McDaniel hadn't built a case against them, and in fact, had dismissed their significance. Kate wondered if he'd begun to reconsider that now, or was there another reason he'd ruled them out?

Pulling to a stop, Kate's phone buzzed in the center console. "Hang on, it's Cam." She answered. "Hey, we're just about to talk to..."

"Is the team with you?" Fisher cut in.

"Yes."

"Put me on speaker. Scarborough's here too."

"What?" she asked. "Why is he there?"

"I need to tell you all something he found. Reid...put me on speaker," Fisher insisted.

"Yeah, okay." Kate set down her phone. "Cam is with Nick, and he has something he wants all of us to hear." Kate felt Duncan's stare from the back seat but only glanced at her with uncertainty. "Go ahead, Cam. We're all listening."

"In 1986, a man by the name of Jason Belgrave, also known as the Pied Piper, was convicted of murdering ten young men. He cut up their bodies and dumped them in Lake of the Ozarks. All the bodies had been recovered when he confessed to their location."

Kate's lips parted as she shot a glance at the team. "Convicted?"

"That's right." It was Nick's voice who replied. "It was part of our case studies back at the Academy. I had to dig way back to find the details. But when I did, I confirmed how he murdered his victims. While he didn't use a reciprocating saw, he did use a hand saw."

"Jeez, that takes some patience. But it's still pretty close," Walsh replied.

"Yeah, that's what I thought," Nick said.

"You have Everette Knapp," Fisher cut in. "Who was convicted in the disappearance of several people—without having found their remains. And now you have another, who was convicted with clear proof, dating back decades." Fisher paused a moment as if to gather his thoughts. "Reid, this could mean that your theory that Knapp was innocent may be more than just theory, especially given the disfigurement on his right hand," Fisher said. "It means someone familiar with the Pied Piper investigation could be responsible for the Knapp murders."

Kate rubbed her forehead, trying to comprehend his implications. "But how does this tie into our hunt for Draker's killer, the murder of Tim Dawes, and now the kidnapping of a young girl?"

"Kate, as I reviewed the files," Nick cut in. "And Fisher filled me in on your investigation with Agent McDaniel, I noticed something. The original Pied Piper killings had references to a bar called The Crooked Creek outside of the Lake of the Ozarks. Apparently, Belgrave had frequented the bar and may have met some of his victims there."

"It's under a different name now," McDaniel jumped in. "Margie and Ray's Lakeside Bar."

Kate nodded, the pieces coming together in her mind. "The same bar where he'd met with Sandra Dawes."

"I don't have a background on Clevenger," Nick said. "But it might be worth taking a look at his history."

"He's in his early thirties, Agent Scarborough," McDaniel cut in. "Much too young to even remember this Pied Piper. Hell, I'd never heard of him either."

"Could be because he was tried and convicted, then killed himself a few years later," Nick replied. "This was a long time ago, but that doesn't mean your current possible suspect, Clevenger, doesn't know about it. If he grew up there, people would've talked about it. It was a major investigation. Interest fades over time, but maybe this guy kept it in the back of his mind."

"Hey, Nick, it's Eva. I'm not sure where Knapp fits into this," she said.

Kate glanced at her. "I don't think he does. I think he was a scapegoat."

Walsh raised his chin. "So you're saying Clevenger could have murdered the other victims that've been recovered...some seven-odd years ago. Okay. And since he was McDaniel's and Draker's informant, it is possible Draker stumbled onto something that revealed Clevenger's past." Walsh narrowed his brow. "But why take the Holland's granddaughter, and possibly murder their son-in-law? And why wait seven years to try to take his next victim?"

McDaniel raised his index finger. "I might be able to help answer that. When we first got in touch with Clevenger, it was Agent Draker who mentioned to me that Clevenger's family was from here. Going back to when Bagnell Dam was built."

"So maybe he knew the history of Belgrave," Kate said. "And Knapp?"

McDaniel shook his head. "I'm starting to think you could be right about him. Back seven, eight years ago, Clevenger would've been in his early twenties."

Kate nodded. "Which fits right along with a typical profile."

"You say the granddaughter's been taken?" Nick asked.

"And the son-in-law, murdered," Kate replied. "Clevenger had to at least know about Sandra Dawes, given his connection to the Hollands, even if we're to believe they never met before the bar that night."

"He'd probably seen pictures around the Holland's house," Surrey replied.

"Could be." Kate nodded. "And then he grew attracted to her; an obsession developed."

"Now, you're onto something," Nick said.

Kate smiled, nodding. "Yeah, okay. Thanks Nick. Cam. We need to get inside and talk to the Hollands. Their granddaughter's life is on the line. But we'll keep you posted." She ended the call, feeling strangely energized, as she had in the old days when she and Nick had worked together.

Kate opened her car door. "Agent McDaniel, if you'd like to take point on this, we're happy to remain in the background. This is your investigation."

"Thank you, Agent Reid. I'll set the stage and see where it takes us."

As they emerged amid a setting sun, they walked toward the ranch-style home with its wrap-around porch and log-cabin exterior.

Kate fell in behind McDaniel as he knocked on the door. It was clear the Hollands had seen their arrival, the door opening almost immediately. An older man stood on the other side with a stocky middle-aged woman next to him. She recognized them from the station when they'd been brought in regarding their other daughter's remains.

"Good evening, Mr. and Mrs. Holland," McDaniel began. "I apologize for arriving unannounced. These people with me are from the FBI in Quantico. Might we ask you some questions?"

Henry Holland stared them up and down. "Surprised to see you at my door again, Agent McDaniel."

"This about your granddaughter," he replied. "We're also here to discuss the man I believe may still be in your employ...Mr. Wayne Clevenger."

At this, the couple traded a glance, and Kate realized they knew exactly what he was asking.

"Come in." Henry stepped aside. "My wife and I have been beside ourselves with worry ever since our daughter told us what happened." As the team entered, Henry continued, "Is that why you're here? You have some news for us?"

"If they had news, Henry," Jean cut in. "They'd be talking to Sandy, not us." She eyed them. "No, I think this is about something else entirely."

"You are partially right, Mrs. Holland," McDaniel said as he entered the living room. "Though it's not entirely unrelated." He tilted his head, fixing his gaze on the wife. "What can you tell me about Wayne Clevenger, ma'am?"

The hefty woman dropped onto the plush brown sofa. "What do you want to know? He used to work for us a while back. Doesn't anymore."

Mr. Holland sat down next to her, taking her hand. "That's right. Helped take care of the property. Fixing fences and repairing odd things around here."

Kate and the others lingered in the background, observing, listening. The elephant in the room was hard to ignore. Everyone here knew what these people did for a living and a sort of dance had begun. And it wasn't going to help them find Ella Dawes. Regardless of who the Hollands really were, a girl's life hung in the balance. Still, Kate couldn't cross the line. It was up to McDaniel to break through.

"Mr. Clevenger seemed to fall off the face of the earth about three, four weeks ago," McDaniel said, taking a seat in a chair across from the couple. "About a week after my partner, DEA Agent Draker, also disappeared. And earlier today, the boat where my partner had met with another man, turned up near the northern shoreline."

"Is that so?" Mr. Holland asked. "Turned up? So, I'm assuming neither your partner nor Wayne were present when you found the vessel."

"No, sir." McDaniel shook his head, rubbing his hands together as he appeared to think how best to phrase his next words. "Among the remains recovered where your daughter was also found, we recovered my partner's remains. So, whoever killed him knew where those bodies were to begin with."

"And you think that was Wayne?" Henry asked.

"It's a question worth exploring because there's some other interesting information that's come out about him too."

"And what's that?" Jean asked, a hint of sarcasm lacing her tone.

"Mr. Clevenger knew your daughter, Sandra...intimately. And now Sandra's husband is dead, and her daughter has been taken from her home—your granddaughter." He glanced back at Kate. "We'd sure be grateful to have a talk with Wayne, if you know where he might be."

Kate picked up on Mrs. Holland blinking several times and tugging down her oversized blouse. She was nervous or upset. Maybe both. And clearly had no idea about Clevenger and her daughter. That much had just become painfully obvious.

"I'm afraid we haven't seen Wayne in some time," Henry answered, seemingly cutting off any response his wife might have.

"Have you tried to contact him over the past few weeks?" McDaniel pressed. "Called anyone he knows, friends or family? Asked anyone where he might be?"

"No, sir," Henry replied. "He was an employee, not family. He didn't turn up one day and that was that. No need to beat a dead horse."

"How long have you known him?" McDaniel asked.

"He worked for us for a few years," Jean said. "It's not the first time he's taken off. Nature of the business, I guess. But I will say, we had no idea he knew Sandy."

Henry side-eyed her. "Well, it isn't like we didn't talk about her around him. He knew we had a daughter. Course he did."

"But he never mentioned seeing her or going out with her?" McDaniel asked.

"No, sir."

Jean let go of her husband's hand. "Are you suggesting Wayne had something to do with our Ella's disappearance?"

Kate found it interesting that neither of the Hollands seemed all that concerned their son-in-law was dead. She gestured to the other others to step back into the foyer. "These people don't care what happened to Tim Dawes. Doesn't that seem strange to you?"

Surrey glanced toward the living room. "This whole thing seems strange. But I think they know where Clevenger is."

"And as far as their granddaughter," Duncan cut in. "The wife was surprised to hear about any sort of relationship between Clevenger and their daughter. She looks as though she's considering the possibility that Clevenger had taken Ella Dawes."

Kate nodded. "Maybe we should be keeping watch over Henry Holland. He might lead us straight to Wayne Clevenger."

❧

A CHILL CLIMBED up Ella's arms as the grew colder. Night was coming. There were no windows down here, only the door at the top. But it was what gave her a sense of time, the scant light that spilled in around it. That light was all but gone now.

It would be her second night here. He'd fed her. Let her go to the bathroom. But otherwise, she'd been stuck down here, and when she'd tried to scream, he came. The cloth he'd tied around her mouth had been dipped in hot sauce, so now, she won't scream again.

The thumping sound came and went with regularity, yet Ella hadn't known what it was or who'd caused it. But she'd heard all the ghost stories about the lake. All the people who'd died here. Maybe it was one of them. She wasn't sure who to be more afraid of, the man who kept her hostage down here, or whatever was making the noise.

Ella moved through the dark, running her hands along the walls over the rough concrete surface. Could there be some way out of this basement prison?

She heard footsteps from above and froze in place. He was coming back. Quickly, she scurried across the floor, reaching the ratty mattress in the corner when the basement door creaked open. Light from his flashlight blinded her as he stepped down, aiming it at her face.

"What are you doing over there?" he asked, his tone calm and measured.

"N-nothing," she stammered.

He marched toward her and grabbed her. No longer calm, he pulled her close. "Don't lie to me."

Ella shook her head, tears filling her eyes once more. "I heard something. That's all. I didn't know what it was."

He let go of her. "What the hell are you talking about? What did you hear?"

18

The idea Nick had played some small part in helping the team...in helping Kate, brought him a sense of purpose. And her voice, the excitement evident in it when a new piece of the puzzle clicked into place... God, how he missed that. How he missed her.

Fisher had briefed him on the rest of the investigation, as though he was part of the team again, both glossing over the fact that it wasn't to be.

Now, Fisher pulled out a bottle of bourbon from his desk drawer, pouring himself a shot. It never bothered Nick when other people drank around him. He'd come to accept the occasional urges, turning to distraction to keep it at bay.

But alcoholism was a disease that could lay dormant, offering a false sense of control over one's life, only to rear its ugly head when least expected. It wasn't an excuse, or maybe it was.

"You still with me?" Fisher asked as he took a sip of his bourbon.

"Yeah, sorry. Just thinking about how the team's doing. If they were able to get any details out of the Hollands." He saw Fisher's expression shift, turning into something akin to regret. "What is it?"

Fisher set down his glass, unleashing a heavy sigh. He reached for a toothpick from the holder on his desk, twirling it around between his fingers. "Cole asked me to back him up on that recommendation that you return to our unit."

Nick felt a catch in his throat. "I'm sorry he put you in that position, Cam. Really." For a moment, he was afraid to ask Fisher's thoughts on this, but he was still a friend. "What did you tell him? And please...be honest."

Fisher placed the toothpick between his lips and leaned back in his chair. "You know I wanted this job since before you came onboard."

"I'm aware," Nick replied.

"And the only reason I got it was because you left...voluntarily, I might add."

"I did. I thought it best for not only the team, but for Kate. It was too difficult to separate the job from our relationship."

Fisher nodded. "I know how that goes, and it was the same reason Eva and I broke it off." He glanced away, regret masking his face. "The thing is, Nick, and you know I love you like a brother... but first of all, I didn't think you'd be interested in coming back here because it would be in a secondary role. And then there's Kate. With you two separated..." He cleared his throat. "Anyway, I didn't give him an answer. Cole asked me to think about it, so I am. He'll need my support if he hopes to sway Bennett." Fisher leaned over his desk. "We're finally gelling, all of us, you know? Things have settled, and it's been a long time coming."

Nick could only nod because he knew Fisher was right. He'd seen it with his own eyes how well they were all doing without him. And he'd been okay with that, growing into his own role with

Unit Two and then the Taskforce. Then it all went to shit through no one else's fault but his own.

"Look, Cam, coming back here..." He surveyed the office. "It would be a mistake. I know that. I couldn't do that to you, and certainly not to Kate. I mean, she's riding the wave all the way to the top. I see that."

"Yeah, I do to," Fisher replied. "You taught her well."

"No." He smiled. "I might've opened the door for her, but Kate...she blazed her own trail. And continues to do so."

Fisher nodded. "So, what the hell are you going to do, man?"

Nick leaned back, crossing his legs. I don't know...maybe a fresh start is what I need. I didn't know I'd get a choice after what happened, but now that I have one..." he shrugged. "It seems like there's really only one option that remains."

~

Henry dropped the curtains when the headlights faded from view. "They're gone." He turned back to his wife. "We gotta find that son of a bitch. If he has Ella, I swear to Christ..."

Jean raised her hands. "Calm down, Henry. We told him to lay low and he has. But the time's come to get to the truth. Call him... right now, you call him and ask him if he dared lay a hand on our Ella."

"And Tim?" Henry asked. "You think he killed Tim?"

"I don't know, but right now, that's not important to me. My granddaughter is what's important."

Henry nodded, picking up his phone. "I'll call him." He dialed the number, listening to it ring. His chest tightened as it hit the third ring and no answer. "Don't you ignore me, now. Pick up the goddam phone, Wayne." He closed his eyes when it went to voicemail, and he ended the call.

It seemed he didn't need to tell his wife this, because she marched straight for the foyer and snatched her keys from the table.

"Where is he, Henry? I gotta know if he has her. You tell me right now."

Henry pocketed his phone. "Come on. Settle down, now. We don't know anything, all right? Why the hell would he take her, huh?"

"Don't be ignorant. You heard what they said...how he was with Sandy. For God's sake." Anger flushed her cheeks. "He always answers when you call. No, uh-uh. No, sir, if he took Ella, I'll see a bullet shot straight through his head. Tell me where he is, Henry."

"Let me call Alex, all right?" He picked up his phone again and, when the line answered, he continued. "Where the hell are you? It's me. I'm gonna need you to give me that location now."

"I thought you said..."

"I know what I said," he shot back. "Things have changed. Now, give me the goddam address."

"Yes, sir."

Henry snapped his fingers at his wife, lowering the phone from his face. "Get me a pen and paper."

She darted away in search of the items, quickly returning and handing them over.

"I'm ready. Go ahead."

"8371 Oak Creek Road. That's where I told him to stay till all this blew over."

Henry jotted down the address, then hung up the call.

"I'm going with you," Jean added.

Henry reached for his jacket. "The hell you are. I don't know what I'll be dealing with, and I don't need you there launching into some tirade."

"She's my granddaughter, too."

He raised his hands. "And if she's there, I'll get her back. I promise you that." Henry marched out the door into the now-darkened skies. He hoisted himself into his truck and peered again at the address. Turning the engine, his foot slammed on the gas making his tires kick up the gravel as he sped toward the road at the end.

The truck's amber headlights cut through the blackness of the narrow two-lane road. The rumble of its old V-8 engine drowned out the drumming of his heart against his ribs. Much more of this and his heart might just stop altogether. But right now, even God couldn't stop him from getting to Wayne Clevenger.

As he pulled onto Oak Creek Road, the tires crunched atop the gravelly lane. Nothing else out here but bare trees and the occasional yellow eyes of nocturnal creatures. Set far back with no other homes in sight, he spotted the house. "That's gotta be it." And as Henry drove on, the numbers mounted on the edge of the front porch's eve confirmed he was at the right place.

Henry stopped, throwing the truck into park and jumping down onto the firm earth. Hiking up his pants, he marched toward the entrance. No lights burned. No signs at all that anyone was here. "Wayne!" he shouted. "Where is she?"

Light seeped between the curtains as they were pulled back, and a shadowed figure appeared. It was Clevenger.

"Where is she, boy?" Henry shouted.

The curtain dropped again, and the front door opened. A man in a white tank top under a flannel shirt and baggy jeans stepped out onto the porch, hands raised. He was gangly with shoulder-length unruly hair. "Whoa, hey Henry. I don't know what you're talking about. Where's who, now?"

"Don't play dumb with me, son. Where's Ella? If you hurt her, I swear..."

Clevenger backed up, stepping back through the open door. "Ella? What the hell you talking about?"

"Ella! My granddaughter. The goddam FBI is out looking for her." Henry scanned the dismal living room. Empty beer cans and fast food wrappers littered the floor. Old, worn furniture was placed sporadically, and it was cold, like it had no heating system.

Clevenger kept his hands in the air. "I don't have your grand-kid. Why the hell would I take her?"

Henry stepped closer, snatching his tank top, twisting it inside his fist. "Because you're not answering your phone. You answer the goddam phone when I call, you hear? What was I supposed to think?" He let go of the shirt, taking a step back. "I know what you did with Sandy, you low life son of a bitch. You took a liking to her, I'll bet. Figured out she wasn't about to leave her husband, then you killed him, didn't you?"

Clevenger shook his head. "Are you insane? I didn't kill Sandra's husband, and I sure as shit didn't take her daughter. I don't know where the hell this is coming from, Henry. I just done what you asked. Kept my head down, just like you told me to. Been stuck out here for weeks."

"They found the boat, you know. The FBI was out on it today." Henry moved in again, raising his chin. "So, you got some-thing you want to say to me, son? Best do it now before I find out for myself."

⌇

UNDER THE LIGHT of the side table lamp, Dr. Shane Fuller reviewed Sandra's patient file. All of his notes, examined with an intensity as though learning about her for the first time.

She had discussed her sex life, or lack thereof. How she had felt taken for granted and overlooked by almost everyone. But it was how she'd felt about her parents that seemed the most tragic. Her husband had insisted she cut ties with them when their daughters were still toddlers. And she willingly agreed. But what seemed to lay beneath that decision was regret.

He assumed that losing Ashley, then being asked to turn away from her parents, that Sandra had felt even more isolated. Disassociated from that part of her family. The part that had included her twin. But it was what, or who, she hadn't mentioned that seemed intriguing. Jacob.

It was only when Ashley's remains had been found that she ever say a word about what had happened to his son, alongside her sister. "You were always so selfish. Self-centered. It was all about you, wasn't it, Sandra?"

Headlights passed by his front window. He stood up for a better look and realized a vehicle had stopped on his driveway. "Shit." Fuller closed the file, hurrying to his bedroom, and tucking it inside a dresser drawer.

On his return, the knock came. He composed himself, straightening his white button-down shirt, smoothing down his thick hair streaked with gray. And on opening the door, he stepped back in surprise at the several people in suits standing before him. He recognized two of them—the woman with the long dark ponytail was FBI Agent Reid. The other, wearing the expensive suit, that was Agent Surrey. "Agents Reid, Surrey, I'm surprised to see you here. Can I help you with something?"

I'm sorry for dropping by." She thumbed back. "We've been helping out the local authorities find Ella Dawes. I'm sure you know she's gone missing."

"I'm aware, and in fact, had gone to join the search earlier today." He glanced down. "Though I don't think Sandra wanted me there."

"May we come in?" Kate asked. "We'd like to talk to you about Sandra."

"Uh, yes, of course, though I kind of thought you and I were done with all that." He stepped aside, allowing the hoard of federal agents into his home. "Please forgive the mess. I'm usually busy with work and don't get much chance to clean." He gestured toward the living room. "Please, find yourselves a seat. Can I get anyone something to drink?"

"No, thank you, I think we'll be fine," Kate replied. "We just need to ask you a few more questions."

"All right." He joined them in the living room, taking a seat on the raised fireplace hearth while they sat on the sofa and chairs. "So, what can I answer for you? Bearing in mind, Mrs. Dawes is a patient, and I am limited as to what I can say. Just as I mentioned before."

"Of course," Kate replied.

He studied the agents in his living room, feeling as though they were circling the wagons. "Go on then. Ask away."

Agent Surrey got to his feet. "I don't suppose I could use your restroom?"

"Uh, yeah, sure." Fuller aimed a finger ahead. "It's down the hall. Second door on the left."

"Thank you."

⌇

Surrey headed down the hall, a soft echo under his feet as the wood floor gave way beneath his steps. While they had no more answers regarding Clevenger's whereabouts, McDaniel insisted on returning to the station for an update on the search for Ella Dawes.

But Kate's intuition wouldn't let go of the idea that Dr. Fuller had known more about Sandra and her possible relationship with Clevenger. And Sandra's concern over the idea Fuller was stalking her, well, more could yet come of this hunt for answers.

The plan had been for him to get deeper into the house and search for anything that might point to Ella or Tim Dawes. Now, while the rest of the team kept Fuller occupied with questions he likely wouldn't answer, Surrey was on the hunt. This wasn't just a legally gray area, this was outright illegal. He had called out Kate for her moral ambiguity more times than he could count. Yet he was traveling down that same path in hopes of finding the young girl. It was a slippery slope, and he was sliding fast. Regardless, something about Fuller had seemed off and Kate wasn't the only one to see it.

The bathroom door was just ahead. Surrey glanced over his shoulder, ensuring Fuller was still occupied. He turned on the light and closed the door, as though he'd gone inside.

But instead, Surrey quietly moved down the hallway. He paused outside a closed door that he assumed led to Fuller's bedroom. Slowly, he turned the handle and pushed the door open just enough to slide inside.

From what he could see in the dark room, it appeared neat and orderly, with few pieces of art on the walls. No picture frames or nick knacks on the dresser or nightstands. Surrey used the light on his phone and moved through the space, opening dresser drawers and rifling through their contents. Stopping for a moment to ensure he still heard voices, Surrey then opened a bedside table.

He shuffled the various items from a watch to a pair of headphones to papers. And then he saw it. Polaroids. A small stack of them. Maybe ten in total. Not the old Polaroids he'd grown up with. These were from one of those new ones all the kids had that printed small pictures, like his own children had received last Christmas.

In each image was Sandra Dawes. Some with her kids, some with her husband. Some alone. But all appearing to have been taken without her knowledge, as though Fuller was a private investigator and he'd taken candid shots of the family.

Footfalls approached down the hall. "Damn it." Surrey returned the photos, returned everything back to its place as best he could remember.

Carefully closing the drawer, he walked to the doorway, craning to see if anyone was there. A figure walked by several feet away. As it disappeared, he darted toward the bathroom, opening the door, and turning off the light.

A quick clearing of his throat, and he returned to the group, seeing that Fuller was no longer sitting on the hearth. He looked at Kate. "Where'd he go?"

"I'm right here, Agent Surrey," Fuller said, returning with a handful of water bottles. "I was getting thirsty. Figured you all might want a drink." He handed a bottle over to him.

"Thanks."

"So, as I was telling Agent Reid, I lost my son at the same time Ashley Holland went missing. They were together, on a date."

Surrey glanced at her. They'd now known about Jacob Fuller, yet the good doctor had said nothing of the fact his son was dead when they'd asked about family at their first meeting. Now, he was admitting that his son had known Ashley Holland.

"So you know his remains have also been recovered," Surrey continued.

"Yes, which is why I assumed you two showed up tonight."

"We were hoping you could shed light on who might've taken Ella Dawes, actually," Duncan cut in. "As we understand it, Mrs. Dawes was concerned by her recent run-ins with you."

"Run-ins? Hardly," he interrupted. "I happened to see her

shopping recently. Offered a shoulder. I hadn't realized it had caused her any distress."

Kate cleared her throat. "Well, Dr. Fuller, I want to thank you for talking to us. As I said earlier, if you think of anything, or recall Sandra mentioning anyone who might be of concern, please contact us." She handed over her business card.

"Of course, Agent Reid," he replied, taking the card in his hand. "And do please let Mrs. Dawes know that I'm terribly sorry if I'd frightened her. Just wrong place, wrong time, I guess."

Kate nodded and headed toward the door. "Thank you again for your time, Dr. Fuller. And I'm very sorry for your loss."

They exited the home, heading back toward the sedan. As they all stood outside the car, Kate regarded Surrey. "Well?"

"Get in," he replied, climbing inside. And when the team and entered the car, he continued, "I found a stack of Polaroid pictures. All had Sandra Dawes as the main subject."

"Were they sexual in nature?" Walsh asked. "As in, was she having a fling with her therapist?"

"No." He fixed his gaze on Kate. "Sandra was right to be concerned. What I saw in those pictures? Fuller was stalking her, and I have no idea how that fits into this investigation."

19

With the Amber Alert having been issued, the local police, and federal agents all on the hunt for young Ella Dawes, there was nothing left for Kate to do tonight. With no indication from Surrey that Fuller had the girl, it seemed more and more likely she was being held captive by Wayne Clevenger, who they had yet to locate.

Regardless of the photos Surrey had found inside Fuller's home, she wondered why he would've withheld the information about his son. The only thing that made sense was if he was their killer. Though murdering his own son?"

Frustrated, Kate paced the few feet between her bed and the door of her hotel room, pondering these questions for which there seemed to be no answers. Worst of all, her own trauma was forcing itself to the surface, amplifying her fear and feelings of help-lessness.

What would've happened to her had she never remembered the past? Never remembered Joseph Hendrickson and what he'd done when she was just a kid. Would he have sought her out again? It was a question she'd tried to resolve with her jailhouse interviews, yet the answers had remained elusive.

As Kate finally dropped to the edge of the bed, she considered the necessity to put a tail on the Hollands. Despite their denial, they must know where Clevenger was holed up. Their granddaughter's life was at stake. Would they not have revealed his location if it could free her?

She scrolled through her messages from Agent McDaniel in search of any new developments, but when she happened upon an earlier message, it struck her. "Shit. The boat." They'd left to pursue the Hollands and now, the vessel had been left unattended. Evidence sitting right there for anyone to erase.

"Screw this. I'm going out there." Kate grabbed her coat and car keys and walked into the hall. She marched to Surrey's door and knocked. Going out there alone wasn't wise and Surrey would take issue with her going against protocol. They all would.

He opened the door, eyeing her car keys. "Where are you off to?"

"The boat," she replied. "It's siting out there, free access to anyone who wants it. Ready to take a ride with me?"

Without a word, he turned around and pulled on a jacket, snatching his wallet and phone from the dresser. On his return, he regarded her. "Let's go."

They said few words to each other, the long day having already taken its toll. But they were comfortable enough around one another that silence usually meant their thoughts were on solving the case.

The quiet drive came to an end when Kate aimed her finger ahead. "Over there."

"Yep," Surrey replied. "Just beyond the clearing."

Kate pulled off the side of road. "Let's go check it out."

They stepped out of the rented sedan, donning coats amid the chilly night air. Before approaching, she scanned the darkened shoreline with only the light of a hazy moon shining down. Searching for signs of movement, the silhouette of the abandoned vessel came into view, partly submerged near the bank. "There it is. Looks like they managed to get yellow police tape around the trees at the shoreline."

"Like that's an effective deterrent," Surrey replied, aiming his phone's light at the ground. "Watch your step."

By the lights on their phones, they made their way to the shoreline. The boat sat several feet out, the waves causing it to sway a little. Kate slipped off her shoes and rolled up her jeans, wading into the cold water. She looked back. "You coming in or what?"

Surrey appeared reluctant as he took off his black dress shoes and cuffed his suit pants. "Great. I just had these dry cleaned."

"Don't be such a prima-donna." Kate sloshed through the icy water, drawing nearer to the boat, but when a rumbling sound traveled over the water, she stopped. Peering over her shoulder, it seemed Surrey heard it too.

"Someone's coming." Kate extinguished the light on her phone as Surrey caught up to her.

"Get down," he said, pressing on her shoulder to keep them out of view.

She crouched down behind the vessel, peering out into the darkness. The water had reached her waist, chilling her to the bone.

The approaching boat stopped, the engine cut. And when the voice of a man arose, she turned to Surrey. "Can you see who it is?"

He craned outward but shook his head.

"I'm here," the man said. "I'll call you back if I find anything." He climbed aboard the boat, making it teeter.

Surrey pulled Kate back from the vessel as it rocked. Relief swept through her as it almost knocked her deeper into the water. The noise would've drawn the man's attention. They waited, Kate's lips beginning to tremble from the cold. They couldn't stay here much longer, but if whoever was aboard this vessel intended to search it for something, they had to know what it was...and who wanted it.

Standing on the deck, the man was on his phone again. "Yeah, just got on board. Haven't found anything yet...No, no one followed me...Okay, I'll dump it as soon as I'm done."

Kate's pulse quickened. Who was this guy, and who'd sent him? As the man ended his call and headed back below deck, Kate turned to Surrey and whispered, "We need to find out who this is."

Surrey glanced up at boat. "If we confront him, we won't know what he's after."

"But we'll know who he is," she insisted.

The vibration of her phone sent a shockwave through her. As she retrieved it, the screen illuminated.

Surrey slammed his hand over hers that held the phone, dousing the light.

"It's Levi," she whispered, placing the phone at her ear. When she didn't say anything, it seemed he knew.

"Kate, are you safe?"

Cupping her hand over her mouth, she replied. "With Jonathan at the boat."

"Goddam it," Walsh sighed. "We've been looking for you guys. We need you back here...now."

~

SANDRA HAD INSISTED YOUNGEST DAUGHTER, Marissa, stay with her friend tonight. The cops had kept a patrolman outside the house for her protection, but even that didn't seem like enough. Whoever had taken Ella could easily come back here. Now, no one knew where Marissa was, except for her and the cops. This left Sandra to do what she needed to do.

She walked outside, glancing left and right, before heading down to the curb where the officer was parked. He noticed her arrival and rolled down his window. "Can I help you with something, Mrs. Dawes?"

"Uh, I need to run to the store. I'm out of a few things. I won't be long. Is that okay?"

He seemed to consider whether this was a good idea, and she wore her best pleading expression. "Honestly, I won't be long. I need to go before the stores close."

He inhaled a long breath. "Yeah, okay. But if you're not back in twenty minutes...by the way, which store?"

The number of grocery stores here could be counted on one hand, so she picked the only one that came to mind. "Byers. It's just a couple of miles away."

The officer drew in his brow as it seemed he'd begun to reconsider. "Maybe I should follow you there."

Sandra glanced back at her house and then turned to him again. "But what if someone tried to get inside while we were both gone? Officer, I'd feel much better if you kept your eye on the house. Nothing's going to happen to me at the store. They'll be plenty of other people there."

Finally, he nodded. "You're probably right. Okay, Mrs. Dawes." He raised his index finger. "Twenty minutes. Got it? Any longer, and I'm coming to look for you."

"Understood. Thank you." Sandra smiled and walked to her car, already wearing a coat and holding her keys, figuring the officer would agree to her request.

Once inside, she backed out of the driveway, offering the

officer a polite wave before heading down the street. Her destination was only ten minutes away. And now that she was alone, only one thing mattered.

Her thoughts were consumed with Ella. Who had taken her. Where she was right now. Was she hurt? Was she scared? Wiping the tears that had again spilled, Sandra kept her eyes on the dark road ahead. She was almost there.

It was the final turn, and she'd reached the house on the end of Lakewood Drive. Sandra's car came to an abrupt halt outside the craftsman-style home. Her hands trembled, almost bone-white from gripping the steering wheel. Her eyes, red-rimmed and growing more frantic, scanned the quiet street before she cut the engine. Sandra stepped out into the chill of the winter air.

The house in front of her, she knew all too well. Warmly lit and inviting, it belonged to Dr. Shane Fuller, her therapist for the past six months. The man knew her deepest, darkest secrets. He'd listened week after week to things that she'd shared with no one else. But tonight, he was not her confidant. In her now-fractured world, he had become her enemy.

The hammering of her heart against her chest drowned out the sounds of the world around her. And her mind, a chaotic swirl of grief and rage, forced her vision to narrow, the periphery, obscured. News of her husband's murder was still a raw, gaping wound, and the disappearance of her daughter, Ella, had splintered her sense of reason.

The police continued their search for Ella, but Sandra had spiraled down into the darkest corridors of her mind, clutching at a suspicion that felt as real to her as her own pulse.

She rang the doorbell and waited, her breath forming small clouds in the cold air. The door opened, and there he stood— Shane Fuller, a look of concern quickly overtaking the surprise on his features.

"Sandra? What on earth—are you alright? It's almost ten o'clock."

His voice, usually calming to her, now struck her as deceitful. Nothing but a shrill sound of lies. Without waiting for an invitation, Sandra pushed past him into the foyer, her eyes darting around as if she might find clues to a conspiracy hidden among the furnishings.

"Why, Dr. Fuller? Why would you do this to me?" Her voice was a cracked whisper, but it rose swiftly to a shout. "You did this! You took them from me!"

Fuller, his initial shock seeming to morph into concern, gently closed the door and faced her. "Sandra, you're upset, and understandably so. But I assure you, I don't know what you're talking about. Let's sit down, and you can tell me everything."

"No!" Her hand flailed out, pointing an accusing finger at him. "You've always wanted me, haven't you? All those sessions, you were just waiting, planning. Stalking me. You took my husband out of the picture, and now my daughter."

"Sandra, please, you need to listen to me," he implored, his voice steady. "I am here to help you, not harm you. Your husband's death and your daughter's disappearance are tragedies, but you are in shock, and your mind is trying to make sense of it all."

Her eyes searched his, desperate for a flicker of guilt, but finding only the calm sincerity that had always made her trust him. Doubt crept in, unwelcome and confusing. She shook her head, trying to dispel the fog of her own grief-stricken presumptions.

Fuller took a cautious step toward her. "You're in pain, and it's twisting your thoughts. Let me help you. We can call the police together, see if there are any updates on Ella—"

"Stop it!" Sandra collapsed onto a chair, her body suddenly devoid of the energy that had fueled her confrontation. Tears streamed down her face as the real weight of her situation settled on her shoulders again. "Why have you been following me, then?"

Fuller knelt beside her, his hand reaching out to tentatively touch her arm. "As I told the FBI agents, who I assume you sent to my door earlier tonight...it was strictly a coincidence, us running into each other at the pharmacy and the market. And then I heard what happened with Ella and I wanted to help. That was why I went out there to the lake this morning, to do whatever I could to help."

Sandra stared at him, her eyes burning from tears. She wanted to believe him, to trust in his soothing words like she had so many times before. But the gnawing doubts remained, chewing away at her fragile psyche.

"It wasn't a coincidence," she said, her voice hollow. "You've been planning this. You wanted my family gone so you could have me."

Fuller shook his head emphatically. "That's simply not true. I care about you as my patient, nothing more."

Sandra scrambled to her feet, fresh hysteria rising inside her. "You're lying."

He slowly stood, raising his hands in a calming gesture. "Sandra, look at me. Breathe. I want to help you get through this, but you have to trust me."

"Trust you?" Sandra scoffed. "After what you've done? You might have the police fooled, but not me. This all goes back to my sister, doesn't it?"

Fuller looked down. "What happened to your sister and my son was the work of a madman. A tragic event that has impacted both our lives."

"You know, Tim said I should've found a different therapist instead of going to you. After all the history between our families." She wiped her tear-stained cheek. "Why didn't you ever ask me about Ashley, huh? I mean, my God, she was my twin. What that must do to you every time you see me."

"Stop," Fuller whispered.

"Or was that why you took me on as a client? You wanted to see me because of her. Because of Ashley." She leaned in, searching his face for some semblance of truth. "Were you jealous of your own son, Dr. Fuller? Jealous that Jacob had Ashley? So, I guess I was your consolation prize then, huh?"

He raised his gaze with eyes now darkened. "I said stop."

She plunged her hand into her purse and withdrew a gun. "I knew it. You're behind all of this."

Dr. Fuller's eyes went wide with alarm. "Sandra, put down the gun."

"Where's my daughter?" She aimed it at his chest, holding firmly with both hands. "Where is she, goddam it. I won't let you take her too, like you took my husband and sister."

"Ashley was murdered right along with my Jacob," he insisted.

Sandra shook her head, nose running, eyes spilling with tears. "Tell me where Ella is, or I swear to God, I'll kill you."

"Please, don't do this, Sandra." Fuller had his hands raised and spoke in an even tone. "I've done nothing to your family. You have to believe me."

"Yeah, well...I don't." Sandra fired the weapon.

～

THE ONLY THING that could've made Kate leave that boat and whoever had gone inside it was Walsh's call telling her someone had spotted Ella Dawes. But was she still with her captor, or had she escaped? No one seemed to know.

She and Surrey had managed to get out of the water and back to the car before the man had reemerged above deck. But neither had gotten a good look at him, so the entire plan had been flushed down the toilet.

"I know you're still pissed," Surrey said as Kate parked outside the station. "But this girl's life is more important."

She cut the engine. "I know, but we didn't even get a look at the guy. We have no idea who he was or what he was doing there."

"Yeah, I get that, but once we're finished here, when daylight arrives, we'll head back. He was looking for something."

Kate opened her car door. "And he probably found it, taking it with him when he left." She walked toward the entrance, not waiting for Surrey. Though being angry with him wasn't going to solve anything. He was right.

Inside, she saw Walsh and Duncan with Agent McDaniel in the lobby. Surrey entered only steps behind her.

Walsh caught sight of them and headed over. "What the hell were you two thinking, going out there alone?"

Kate raised her hands. "It was a last-minute hunch, all right? I dragged Jonathan with me.

Surrey thrust his hands in his pockets. "We did see someone, but couldn't get an ID. It was too dark."

"He was looking for something," Kate added. "Anyway, we got your call and dropped back."

"Goddam it." Walsh glanced away. "You should've stayed. I didn't know..."

It's okay." She eyed him. "So what's going on? Do we have Ella Dawes? Is she safe?"

"Come on. Everyone's over here." Walsh waved them over. "A call came in from a man who was driving home from work an hour ago. He'd stopped at a gas station and said he saw a girl who matched Ella's description. Apparently, he'd taken part in the search yesterday morning and knew who to look for. Anyway, he tried to get her attention, but she ran from him, disappeared around the back of the building. He thinks she got into a car and drove off but had no details to that effect. Called it into the station right away."

"Did he get a good look at the car?" Kate asked.

"That's all we got," he said. "McDaniel reached out to me and asked if we'd come down, thinking they'd manage to find her."

Just before they reached the others, Kate stopped and squared up to Walsh. "Did they already send out units to that location?"

"About twenty minutes ago," he replied.

Kate followed him as they continued toward the bullpen. She wondered...if the man on the boat had been Clevenger, and assuming he did take Ella, would that have given her a chance to escape? But then, who helped her? And why would she run away from someone offering help?

"No sign of the girl yet," Duncan said, seeming to know that would be Kate's first question.

"So we're playing a waiting game," she replied. "We were at the boat, and we weren't alone. Someone else showed up, but we don't know who."

Duncan set her gaze on Kate. "You didn't get a good look?"

"It was dark, and we were doing our best to avoid detection, so, no, we didn't see his face. But it was clear he was there on someone else's direction. He was on the phone, talking about getting rid of something."

"We've all considered the idea Clevenger is behind the girl's abduction," Surrey added. "So if it was him, it starts to make sense that someone had spotted Ella Dawes. She might've had an opportunity to make her escape while he was out."

McDaniel approached them, pocketing his phone. "Son of a bitch."

Kate turned to him. "What is it?"

"A unit was dispatched to a 'shots fired' call," he continued. "It was at Shane Fuller's home."

Kate's lips parted; her breaths shallowed. "Oh, God. Is he dead?"

"We'll know shortly," he replied, his attention drawn to an approaching officer.

"Agent McDaniel?" the officer asked.

"Yeah? You have news on Fuller?"

With his gaze downcast, he continued. "It wasn't Ella Dawes. The sighting that came in...it wasn't her."

"For God's sake." McDaniel rubbed his beard. "Then who the hell was it? The caller saw someone."

"Uh, we don't think so, sir. It appears to have been a false tip. The guy was looking for attention or something. He did volunteer in yesterday's operation and, who knows, I guess he figured he wanted to be in the spotlight. Anyway, he's in custody now. Our people are trying to get to the bottom of it."

McDaniel looked up, appearing resigned. "So we still have no idea where Ella Dawes is."

Frustration tightened Kate's chest. "And now we have no idea what the hell's just happened to Shane Fuller."

20

Lights on patrol cars swirled red and blue, standing in stark contrast to the clear night sky. Neighbors stood on their porches, wrapped in coats. Officers meandered the property, some standing in the open doorway to Dr. Shane Fuller's home.

Word had reached McDaniel on the drive over. Fuller was dead. And as the team stopped along the curb, observing the scene, only one person sprang to Kate's mind as to who'd committed this murder. The one person who'd suffered more than her share over the past few days, and was probably at the end of her rope, searching for her daughter. Still, reserving judgement for now, Kate needed to get inside and see for herself.

The house looked different. Cold. Empty. Fuller's body lay in a pool of blood on the wood floor of his living room, the very room she and the team had been in only hours earlier. No doubt Fuller was obsessed with Sandra Dawes. Surrey had confirmed as much when he found the Polaroids. But Sandra must've come here believing he'd had her daughter. Kate should've realized how desperate Sandra had become.

"Shot almost point blank," McDaniel said, examining Fuller's body and the gaping hole in his chest.

"If anyone has another suspect in mind besides Sandra Dawes, I'm all ears," Kate said. "The photos Jonathan found. The fact she came to me, afraid he'd been stalking her, and was even at her home..." It was all she could do to quash her guilt for not stopping the ticking time bomb that was Sandra Dawes. "With her daughter missing, we can assume she wasn't of sound mind. Probably came here to confront him."

"And yet, the girl isn't here," Duncan said. "So who the hell has her?"

"The one person we can't seem to find." Kate walked outside, heading toward the separate entrance used by Fuller's clients. She jiggled the handle, but the door was locked. "Damn it." Turning back to find the key, it seemed Surrey had the same thing in mind.

"You looking for this?" he asked, holding it in front of her.

A wry smile curled her lips. "Where'd you find that?"

"In his bedside table. I'd seen it there earlier, so I just ran back to look. Figured it could be the key to this door."

She took it from him. "It's best if we get in there before all these other guys." Kate stepped inside, turning on the lights. "If he was hiding something, I think will be in here."

Just inside the door lay a small waiting area with a few chairs. Books and crayons for kids. As they pressed farther, they entered Fuller's office. Shelves were stacked with self-help books, Psychology Today magazines, and other books on counseling. A large oak desk was situated in in front of the bookshelves. Clean, except for a laptop and pad and paper.

"Let's see what we can find," Kate said. "We know Fuller's son was identified with Ashley Holland, but did they know each other? And if so, is that why Fuller was obsessed with Sandra?" She made her way to the desk and began rifling through the drawers.

"Hey, Reid, come look at this." Surrey stood at the bookshelves, holding a manila folder.

Kate crossed the room and stood beside him, looking over his shoulder. Inside were a few local newspaper clippings about a young man and woman who'd gone missing seven years ago. The young man's name was Jacob Fuller - Dr. Fuller's son. And the woman...Ashley Holland.

"They were together, according to this," Kate said.

"Why would Sandra Dawes hire Fuller to be her therapist when they shared this kind of connection?" Surrey asked. "Her twin essentially died with his son. Jesus."

"Could've been the start of his obsession with Sandra," Kate added. "Her twin was the last person seen with his son."

Now, more than ever, Kate regretted turning away from the man she now suspected could've been Wayne Clevenger. Deciding instead to come here to witness the tragic end of Shane Fuller's life. He didn't have the Dawes' child. But what if that man at the boat did?

"If we don't find Ella Dawes," Kate said. "We both know what happens next. I'm not sure we should be the ones to track down Sandra."

"What are you thinking?" Surrey asked.

"If Ella has been taken by the same person who murdered Draker, and we think that could be Clevenger, then she might already be lost."

"And if he didn't take her?" Surrey asked. "How do we find her?"

She fixed her gaze on him. "The Hollands...They must know where Clevenger is, maybe even ordered him to kill Draker."

"We've already talked to them." He shrugged. "They claim ignorance regarding his whereabouts. And even so, if they thought he had their granddaughter...no way they'd let that slide."

~

WHILE THE LOCAL authorities worked to bring in Sandra Dawes for questioning, there was only one place Kate wanted to go—back to the boat. Fuller's involvement in Ella's disappearance was now resolved. But what wasn't? Wayne Clevenger, because he was the only person Kate believed had reason to take the girl. And if they found him, they'd find the person who killed Agent Draker...the only reason they were all here right now.

It was time to split up. Dawn had arrived. Kate and Duncan drove back to the vessel to search for anything that might reveal who murdered the agent. And determine what the man might've removed last night.

Surrey and Walsh were already on their way back to the Hollands. They now had leverage they hadn't earlier. Sandra. So if they wanted to help their daughter, who likely just murdered someone, they'd come clean regarding Clevenger's whereabouts.

"We're running out of time for that little girl," Kate said, heading out toward the lake again.

"I'm aware," Duncan replied. "And word about Fuller will spread quickly...probably to the kidnapper, himself. I don't know if that'll change anything, but if it is Clevenger, the guys will have the best shot at finding her."

"If Clevenger is our unsub, how the hell is he tied to the Pied Piper or Everett Knapp for that matter?" Kate replied. "Because whoever dumped Draker's body...."

"Right," Duncan said. "Preaching to the choir, here."

As they made their way along the still gray, shadowy roads, she felt Duncan's eyes lingering on her. "You might as well say what you want to say."

"I was just thinking... you know...have you thought about what's going to happen to Nick?"

Kate scoffed. "Oh, I've thought about it, but there's nothing I can do. It's his decision."

"Kate, I know you've been to see him a couple of times. The call he made earlier...I saw the look in your eyes." Duncan turned her sights toward the road ahead. "Do you think you can get past what happened?"

"I don't know," Kate conceded. "I did go see him after the hearing. We just talked, nothing else happened. I'll admit that it felt good being around him. And I was careful not to let my emotions take over." She felt her eyes sting. "On one hand, we have a lot of history. I still love him; that was never in question. But our jobs are hard. Our lives are sometimes on the line. That part, not for him anymore so much. But just to get a sense of how critical it is for us to keep our focus. To not let the personal stuff get in the way. So for him to have ignored the consequences of his actions...despite his reasons, I'm just having a hard time accepting that."

"We all screw up," Duncan added. "I know the decision he had to make that day."

Kate shot her a look. "It's no excuse for risking not only your life, but possibly the lives of others. He got behind the wheel and he could've died, Eva."

She grunted. "So maybe that's the heart of this thing...you could've lost him that night and he didn't think of that. He didn't think of you when he made that decision."

"No, he didn't," Kate said, her voice cracking. "And I'd only just found out I was pregnant, and I thought...Jesus, would he make a decision like that if he'd become a father?" She wiped away the tears that finally came. "I was pissed."

"I get that." Duncan's tone softened. "When Cam and I broke up, we didn't have all that to consider. It was really us deciding what was best for our careers and for the team."

"Exactly. You considered everything in that decision," Kate replied. "Nick failed to do the same."

"I don't envy your situation." Duncan's voice fractured with emotion. "But if anyone can work through something like this, it's you two."

Kate returned a half-smile, trying to disguise her pain. "What, are you looking to get rid me already? Am I that hard to live with?"

And Duncan did the only thing she knew how to do to help Kate, she reached for her hand. "No, of course not...Well, maybe a little."

"This is it, up here." Kate veered off to the shoulder, the rented sedan slogging through the forest floor. She came to a stop just before the woods thickened. Through the bare trees, illuminated by the gray morning light, the boat was visible, listing in the water only feet from the shoreline. "I should've stayed here. It could've been Clevenger, and I didn't know it."

Duncan prepared to step out. "We can't think about that now. This is our shot at getting more information."

Kate stepped out to join her. "I wish I had your confidence. If we take the GPS, we'll know for certain whether this boat was ever at the grounds where the remains were dumped, tying the owner of this vessel to the other murders."

～

Nick shot up from his bed, forehead damp with sweat, heart pounding. He snatched his phone, peering at the time. "five a.m." Swinging his legs to the floor, he flipped on the bedside lamp. His eyes stung a moment before they adjusted to the harsh glow as he swiped open his phone.

Kate's phone number appeared. His finger hovered over it, knowing he had to tell her what he saw. While he slept, his mind mulled over the old case file he'd once studied—the Pied Piper investigation. And what jolted him awake was his recollection of something she had to know.

But maybe it was best to call Surrey instead. "No, just call her. She's still your wife, for God's sake." Nick pressed the button, putting the phone to his ear. The line rang. Once, twice. He drew back his shoulders when she answered. "Kate, it's me. Did I wake you?" He closed his eyes, wincing at the stupid question.

"No, Eva and I are back out at the boat. A lot's happened since we talked. I can't get into it now. What's wrong? Are you okay?"

He figured she thought he was calling because maybe he'd done something stupid—again. "I'm fine. Listen, I woke up, recalling something about that case…"

"The Pied Piper?" she asked.

"Yes. I don't know why I didn't remember this before, but when we studied the files—the profile of the killer—all of that, there was something he left on the bodies before dumping them."

"I'm listening."

"A carving, like a tattoo." He got up, wearing only his boxers, and paced the darkened bedroom, as if the steps made him think more clearly. "The bodies you found were already decomposed, leaving only bone. Except for one…"

"The DEA agent," she said.

"Right. The Bureau never released to the public the information on this carving." He stopped, peering at the early morning sky through the bedroom window.

"So if the agent has this carving," Kate began. "Then whoever killed him has intimate knowledge of the Pied Piper, which could only mean one thing—"

"Your killer knew Belgrave and emulated him," Nick cut in. "Family. Friend. My guess is family considering how long ago this happened. Have Dr. Bailey look at the agent's body for the sign of the Freemasons."

"The Freemasons?" Kate asked.

"That's right. His victims were branded with the symbol. Many of the towns that were flooded out when the dam was built had several Freemason members. If your agent has that symbol, and it'll be small, then..."

"I can look for a connection to Belgrave, which I think I already have someone in mind." She was quiet for a moment.

"Kate, you still there?" he asked.

"Yeah, yeah, I'm here. Thank you for this, Nick."

He sighed, placing his hand on his cheek, nodding. "I hope it helps. Good luck down there. Please be safe."

"I will."

Nick closed his eyes, wanting to say the words, but terrified of her response. He swallowed hard, deciding to lay it on the line regardless. "I love you, Kate." She went quiet again.

"Thank you, Nick."

She ended the call, and he peered at his phone. She didn't respond in kind, but at least she knew how he felt.

～

KATE POCKETED HER PHONE, her thoughts consumed by the news.

Duncan stood before her, snapping. "Hey, are you good? What's going on?"

She returned to the moment. "That was Nick. He remembered something about the Pied Piper. Something that could help us."

"Hey, I'm all ears." Duncan stood in the water, ready to board the vessel.

"He said in the case files, the Bureau noted on the victims a symbol carved into their bodies. The Freemasons symbol," Kate replied. "With only Draker's remains still containing any tissue, he suggested we ask Dr. Bailey if she'd made note of a small carving."

Duncan set her hands on her hips, nodding. "But we know Jason Belgrave was murdered in prison. So, who else knew if the Bureau kept a lid on that detail?"

Kate looked out over the water, her breath visible in the cold morning air. "Someone who knew Belgrave. But one step at a time because we don't know if any such marking was found on Draker. You'd think Bailey would've made mention of it."

"That is true," Duncan replied. "Look, it's cold as hell out here. Let's put a pin in that and do what we came here to do. Otherwise, we're getting bogged down with distraction."

"I agree. We'll follow up after this." Kate led the way through the icy waters, wading in up to her knees, until she reached the ladder on the side.

They boarded the boat, stepping onto the bow. The smell had grown worse and was almost caustic now.

"They need to get this out of here sometime this morning. It's not safe," Kate said.

"Now you tell me," Duncan replied with a wry smile.

Kate turned on the flashlight feature on her phone and aimed it at the interior cabin. "For now, we remove the GPS and get it back to the station."

"You don't want to check to see if this guy you saw took anything?"

The vessel swayed as Kate looked around. "I'm not sure we'd have any idea what was here or not. Besides, if we discover this boat was at the scene? I think we'll have our answer as to who else was there. For now, we take care not to destroy any potential evidence by ensuring they get this thing out of here." But as they started toward the wheelhouse, a rumbling sounded in the distance.

Peering at Duncan, Kate raised a finger to her lips. She pointed outward. The rumbling grew louder. "Shit. I think he's back," Kate whispered. "Must've had the same idea as us."

"Coming back when there's light. We need to get off this boat." Duncan clutched Kate's arm, tossing a nod toward the stairs that led to the upper deck. She started ahead, climbing the ladder, keeping low while Kate trailed steps behind her.

Kate stared out over the water, a dull shimmer of gray light bouncing off the ripples. "I see it. We have time to get out of sight."

They hurried to shore as the other vessel drew near. A grouping of Oak trees lay ahead, their leaves having fallen, but their trunks, thick enough to conceal them. "Take that one." Kate aimed a finger at the tree on the right. She thumbed back to the nearby tree on her left. "I'll take this one."

They took shelter behind the trees, both with hands on their sidearms as the approaching boat's engine cut and moored next to the damaged vessel.

Was this the same man Kate had seen earlier? She glanced back, wondering if their car was in view. Feeling confident he wouldn't be able to see it from the boat, she peeked around the tree trunk, watching the lone man disembark. His face was obscured by shadow, but he didn't seem the same. He moved slower, appeared larger.

She felt Duncan's eyes on her, awaiting her signal. Kate shook her head slightly - not yet.

The man boarded the grounded vessel and disappeared below deck. After a few minutes, various rummaging sounds drift toward them. He was searching for something and didn't take care to keep quiet. Then again, he probably wasn't expecting company.

When he re-emerged, Kate caught a glimpse of something metallic in his hand - was it a knife? Tough to know for sure in the morning haze. He'd gone back and forth a few times, each time emerging with hands full. He was cleaning house.

Finally, the man appeared again, this time holding a small duffel bag. Kate stepped out from behind the tree and leveled her gun. She glanced at Duncan, who gave her a subtle nod before drawing her own weapon. They moved silently from behind the trees. The man had his back to them as he descended the ladder, standing in the knee-deep waters.

"FBI. Put your hands where we can see them," Duncan called out.

The man turned to them, startled, nearly losing his balance.

Kate let out a slight gasp, recognizing him. "What are you doing here, Mr. Holland?" Was he the person she saw earlier? No. it couldn't have been. She was certain the man from earlier was taller. Younger.

Duncan flicked off her safety, an audible click that cut through the air. "Answer the question, Mr. Holland. Now."

"It belongs to me, okay? The boat was taken without permission. Then y'all said it had been found. I had to see what happened to it."

"Why didn't you tell us it belonged to you?" Kate asked.

"Look..." He darted his gaze between them, still standing in the water. "I'm trying to find my granddaughter, all right? Which is a shit ton more than what you people are doing."

He was lying. Kate glanced at Duncan, and it seemed she realized it too. "It's very early in the morning, Mr. Holland. An odd time to come and collect your things. Especially since it's part of an investigation into the murder of Agent Draker." She kept her gun trained on his chest. "Why don't you tell us why you're really here?"

21

Plans had changed when Surrey and Walsh had arrived at the Holland's home once again. News about what Sandra had done—murdering Dr. Fuller—had already reached Jean Holland. Their leverage, it seemed, was gone. However, the wife was cagey regarding Henry's whereabouts, setting off alarm bells in the agents.

Nevertheless, Jean had insisted Clevenger's location remained a mystery to them. She'd even gone so far as to insist Sandra was a lost cause now, and that she intended to focus on finding her granddaughter.

Whatever the two had hoped to gain by driving out there had vanished and they were back at the beginning.

Having returned to the station, McDaniel awaited them both. "Listen, the local authorities found Sandra. I suggested we bring her in."

"Why is that?" Surrey asked.

He regarded them. "Because we know about her involvement with Wayne Clevenger. If she can reveal more, then it might help us find him, and find her daughter as a result." McDaniel glanced back at the bullpen. "And I gotta be honest with you, I'm not sure these guys are going to be able to keep her from doing something stupid, you catch my meaning?"

"He might be right." Walsh rested his hand on Surrey's shoulder. "You go with him. I'll stick around here and wait for Duncan and Reid to get back with the GPS, so we can process it ASAP."

"Yeah, okay," Surrey replied. "Let's get this over with."

~

SANDRA DAWES STOOD in her foyer, the front door, open. Her eyes were wide, and blood splatters painted her face like a macabre abstract. She clutched her youngest daughter, Marissa, whose arms were wrapped around her mother's waist.

Surrey had joined McDaniel on the front porch and regarded the woman. She hadn't bothered to clean up and God knows what her daughter must've been thinking, seeing her mom covered in blood. An overwhelming sadness fell on his shoulders. This woman had made the biggest mistake of her life, and she knew it. It was written all over her face.

The little girl sobbed, calling her mother's name while they entered the home.

"I didn't mean to do it. I swear, I didn't." Sandra held a gun in her right hand, aiming it down at the floor. Presumably, the murder weapon.

McDaniel took a cautious step forward. "Mrs. Dawes, I'm going to need you to hand me the gun, all right? Give me the gun."

She gazed down at it, almost as though she'd forgotten it was there. A sort of shockwave seemed to run through her, and she gasped, placing it in McDaniel's hand.

"Okay. Good." He gave it to Surrey, casting a glance at the

young girl beside her mother. "Mrs. Dawes, did you go see Dr. Shane Fuller last night?"

"Mommy?" The girl tugged on her mother's blouse. "Mommy, where's Daddy? Who are these people?"

Surrey had to get this girl away from Sandra. While she'd handed over the gun, something in her eyes spoke to a mind barely clinging to reality. "It's Marissa, right?" he eyed the girl, who nodded her reply. "Would you show me to your kitchen? I'm so thirsty and would love a glass of water."

Sandra's fingers dug into the girl's shoulder. "No. She stays with me." Her eyes met his. "Is he dead? Did I kill him?"

"Mommy?" Marissa's tone was soft and small.

McDaniel licked his lips, appearing hesitant. "I'm afraid so, ma'am."

Surrey watched the scene unfold like a tragic nightmare. And what was worse, Fuller didn't have Ella, Sandra's missing daughter. She wasn't there. Local authorities had searched the entire place, and no sign of the girl.

"Mrs. Dawes, I'm going to need you to come with us now, okay?" McDaniel eyed Surrey, a silent request for assistance.

"You're not taking her from me," Sandra said flatly.

And then something inside Surrey took over. A fatherly instinct he didn't often get the chance to express. "Hey, there, Marissa. I'm Jonathan. Your mom is going to be just fine, okay?" He offered his hand. "Why don't you come with me? We'll follow right behind your mom, and you can see her when we get to the police station."

He waited, eyes on Sandra, praying she wouldn't make a bad situation worse. Her fingers still dug into Marissa's shoulder. He tilted his head. "I have two kids. Not much older than yours. Please, Sandra..."

Her eyes reddened and tears fell, leaving salty trails through the blood spatters on her cheeks. She looked at Marissa. "He's right, baby. You can go with him. I'll be okay."

"What about Ella?" she cried.

"They're going to help us find her." She looked at Surrey, a flicker of lucidity having returned. "Thank you."

Relief swelling in his chest, he grabbed hold of the girl's hand and led her outside while McDaniel took Sandra Dawes into custody.

"Sometimes, I really dislike this job," he whispered. "Come on, Marissa. We're going to get into that car there and we'll follow your mom."

She nodded, sniffling and wiping her nose. He felt Marissa's grip on his hand tighten, and an unexpected longing surged in him. He desperately missed his own children in this moment.

As he loaded her into the back seat, his phone buzzed in his pocket. Surrey answered the call. "Yeah, Reid, hey, are you guys still out at the boat?"

He closed the door with the girl inside. "I'm here. I can barely hear you. You're breaking up on me," Surrey said. "Reid, you still there?"

Muffled, indiscernible noise ensued. Surrey shook his head. "Where are you? Reid, I can't hear you." The call was cut off. "Goddam it. What the hell?" He walked to the other vehicle, where McDaniel had helped Sandra inside. "I just got a call from Reid. She and Duncan are at the boat, but the call broke up on me. I don't know, but I'm not getting a good feeling here. I need to get down there."

"Go," McDaniel replied. "But do me a solid? Take the girl to the station first? It'll take too long for me to get another unit out here, and she can't be in this car."

"Understood." Surrey nodded and picked up his phone again. "Hey, Walsh, I need a favor."

"Name it," he replied.

"I think we might have a problem." He stepped into the car with the girl. "I'm heading your way now to drop off Sandra Dawes' other daughter. We have Sandra in custody. Then, you and I need to head out to the boat. Something's wrong."

⁓

"WE SHOULD'VE SENT a patrolman with them," Surrey said, gripping the steering wheel as he sped back to the lake, Walsh next to him.

"They were only supposed to get the GPS unit off the boat, then head back to the station. Now, neither are answering their phones," Walsh added. "Which doesn't leave me with the warm fuzzies." He glanced at Surrey. "You seem a little shaken after dropping off Marissa Dawes."

"Just hard to imagine what's going to happen to her now. Whether her sister is still alive, I don't know, but if she is, those two will be on their own. And worse-case? The youngest will be completely alone."

Walsh focused his gaze on the road ahead. "You didn't pull that trigger, man. Sandra Dawes did. But who knows, she clearly wasn't in her right mind. They might be able to get her to plead out."

"Still won't help those girls," Surrey added.

"No, but maybe it'll force the grandparents—the Hollands—to reconsider their lifestyle. Because I can't discount Kate's theory."

"That Ella Dawes was kidnapped because of her grandparents?" Surrey asked.

"Sure as shit didn't help matters, I'll tell you that much."

"No, it did not." Surrey narrowed his gaze. "Is that their car? Over there, about two hundred yards ahead."

238

Walsh peered through the windshield. "Yep. That's it. Pull up behind it."

When he came to a stop, it didn't take long to realize the car was empty and there was no sign of anyone nearby. "Christ, I'm not feeling good about this. They're still here. Somewhere."

"I don't like it either," Walsh replied, checking his weapon.

In the growing morning light, they stepped out of the car, weapons aimed ahead. Surrey walked toward the other vehicle, scanning it for any signs of trouble. "Nothing."

Walsh glanced at him. "Then they're still at the boat. Let's go."

Alert, quiet in their steps, they moved with caution, approaching the vessel just beyond the shoreline. It rocked in the water, appearing empty.

Surrey waded in, Walsh close behind. They reached the ladder and climbed aboard. The boat creaked, and moaned as they searched it.

"They're not here, man." Surrey felt panic rise in his chest.

Walsh stood near the wheelhouse, peering inside. "They got the GPS unit." He looked back. "But there's no sign of them."

~

WHEN KATE's call to Surrey had cut out, a split-second decision had to be made. They'd brought down Henry Holland from the grounded vessel, but their odds turned on a dime when they'd realized he wasn't alone. Wayne Clevenger had accompanied Henry, and it seemed it had been against Henry's will.

Clevenger was armed, giving Kate and Duncan two options. Kill him where he stood, leaving them with no more answers than when they'd started, or let Clevenger believe he'd had the upper hand. They'd chosen the latter.

Now, as the engine stopped and the boat steered toward the

dock, the time had come for them to put their plan into action. Sitting on the bench that lined the bow, Kate glanced at Duncan and whispered, "Be ready."

"Always."

Wayne Clevenger made his way toward them, carrying on to the side and tying off the vessel. He turned back to the agents, his gun visible in his waistband. "Sit tight, ladies. This is almost over." Henry Holland was in the wheelhouse, helping to dock the boat.

Kate didn't recognize their location. While the sun rose higher in the sky, no other boats were in sight. They must've been in some hidden alcove of the lake. No houses, nothing. "Where is she—the girl?"

"What girl?" Clevenger replied, knotting the rope around the dock cleat.

They could easily end this right now. Even though Clevenger had taken their weapons, he had no idea who he was up against. But then, Kate might never know where to find the girl because she was certain this man had her. And it was the only reason she and Duncan were here now, running the risk that this could still go sideways. "Does he know?" Kate nodded toward Holland, who was still at the helm.

"I'll bet he doesn't," Duncan replied. "Why'd you take her?"

Clevenger scoffed. "Shut the fuck up. You don't know what you're talking about."

"You've already murdered a DEA agent," Kate added. "You think taking the lives of two more federal officers is a good idea? You know how many they'll send for you now?"

Clevenger didn't respond, instead retrieving a phone from his pocket. "This one must belong to you, Agent Reid." He held the screen so she could see it. "Looks like you've had a few missed calls. I'll bet they're starting to panic now. Wondering where you two are."

A single thought ran through Kate's mind. Ella. Never mind the rest of the team she was certain was on the hunt for them now. Eyeing Clevenger, she had to keep him engaged. "They'll find us. And when they do, you'll wish you would've killed us back in the woods."

Clevenger smirked. "I don't plan on keeping you alive long enough to be rescued, Agent Reid."

A silent look passed between Kate and Duncan – each prepared, trained, ready to get themselves out of the situation. Clevenger was dumb enough to take them in the first place. He deserved what was coming to him.

Whatever he'd had planned, it seemed he'd prepared to initiate it. Grabbing Kate's arm, he yanked her to her feet. Duncan stood quickly to join her. Coming face to face with people like Wayne Clevenger was nothing new for either of them. Kate often blurred the lines between her investigative profiling and hunting down killers. But she was good at it. They all were.

As Clevenger shoved Kate off the boat and onto the rickety dock, she stumbled but quickly regained her footing. The dock led to a dense forest with no signs of civilization in sight.

He grabbed Duncan next, forcing her onto the dock next to her.

Fighting back her instincts, Kate nodded at Duncan, silently acknowledging they had to wait this out for as long as possible. Long enough for this asshole to tell them where to find Ella Dawes.

From just outside the wheelhouse, Henry Holland called out, "Wayne, get over here."

It would've been better for Holland to step onto the dock and join them, but Kate knew they couldn't afford to let Clevenger back onto the vessel. He might just leave them there, still having no answers about the girl.

But Holland just left them an opening, distracting Clevenger. In one swift motion, Kate spun around, delivering a sharp kick to Clevenger's hand, knocking the gun from it. It clattered onto the dock and Duncan charged after it. Her hands zip-tied, she struggled for a moment, then finally grasped it.

Clevenger recovered quickly, pulling a knife from his belt. "You think I didn't come prepared?" He lunged at Kate.

And now, Holland was on the move, heading toward them. But the old man was slow, and Duncan rushed to stop him. "No, don't!"

Clevenger swiped his blade, barely missing Kate's stomach. And when he swept it again, a wide swing, she stepped inside his reach and slammed her palm up into his chin in a brutal uppercut. His head snapped back, and the knife dropped from his fingers.

Before he could react, she sent her knee to his groin, and he doubled over. She grabbed him by the hair and slammed his face down hard onto her rising knee, breaking his nose with a nasty crunch.

Duncan aimed the gun at Holland. "Don't move." She walked toward Kate, turning the weapon onto a bleeding Clevenger. "Go over there, next to Holland." When he did as she'd instructed, Duncan looked back at the surrounding tree line. "The girl might be around here somewhere."

"Agreed. I think he wanted to come here to get rid of all of us." Kate turned her attention to Clevenger. "Give me my phone." She took it from him and checked the screen. "I have a signal. It's weak, but I'll try to get Jonathan. With the phone at her ear, a smile spread on her lips as it rang. He quickly answered. "We're okay. Where are you?" She jumped in without waiting for him to speak.

"Oh, Christ, Reid," Surrey replied. "What the hell's going on? We're at the grounded boat. You're not. What the hell happened?"

She surveyed the area, sunlight shining down through the bare trees. "I have no idea where we are. Wayne Clevenger took Henry Holland hostage, forcing him to drive out to the boat to collect the GPS, and any other evidence tying Clevenger to the murders, most likely. We were confronted, and for the safety of Ella Dawes, we planned a way to get to her. Best guess is Clevenger brought us here to kill us all. We think the girl could be here somewhere."

"Okay. Listen, one of you needs to get back on that boat that brought you there and look at your location. Give me the coordinates and we'll be there ASAP."

Kate eyed her partner. "Can you check the coordinates?"

"On it," Duncan replied, handing her gun to Kate. "I'm not entirely certain you can trust Holland." As she started on, she regarded the men. "Don't do anything stupid. She will kill you."

"Eva's checking..." Kate stopped cold at the faint sound in the distance. It seemed her silence alarmed Surrey.

"Reid?" he asked. "You good? Reid, you still there?"

Taking her eyes off these men would be a mistake, but the sound...like a child. "Yeah, sorry. I'm here." Whatever Surrey said to her after that, she didn't catch. A waft of cold air went right through her, then she spied Duncan's return, calling her name.

"Hey, you all right?" she asked.

"Yeah, sorry," Kate replied, shaking out of her trance.

She handed over a slip of paper. "Coordinates."

"Thanks." Kate relayed the information.

"Got it," Surrey replied. "We'll be there as soon as we can. Sit tight."

"Will do." Kate ended the call, pocketing her phone. She returned her attention to Clevenger. "Tell us where she is."

Holland turned to him, narrowing his gaze. "I knew you had her, you son of a bitch."

"He took your granddaughter, Mr. Holland," Kate said. "I have no doubt about that. Probably murdered your son-in-law too.

But what we still need to know is what happened to the DEA agent. How'd you know where the boat was, Wayne?"

"I didn't kill anyone. I didn't take that girl either. You're wrong about this," he replied.

It wasn't lost on Kate that he didn't answer the question. "You're in love with her, aren't you? Sandra Dawes?" she pressed, realizing if she pushed in the wedge deeply enough, he'd crack wide open. "You know she killed her therapist, Dr. Fuller. She'll be going to jail for a long time."

Clevenger's expression remained firm. He wasn't going to confess to anything. Not here. That might change when they find Ella and gather evidence against him.

"If they don't kill you, I will," Holland said to him.

"Settle down, old man," Clevenger replied.

Duncan nudged Kate as she glanced over her shoulder. "Hey, over there. I see a light coming from that direction."

In the glare of the morning sun, it was hard to see anything through the trees, but Kate squinted and finally noticed the faint light. "Is that a house? I thought I heard something a minute ago. Like a voice." Kate turned back to Clevenger. "You have a place out here? Is that why we're here? Does Henry know you planned on killing him along with us and his granddaughter?" She peered over her shoulder again. "We can't wait for backup."

"You go," Duncan said, taking the gun from her. "I've got this."

Kate turned on her heel and headed to the direction of the light. As she traversed the uneven terrain, an overwhelming sensation of being followed consumed her. It was like her dreams—the ones she used to have that forced her long-buried childhood memories to the surface.

Kate pressed on through the thickening woods, shadows closing in on her. Her breath caught in her throat as the light came into focus. Her thoughts were on finding Ella, but the familiar sense of uncertainty made her skin crawl.

Kate moved swiftly through the trees, her pulse quickening as she closed in on what looked like an old cabin in the distance. She could almost feel Joseph Hendrickson's cold hands grasping at the back of her neck. Suddenly, she was six-years-old again.

She had fought him with all her tiny might, kicking and scratching wildly. When he stumbled on the rutted floor, she had wrenched herself free and sprinted for the basement stairs. She could still hear his enraged shouts echoing through the trees as she burst through the front door and ran barefoot through the forest.

Kate had run blindly into the woods, branches whipping her arms and face as she went. She could hear Hendrickson crashing through the underbrush behind her, yelling after her.

She had run for what felt like hours, her feet bleeding and her lungs burning, the blindfold he'd forced her to wear, still around her neck.

"Stop," she whispered. Up ahead, a porch light burned from a small cottage off a narrow lane. Kate slowed down, approaching with caution, all her senses on high alert. She swept the perimeter, looking for signs of Ella or anyone else. But something told her the girl was here.

Kate peered through a dirty window but could barely make out anything in the dark interior. She turned the knob of the front door, but it was locked. The only solution was to break a window. She pulled off her coat, wrapped it around her hand, and punched through the glass. The sound echoed all around her, and then she heard the cries for help. Distant. Almost indiscernible.

Inside, Kate swept her flashlight around the living room. An old sofa and a small round table near the open kitchen. Beer cans and food wrappers strewn around. "This belongs to Clevenger. It has to."

She moved farther inside, looking for any sign of the girl. The small kitchen held a small cooktop and a microwave. A couple of cabinets with doors hanging from their hinges. Kate moved slowly through the home, clearing the corners. The bathroom was empty. "Ella? Ella, are you here?"

Returning to the living room, she peered at the wood floor and then she spied it - a trapdoor partially hidden by an old rug. Kate crouched down and pulled open the chain. A narrow staircase led down into inky darkness.

Kate descended cautiously, the air growing colder and danker with each step. At the bottom was a heavy wooden door secured with a padlock. Kate kicked it, over and over, until the old door splintered open, giving way under the pressure.

The cries grew louder in the dark, and Kate called out. "Ella? Are you in here? I'm here to help you."

"Over here." A tiny voice replied. Ella, handcuffed to the bed. Terrified but alive.

Kate rushed to the sobbing girl. "It's okay, I've got you. You're safe now."

22

It would be all too easy for Duncan to pull the trigger, ending the lives of a killer, and a drug-trafficker. The world would be better off without them. But in all her years, coming across far worse monsters than these, she'd never crossed that line.

But were they right in their assumptions? Did Wayne Clevenger murder Agent Draker? Well, the boat covered with the agent's blood sure seemed to point in that direction. And the fact he'd gone there added to her certainty.

While she'd kept Clevenger under control, a gun aimed at him, she wondered if Kate was okay. If she'd found the girl. And how long before Surrey and Walsh would arrive? A part of her didn't fully trust Henry Holland. This was a man who'd used Clevenger as a drug runner. How'd it come to pass that Clevenger had turned against him, forcing him out onto the vessel to recover potential evidence? Too many questions remained unanswered, but she had to keep her focus on Kate, monitoring how long she'd been gone. Too long...and trouble would be all but certain.

The minutes ticked away. The cold air on her skin was like a frosty layer on a car's windshield. Finally, Duncan fixed her gaze on Clevenger. "Might help your cause if you tell me where you're keeping Ella Dawes."

He looked down, scoffing under his breath. "I don't know what you're talking about."

Duncan moved toward him. "Sure you do. His granddaughter. The man sitting right next to you. I'll bet he'd like to know."

"I swear to Christ, Wayne, I'll kill you," Holland said.

"How did you know where to dump Agent Draker?" she asked Clevenger.

This time, he raised his gaze, furrowing his brow. "I didn't kill him. I didn't kill anyone."

"The hell you didn't," she shot back. "You were one of their informants, and I think Mr. Holland, over here, found out. So you did what you thought necessary and killed the agent. You know, there's evidence all over that boat. Draker's blood. Your blood, no doubt. That's why you went back there. To clean up your mess."

Faint lights appeared out over the water. Duncan set her gaze outward, trying to decipher if it was a boat or just the sun's reflection. But soon, the sound of an engine reverberated. And then...a boat. It was the Missouri Water Patrol. "Well, our time's up, boys."

Walsh stood on the bow. While the officers secured the ropes to the dock, he jumped down, immediately drawing his weapon. "You okay?" he asked Duncan.

"Fine." She tossed a nod over her shoulder. "Reid's out there somewhere. We think the girl is nearby, but Clevenger isn't talking." Her eyes were drawn back to the boat, where Surrey and Agent McDaniel disembarked and headed their way.

"Where's Reid?" Surrey asked, marching toward them.

"In the woods," Duncan replied. "We'd seen a light. She followed. It's been a while. Twenty minutes or more."

~

THE GIRL WAS ALIVE. She was safe. But this was far from over. Kate had to free Ella from the bed. She tested the handcuff that was locked in place around the low metal frame.

Kate grabbed her phone, praying she would get a signal in here. "One bar." She pressed Duncan's number, and the call was answered. "I have her. She's alive and she appears unharmed."

"Kate, it's me," Surrey replied. "I have Duncan's phone. She's fine. We just arrived and McDaniel and Walsh are taking these guys into custody."

Relief swept through her. "Thank God."

"Where are you?"

"A small cottage off an old gravel road. Look, Ella's handcuffed, and I have nothing on me. You need to get here and help me set her free."

"Drop me a pin before we lose the connection," he said.

She sent it to him. "Done. Now get here as fast as you can." Kate ended the call and set her gaze on Ella once again. "Help's coming, okay? How you doing?"

"Where's my mom and dad?" she asked.

The answer to that question wasn't going to be easy. "Your mom's waiting for you, so is your sister. Everything's going to be all right now."

Ella's eyes darted around. "Is he coming back?"

"No. He's been arrested. You never have to see him again." Kate took in the girl's features. Her dark hair, her brown eyes. While she was a little older than Kate had been when she'd been abducted, the resemblance was there.

"No, I mean the boy. Is he coming back?"

Kate narrowed her gaze. "What boy? Is there someone else here?"

Ella peered around the basement, lit only by the open door above. "I heard him. I was sure someone was here, thumping and making noise. He didn't believe me..."

"Who didn't believe you?" Kate pressed.

"The man who took me. He got mad when I said I heard something."

Kate walked around the room. "Honey, no one's here. I can check outside when everyone else gets here, okay?"

Her lips pressed together. "I think he was here to help me. To tell me I wasn't alone."

Kate returned to the bed. "I'll make sure we all look around for anyone else, okay?" She wondered who it was the girl had heard. She'd swept the perimeter on her arrival and found no one else. Maybe the stories about this lake were true, if Kate were prone to believing in such things.

She feared for what lay ahead for Ella. Her father was dead. Her mother, probably going to prison for a long time. And after what she'd just suffered, how would she survive? This wasn't a memory that would bury itself deep inside, never to resurface. Ella was too old for that. No, she would be forced to recon with all that has happened from this moment on.

Light shown through the open basement door, drawing Kate's attention. She squeezed Ella's hand. "They're here. Help is here." She walked to the bottom of the staircase. "We're down here!"

Footsteps made the floor above tremor until finally, she saw him. Surrey ran down the steps.

"We have to get her free," Kate said. "You have the key?"

"No," Surrey replied. "This place belongs to Clevenger. McDaniel called in to his office to pull records. But Clevenger refuses to admit to anything right now."

"Goddam it. He's looking for a deal, knowing we have her," she replied. A part of her felt vindicated, certain he had been the one to take Ella, but the question she wanted to ask—the question of Tim Dawes' killer—couldn't be asked in front of the girl.

"More backup is coming," Surrey added. "Two state police were right behind me. They'll have something to cut those off." He looked at Ella. "Hi. I'm Jonathan. I'm very glad to meet you."

She smiled through her tears, seeming to realize this nightmare was almost over. "Can I go home now?"

~

IN THE MIDDAY HOURS, Kate stood outside the old cottage-like cabin that belonged to Wayne Clevenger, the team surrounding her. Local authorities had arrived, taping off the scene.

She glanced at the sun that shone through a few white clouds as the air began to warm. Turning her attention to the front porch, a woman from Child Protective Services was talking to Ella. Kate's heart broke for the young girl. But she was alive, and that was all that mattered. In time she would heal, just as Kate had.

"Reid, are you okay?" Surrey asked.

Kate shook away the unsettling thoughts. "Yeah. I'm all right. You know, she mentioned she'd heard a thumping sound in that basement."

He turned down his lips. "Huh. Any idea what it was?"

"I didn't see anything or anyone. Who knows? Maybe this place is haunted."

He smiled at her. "You don't believe in things like that."

"No, I guess not." Her gaze turned to Duncan and Walsh, who were now approaching. "Did we get the GPS? It needs to go to analysis."

"McDaniel has it. He'll send it to his field office for analysis," Duncan replied. "You want to tell them what Nick said?"

Surrey tilted his head at Kate. "You talked to Scarborough?"

"I did," she replied. "He called just before Eva and I searched the boat, remembering additional details about the Pied Piper."

"Such as?" Walsh asked.

"He'd carved the symbol of the Freemasons on the bodies of his victims." Kate waited a moment while the words settled around them. "He said the Bureau never released that information."

"None of the remains that have been recovered have any tissue left," Surrey replied. "How does this help us?"

"Draker," Kate said. "We need to ask Dr. Bailey if she's seen any such marking on his body. Obviously, Belgrave—the Pied Piper—is dead, but if there is this symbol on Draker, it means the person who killed him knew Belgrave in some form or another."

Walsh nodded. "Makes for a better explanation than Everett Knapp. Do we think it's Clevenger, then? All things considered."

"Let's get Bailey's confirmation before we go too far down that road," Kate continued. "But it's worth asking about. And digging deeper into Wayne Clevenger's history."

Surrey grabbed his phone from his jacket and dialed the lab. "Then let's find out now." After a couple of rings, Bailey answered. "Dr. Bailey, it's Agent Surrey. I've got you on speaker with my team. I'm following up on the remains of DEA Agent Draker, and I have a question for you."

"I'm all ears, Agent Surrey," Bailey replied.

"Did you make note of a symbol carved or tattooed on his body? Specifically, a Masonic symbol?"

"Interesting that you ask that..."

Surrey's brow raised. "And why is that?"

"Because only yesterday, when we'd received the agent's other arm, a member of my team noticed a faint marking on the back of the shoulder. In fact, it's very near where the arm was severed. It appears to be a square and compass symbol tattooed into the skin."

"The symbol of the Freemasons." The corner of his mouth raised. "Don't suppose you could text me a picture?"

"Of course, I can send it to you now. But you should know that no other symbols were seen elsewhere on the victim, nor on any of the victims. Though, it's impossible to know whether the other victims shared such a symbol given their state of decomposition."

"Of course. Thank you, Dr. Bailey. This is a huge find. I'll await the image." Surrey ended the call. "What do you know? Scarborough's memory came in handy. Bailey's sending over the image now."

Agent McDaniel walked out of the run-down cottage and joined the team. "I think this is where Tim Dawes was taken before he was killed."

Kate regarded him. "How do you know?"

"Dawes' body was found only a few hundred yards downstream from here. And one of the officers found this inside." He held an evidence bag containing a knife. "No doubt we'll find Clevenger's DNA on this."

"The knife used to stab Dawes in the back and cut his face," Kate replied. "We can also cross-reference it with the DNA found in the grounded boat. Clevenger knew where the boat was, so I have no doubt we'll find his DNA in there too." She set her hands on her hips. "That makes Bailey's find all the more interesting."

"Sorry?" McDaniel asked.

"Long story," Walsh cut in. "But the gist is, your partner, Agent Draker; his other arm they'd recently recovered was found to have the symbol of the Freemasons carved on it."

"Carved?" McDaniel said. "Not a tattoo? Though I'd never seen a tattoo on him."

"No, it was carved," Walsh replied.

"So, I guess we know to look for Clevenger's connection to the Pied Piper. He knew where the bodies were. He carved the same symbol into Draker's arm," Kate said. "We could have our killer in custody right now."

Ella was being ushered down the porch steps and Kate locked eyes with the girl for a moment. "Did anyone tell Sandra Dawes we found her daughter? Is she in custody?"

Surrey nodded. "Camdenton PD has her. She's at the station waiting for her lawyer. I don't know if she's aware yet that you found Ella."

Kate kept her eyes glued on the little girl and soon felt Walsh taking her arm, ushering her away.

"She's a survivor, Kate, just like you," he said.

Her eyes stung in an instant. Kate had long ago stopped believing herself a survivor. Not because she wasn't one, but because it was a time in her life that she'd chosen to shut off. Lock away. But Walsh knew better. He knew her reasons for wanting to interview the monsters, to understand their motives and desires.

But this? This one was easy. Clevenger had been obsessed with Sandra Dawes and killed her husband. Now, it was only a matter of fitting the pieces together before they tied him to the Pied Piper.

~

AFTER WHAT HAD HAPPENED with Ella, Kate couldn't shut off the inexplicable need to replay the events of her own past trauma. Too many similarities to Ella Dawes had triggered a resurgence of memories.

It had been a long time, years, in fact, that she'd relived those dark days so vividly as she was right now. Never mind that, as an adult, he'd come after her again. And he'd died as a result. She'd had the ultimate revenge, yet somehow, it had never felt that way.

Maybe because of all the little kids who weren't as lucky as she had been.

And then...the sound that had come to her in the woods. *What was that?* She wondered if she'd imagined it. But Ella had heard something, too. And that something offered her hope. Maybe giving her just enough hope that she wanted to survive.

Ghost stories abounded here in the Ozarks, yet Kate wasn't prone to believing in such things. Never mind. They had Clevenger in custody. Now, they had to prove his guilt. "Hey, Eva, do you know where McDaniel's file on Clevenger is?"

Duncan reached into one of the boxes and sifted through it. "Here." She tossed it over to Kate. "But what you're saying is that you are certain Clevenger killed Draker."

"You don't think so?" she asked.

Duncan sat back down. "Well, if we're to assume he also killed Tim Dawes, then why deviate from the M.O.? That's not usually how these guys operate."

Kate opened the file. "You're not wrong."

The only hope for answers was in his history here—his family. Kate scoured the file, coming across some of McDaniel's notes. "Hey, take a look at this." She moved her chair closer to Duncan. "According to this, Wayne Clevenger originally hailed from Linn Creek."

"They rebuilt that place, right?" Duncan asked. "After the flood."

"That's my understanding. The town had been flooded in the 1930s when the Bagnell Dam was built to form the lake. The residents were forced to relocate, and a new Linn Creek was built."

Duncan turned to her laptop. "Let me take a look at something here." She keyed in a few commands and nodded when the screen populated. "Old census records list the Clevengers as residents there going back to the late 1800s. Wayne's grandfather, Elias

Clevenger, was a store owner before the flood," she continued. "Looks like his brother, who would've been Wayne's great uncle, moved to Osage Beach, but Elias remained to help rebuild the new Linn Creek."

Kate leaned back. "None of that ties him to Jason Belgrave, the Pied Piper."

"According to these records, they were Freemasons." Duncan raised her brow. "The Clevenger family, dating back to Wayne's great-grandfather were members of the local Masonic lodge in Linn Creek before it was flooded."

Kate perked up. "Okay. That's something."

As Duncan read on, she stopped cold. "Oh, wow."

"What is it?"

"His isn't the only family who's been here for generations," Duncan replied. "Crawford. Coast Guard Lieutenant Dean Crawford. His family has lived here for over one hundred years. Let me see what else I can find about him."

She tapped on her keys while Kate waited.

Both Surrey and Walsh had taken the images of Draker's carving sent by Dr. Bailey to Agent McDaniel. They were with him now, reviewing the details with State Water Patrol, leaving her and Duncan to figure out if Clevenger was the man they'd been searching for. The few missing puzzle pieces still needed to click into place. And that was sometimes the hardest part.

Duncan regarded Kate, a look she immediately recognized. "Interesting factoid here...the Crawfords and Clevengers had intermarried at various points in time."

The strands were starting to intertwine. "The Freemasons, Linn Creek, the Clevenger and Crawford families," Kate replied. "But no mention of Belgrave. Where does he enter in all this history?"

~

Henry Holland had wasted no time in marching over to Clevenger's trailer that was parked on his property. Before Clevenger had been told to lay low at the home where his grand-daughter had been found, he'd stayed here. Not that Henry had revealed that fact to the cops or those feds.

He was angry with himself for not seeing Clevenger for who he really was. And what his obsession with Sandra had done. There was no doubt in his mind that Clevenger murdered his son-in-law. Then the son of a bitch took Ella, keeping her in his basement. For what reason? What did he think that would do? If he could've killed him before the cops took him, he would have. Though he'd expected Clevenger to shoot him down when they arrived at the boat. He probably would have had the agents not been there.

Clevenger had maintained his innocence in the death of Agent Draker, insisting it was Alex Medina who'd met with the agent last, taking the boat that had belonged to Henry without his knowledge. Henry knew Medina was talking to the agent, as well as Clevenger. That was intentional. Feeding that agent informa-tion to send him looking elsewhere. And it had worked, till someone decided to kill him. Now, Henry's life was a goddam mess.

What the hell Sandra had seen in Wayne Clevenger was beyond comprehension. It seemed more likely that Sandra was acting out, using Clevenger as a means to get back at her husband for whatever troubles they'd had in their marriage. Henry was never privy to any of that because Sandra had wanted nothing to do with him or her mother.

As he made his way to Clevenger's bedroom inside the small trailer, his obsession with Sandra became immediately clear. He'd kept photos of his daughter. The two, engaged in acts he couldn't stomach looking at. Sandra had been with him more than once. The images proved it.

Henry tossed them aside, disgusted.

But what he hadn't yet found was proof Clevenger had murdered the agent. So was he telling the truth? Was it Alex Medina who killed him?

Henry walked through the tiny galley kitchen, searching the cabinets. Searching every bit of storage in this shithole. And as he returned to the living room, a book lay on one of the cushions. "Since when the hell you read, Wayne?" He picked it up, opening the cover when a photograph slipped out. "The hell is this?"

It had fallen to the couch and Henry picked it up, recognizing the man in the picture. "Agent Draker."

In the photo, he was sitting behind the wheel of his car, but he wasn't alone. This was gonna require a closer look, so Henry slipped on his reading glasses and the passenger's face became clearer. "Oh, shit. I know who you are."

～

AGENT MCDANIEL ENTERED the conference room where Kate and Duncan continued their research. Walsh and Surrey trailed in behind him and all appeared pleased about something.

"What happened?" Kate asked.

"We just got a confession from Wayne Clevenger," McDaniel said.

Her eyes widened with anticipation. "To killing Agent Draker?"

"No." McDaniel shoved his hands into his pockets. "To killing Tim Dawes. So, now we got him on murder and kidnapping. He's going to prison for a long time."

"Was a deal in play?" Kate pressed. "Say, to get something tangible on the Hollands?"

"Tim Dawes' DNA was found on the knife, and inside the cabin, handing Wayne Clevenger over on a silver platter," Surrey cut in. "So when confronted with that proof, he said he didn't do it. That his partner did."

"And who was that?" Duncan chimed in.

"Alex Medina," McDaniel replied. "My other informant, who went off-grid not long after my partner went missing. And, in fact, was the one who'd had that final meeting with him."

"The one you said took the boat," Kate continued.

"That's right. But then Clevenger's lawyer stepped in and halted all questioning," McDaniel added. "Ended up convincing him to plea to a lesser murder charge if he admitted to killing Dawes."

"Can we prove Clevenger was on the boat?" Kate asked. "That's the million dollar question no one seems to be able to answer."

"Not until we get the analysis back," McDaniel replied.

"Excuse the interruption." An officer walked inside, holding a sheet of paper. "Agent McDaniel, this just came in. I believe you were waiting on the data from the boat's GPS. I followed up with your team, like you asked."

He took the report. "Thank you. This is great."

"I also circled the coordinates where the bodies had been recovered based on the Coast Guard's information," the officer added.

Kate got up from her chair to take a look. Peering over McDaniel's shoulder, she nodded. "It was there. The boat was there at the dumping ground. So whoever was in that boat with Agent Draker, killed him, then dumped his body."

"Alex Medina had the meeting with Agent Draker,"

McDaniel said. "They'd met on this boat that belonged to Henry Holland. That much we know. And he's since gone dark. Hell, he could be dead for all I know. So how to prove Clevenger was there, too, without the blood analysis back?"

Kate walked to the whiteboard. Grabbing one of the markers, she wrote a name and then other names below it, connecting them with a line. "We all want to believe Clevenger was on that boat too, and that he's our killer. But what we don't have is evidence to that effect." She circled the names. "Each one of these families has been here since before the dam was built. They know each other."

Surrey folded his arms. "What are you getting at, Reid?"

"I'm convinced one of these people murdered not only Agent Draker, but the rest of the victims discovered at the bottom of the lake. And it's someone who knew or knew of Jason Belgrave—the Pied Piper because we now know about the Freemason's symbol."

Duncan got up and joined Kate at the board. "So, Reid and I have been looking into historical records from the surrounding areas." She grabbed the marker and placed an asterisk by two of the names. "These families here have been here the longest. And, at various points throughout history, they've even been married to each other."

"And both families have had extensive connections to the Freemasons, just as the Pied Piper had. Among these names, who haven't we looked into?" Kate aimed the marker at the name on the top. "This guy."

McDaniel laughed. "What? Are you serious? Lieutenant Dean Crawford? Coast Guard Lieutenant Dean Crawford?"

Surrey walked to the board, examining it carefully. "If Clevenger had killed Draker, would he have confessed to it as he did with Tim Dawes?"

Kate set down her marker. "If he thought it would've helped him with a deal, but that's questionable."

"But he did know where the boat was and took Holland to it to clean house," Surrey continued. "Making him look pretty damn guilty."

"Agreed," Kate replied. "Maybe Medina told him where it was. But setting all that aside, there's that other name on here, which needs to be explored. Because the thing is, Tim Dawes was stabbed and drowned. Nothing about his murder connects in any way to the other killings, including Draker." She turned to the team. "That cannot be ignored."

"So you want to haul in a Coast Guard lieutenant and tell him we suspect him of murdering countless people over the past five to seven years?" McDaniel set his hands on his hips. "This is some bullshit."

23

They had the boat's GPS, proving the vessel had been in the vicinity of where the bodies were recovered. So, if Kate was right, how did Crawford end up on the boat, taking it to that location? More importantly, why? She had to prove both facts and had no idea how to go about it yet. "How long have you been after the Hollands?" she asked, looking at McDaniel.

"Like I said, we had bigger fish to fry, but after vetting them, I do know that they were on the Coast Guard's radar for a while."

"So they were aware of the Hollands' activities yet weren't able to come up with enough to bring charges," she said, almost as if making her earlier point. "Who brought you and the DEA in?"

McDaniel tilted his head. "Coast Guard Senior Chief Lyons. Along with the Missouri Water Patrol. There'd been several overdoses the previous summer and the drugs were traced back to this area. A joint Taskforce was established. I was assigned as well as Draker."

"Hey, guys?" Duncan said. "I found something you might

want to see." She got up from the chair and carried her laptop to the end of the table, setting it back down again for everyone to see. "Dean Crawford graduated from Camdenton High School in two thousand ten." She eyed Kate. "The same year as Sandra and Ashley Holland. Oh, and Jacob Fuller."

"Shane Fuller's son," Kate said. "Interesting. What would really be interesting to learn is whether Crawford and Clevenger knew each other. We know their families had been married in years past, but that doesn't mean those two hung out in the same circles."

"Let me see what I can find out about him." Duncan keyed in another command and waited. "Here we go. Wayne Clevenger went to high school at—"

"Camdenton," McDaniel cut in.

"You already knew this?" Kate asked.

He nodded. "He'd graduated years later, though. Wayne is twenty-eight."

Surrey perched on the edge of the conference table. "We can't ignore that Crawford went to school with two of the victims, long lost for the past five years or so. Maybe he'd been bullied or spurned by one of the Holland girls. We already know Ashley Holland and Jacob Fuller had been on a date when they both went missing."

"Agent McDaniel," Kate pleaded. "You can get this information from Clevenger. He's going down. He has no reason to protect anyone. So don't you think it's worth asking if he knew that Dean Crawford was on that boat with your other informant, Medina?"

Duncan raised her index finger. "And did I mention Crawford also has ties to the Freemasons?"

Walsh grunted. "Does anyone know how to find Crawford? Our best shot at keeping him from getting a whiff of what we suspect is to make sure everyone else thinks our focus is on

Clevenger." He raised his hands. "I'm not ready to take Clevenger out of the equation, but damn if it's not a good idea to have a word with Lieutenant Crawford."

"I'll call him," McDaniel replied. "But we're going to need something concrete if you even think about bringing this guy in."

Kate knew he was right. The man was a ranking member of the Coast Guard, another law enforcement official. "Crawford's DNA will be on file with the Coast Guard. Run it against the samples on the boat."

"The boat is with the forensics team," McDaniel replied. "It'll take time, days, possibly, before we get answers."

Kate considered their options. Relief at the fact young Ella had been rescued and was safe quickly gave way to dread about bringing in a senior Coast Guard official for mass murder. "I need to see Clevenger. I have to ask him what he knows about who was on that boat. He might be more willing to talk if he doesn't want the blame for those mass murders."

McDaniel gestured back. "Have at it, Agent Reid. Good luck. But don't hold your breath."

She headed toward the door. "I've broken harder men than Wayne Clevenger, Agent McDaniel." Kate strode down the hall of the police station, her low-heeled shoes clicking on the tiled floor.

An officer was at his desk when she arrived at the holding cells. "I need to speak with Wayne Clevenger." The fact his lawyer wasn't present would hinder her progress, but it also depended on how desperate Clevenger was to aim the finger of multiple murders away from himself.

The officer unlocked the door to the small, windowless room where Clevenger sat waiting. He appeared far less intimidating without a gun in his hand, aimed at her. His long hair had clumped around his neck and his gangly frame hung off the chair.

"Nice to see you again, Wayne," Kate said as she sat down

across from him. "Your first mistake was in taking that girl. You get that, right?"

"I have nothing to say to you, Agent Reid."

Kate placed her hands flat on the table and met his gaze. "Dean Crawford. I want to know about your relationship with him. And I want to know if he was on that boat with you and Alex Medina."

"What makes you think I was there?" he asked.

She smirked. "Well, you knew where it had been found. You tried to get rid of any evidence that connected you to the murder of Agent Draker...and I know that your family and the Crawfords have ties that go way back."

"What the hell does that have to do with anything?" He pulled up in the chair. "Look, I didn't kill that agent, all right?"

Kate leaned in. "Just tell me if Lieutenant Crawford was there." When he refused to answer, she had to find another angle. Something that would get him to talk. "You were in love with Sandra Dawes, weren't you?"

His eyes softened just a little at the mention of her name.

"And because of you, she killed Dr. Shane Fuller." A flicker of guilt flashed on his face. "She thought he had taken her daughter. Refused to believe it when he said he didn't. She put a bullet in his chest." Kate leaned back and let her words envelope him. "All that, and it was you who had the girl. Now, Sandra will spend the rest of her life in prison. This woman, who I know you care about."

He was quiet, but she could see thoughts swirling in his mind. He couldn't look at her, revealing a slight tremor in his lips and a clenched jaw.

"She didn't love you, Wayne. She loved her husband. You..." Kate eyed him up and down. "You were a distraction. A lonely young, beautiful housewife who only wanted to feel desired. But it was her husband she chose. And you didn't like that."

He looked away; jaw still clenched. His hand balled up into a fist. Now was the time to strike. "I wonder if you didn't already know that Crawford had murdered Sandra's twin sister years ago? Dumping her remains in the lake, along with all the others."

His face masked in momentary confusion, but he remained quiet.

Kate grew frustrated. "The boat belonged to Henry Holland. Medina took it. Somehow, he's vanished into thin air. Did you kill him too?" She paused a moment. "Wayne, you will go down for all those murders in addition to Tim Dawes' murder. So, it's up to you now. Tell me what you know about Dean Crawford."

⚬

HENRY HOLLAND SAT on his front porch, mulling over his approach to this discovery. In his hand, he held the photograph. DEA Agent Darker, and Dean Crawford, an officer with the US Coast Guard. In a car, together. The photo? Taken by Wayne Clevenger, seemingly without their knowledge.

"You were watching them two, why?" he asked no one in particular.

The only thing that made sense was that the Coast Guard was in on the DEA's operation, along with the FBI. Did Wayne know? Had he intended to use this as some sort of leverage?

Henry got up from the rocker and stared out over the sprawling land before him. He walked back inside the house. "I need to run an errand."

Jean stood at the kitchen sink and turned around. "Where? You really need to go somewhere now, do you?"

"Yeah, I do." He turned on his heel, making his way to the foyer, where he grabbed his keys and snatched his coat from the rack.

Returning outside, he climbed into his truck, firing up the

engine. A waft of white smoke billowed from the exhaust, visible in his rearview mirror.

He saw Jean peer at him through the kitchen window. "Don't worry. Ain't nothing gonna happen to what's left of this family." Henry pressed hard on the gas, spinning the tires on the gravel before heading down the long driveway in the afternoon sun.

There was only one place for him to go. Henry had lived here his entire life. He knew most everyone's secrets. It was how he'd managed to become successful in his line of work. And the Crawford's secret? That one was a doozy. Though he often wondered, had Ashley still been alive, would he be doing what he was doing?

Then again, if Ashley was still alive, he wouldn't be in this situation. None of them would be.

He drove out toward the lake, to an old bridge with a storied past. It was said that those who crossed it after midnight never returned. These days, it was surrounded by marinas, yacht clubs, and condos, but its haunted history was a draw for the tourists.

There was much about this lake they say was haunted, but as far as Henry was concerned, the bridge wasn't among them. But his reason for going there was to find what had been hidden long ago.

Within minutes, he'd arrived, parking near the condos. It was quiet here this time of year, so he walked down toward the base of the bridge. He approached the muddy bank beneath it, the cold air stinging his face. He looked around before stepping down to the water's edge. This was the place. The spot where he'd put the items Franky Crawford had found that day belonging to the Pied Piper's victims all those years ago.

As he neared the bridge, he scanned the shoreline, searching for the hidden entrance he knew was there. In his younger days, he had discovered the narrow opening beside the foundation, just big enough for a child to squeeze through. It led to a small chamber built from rock and hard earth.

He had used it as a secret hideout for years, stashing treasures like comic books, candy bars, and dirty magazines. He reached inside, gripping the bag that he knew would still be there.

With some effort, he hauled it out, the contents landing with a thud on the ground. Decay had started. The air, the water, the humidity...it all took its toll on the burlap sack now resting at his feet.

Inside were wallets, driver's licenses, car keys, and other various items that had been taken from the victims and placed in this bag. Now, all he had to do was plant it somewhere the cops would find it. Somewhere near Dean Crawford's home, Franky's son; a place he knew well.

$\sim$

SUMMER, 1986

In Camdenton, Missouri, Henry Holland had just graduated high school, along with his best buddies. The group of teens headed out for a day on the Lake of the Ozarks as summer kicked in to full swing.

It was Henry's last hurrah. His friends would be heading off to college, leaving him behind to go work for his father at the accounting firm. He would eventually be expected to take over the business, where his mother also worked. But Henry was no accountant, and he never wanted to be one.

Never mind that now. It was time to get the party started.

The four friends drove out to the lake in Henry's beat-up old pickup truck, the bed loaded down with a cooler full of beer, fishing rods, and a small tent. When they arrived at the shoreline, they quickly set up camp - unfurling their sleeping bags under the tent and cracking open a few cold ones as Franky Crawford got a fire going.

Laughter and jokes filled the air as the afternoon sun beat down. They took turns daring each other to do crazy stunts like swimming out to the farthest dock or chugging an entire beer in one go.

"To good friends and our last epic summer together!" Henry cheered, raising his bottle. The late afternoon sun glinted off the rolling waters as they clinked them together.

"Hey, guys." Will Clevenger leaned over, his elbows resting on his thighs. "You sure it's safe out here? Y'all heard about those dead bodies they found reaching the North Shore, right?"

"Yeah, so what?" Franky Crawford replied. "That's nowhere near us, man. Don't be such a downer, dude."

Henry glanced at his younger brother, Mike, only a junior in high school, before turning back to Will. "Yeah, I heard he chopped them up and dumped their bodies in the lake."

"But like, he's been arrested, right?" Franky asked, tucking his shoulder-length brown hair behind his ears.

"Yeah, man. He's in jail, I heard," Henry added. "Still, they don't know who those people are yet. They can't find all the parts of them."

"We should totally drive over where they found the bodies," Mike said.

Mike's suggestion sent a chill down Henry's spine, but also sparked his sense of adventure. After another round of beers, he was ready to take the bait.

"All right, let's do it," Henry declared, crushing his can and tossing it into the cooler. The other two whooped and hollered, intoxicated by both the alcohol and the thrill of doing something daring.

"I don't know, man. That seems kind of morbid," Franky said.

But Mike was adamant. He had always been the more adventurous one, always up for pushing boundaries.

Henry looked at Franky and Will. "Come on, guys. It'll be fun."

Franky shrugged, a mischievous smile tugging at his mouth. "I mean, it could be cool to check out...I guess."

They hopped back into the pickup truck, blasting music as they sped along the winding lakeside roads. The sun was sinking toward the horizon when they arrived at the northernmost tip of the lake. Police tape still cordoned off the area where the dismembered bodies had washed ashore weeks earlier.

"This is so creepy," Will muttered, hanging back from the water's edge.

"Don't be a wuss," Mike teased. He waded into the lake until the water reached his chest. "Come on, let's search for body parts!"

Spurred on by the prospect of morbid discovery, the other three joined Mike in the water. They fanned out, peering through the murky depths for any sign of the victims. Franky swam farther out, diving under periodically. Soon, he emerged, holding a canvas bag, waterlogged and covered in slimy algae.

"Dude, no way!" Mike exclaimed as Franky held it up. "That could totally be from one of the victims! What's inside?"

The boys swam over toward the shore to get a closer look when Franky opened the bag. He perched on the edge of the water and reached inside. "It's like...car keys and shit. IDs." He dumped out the rest of the bag's contents.

"What the fuck?" Henry asked. "It's like... people's stuff. You think it could be from the people that dude killed?"

"Should we take it to the cops?" Mike asked.

"They already arrested him. What the hell's it matter now?" Franky scoffed.

"Let me see!" Mike said, snatching it back from Franky.

"Just leave it, man," Franky shot back. "Let's just go, all right? Get the hell out of here."

"Franky's right," Henry said. "It's getting dark. We should go." He looked back at Franky, noticing he still held the bag and seemed fixated on it. "Hey, let's go, man."

~

It was years later, when Franky Crawford lay in a hospital bed, his body, riddled with cancer, that he'd told Henry he'd kept that bag all those years. Henry didn't ask why because he'd seen something in Franky that day. A strange obsession, like the bag had some kind of power over him.

Franky revealed he'd hidden the morbid contents in a coffee can in his garage. He'd wanted Henry to get rid of it because he'd believed his son, Dean, had found the can. Henry didn't question Franky more on it, figuring Franky had seen the same obsession in his son as he'd had...and maybe it scared him.

Instead, Henry had gone to the Crawford home, found the can, and took the bag here, to the bridge. A place every one of his friends and his brother knew about. But none of them were left. Not even his brother, Mike, who'd died in the Gulf War some years later.

The entire thing had been all but forgotten, until now. Even when Ashley went missing, Henry figured she'd been taken, like so many others had in years past. Her body, never found. No one ever found any more people chopped up into pieces and dumped into the lake. But now? Now, he wondered, seeing that picture of Dean Crawford and that dead DEA agent... the time had come make sure no one else in his family would suffer the way his daughters had. He couldn't help Sandra, but he could still help his grandchildren.

It was time to make sure all eyes landed on Dean Crawford because Dean knew a whole lot about Henry's operation. It wouldn't have been possible otherwise. People start thinking he's a serial killer, well, they won't care what he had to say about anyone or anything else. And if he is? If he killed Ashley?

Henry couldn't think about that now as he drove away from the lake, heading toward Dean Crawford's home. Planting these things...mementos left by the Pied Piper...they'd have no choice but to question how and why Dean had had them.

No one knew the Pied Piper, Jason Belgrave. His family wasn't from around here. He had no connections to anyone in the Ozarks, as far as Henry knew. Then again, Henry was only a smart ass teenager in those days, not paying much attention to what was around him. Unless it wore a skirt, or threw a ball, he didn't care. But he cared now.

Franky's been dead a long time, but Henry was sure a switch had been flipped in him after those Pied Piper killings. Little things he'd done that seemed peculiar. Was it too far a stretch to think that same switch had flipped in his son, Dean?

Henry couldn't be sure of anything, but it started to make sense. Retribution for the death of his beloved daughter, Ashley, and the destruction of his entire family was about to come to fruition. He made the turn onto the neighborhood street that was home to Dean and his family. A wife, but no kids. In light of things, that tracked.

He came to a stop at a house a couple of doors down and stepped down from his truck. With the bag in his hand, he approached the home with caution in his steps. No sign of Dean's vehicle, but it appeared his wife was home.

Placing the damning evidence would take some thought. Henry couldn't just leave at the front steps. No, it had to appear as though Dean had kept it hidden for years. So, he walked to the side of the house, careful not to cross in front of any windows. A gate lay before him, leading to the backyard.

Henry passed through it and continued along until he reached the rear of the home. Overgrown with leggy shrubs, dried grass, and weeds, he spied an empty planter. "Perfect."

~

KATE STILL HADN'T CONVINCED Agent McDaniel of her theory, but when the tip came in about Crawford's unusual activities at his house, he'd conceded.

When they'd had dinner with the lieutenant, he'd seemed casual about the investigation. And while Kate hadn't picked up on any notion that he could've been responsible for the current discovery of bodies, she did question why he'd gone along with the arrest of Everett Knapp. They'd had virtually no evidence, save for some DNA of one of the victims in Knapp's truck.

"Lieutenant Crawford is currently on patrol," Kate began. "Agent McDaniel, you keep him occupied, questioning him about Wayne Clevenger. Meanwhile, my team and I will search his house for evidence."

McDaniel handed Kate a document. "This is the warrant, so do what you have to do."

"You, too," she replied. "We'll need as much time as you can give us. And we can't afford to alert Henry Holland. We don't know his role, if any, in this, so we don't want him destroying potential evidence."

"Copy that." McDaniel started away. "Keep me posted."

With a final nod, Kate huddled around her team. "We have the warrant. Now, we just need to find proof."

"Best get going, then," Walsh said.

Crawford's modest two-story home was only minutes away.

Having arrived, Kate parked, and the team stepped out. If any neighbors were around, they'd wonder why all the suits were walking up to a Coast Guard lieutenant's driveway. They were not inconspicuous.

Kate led the way to the front door. "I'll take the lead with Mrs. Crawford. You all just need to be ready to start searching the premises as soon as we have her under control. We have no idea how she'll react to any of this."

She knocked on the door. After a moment, it opened to reveal Marcia Crawford, the lieutenant's wife of four years. She had a pleasant but worn face framed by short blonde hair.

"Hello, may I help you?" she asked.

"Mrs. Crawford, I'm Special Agent Kate Reid. We have a warrant to search your home for evidence related to your husband's involvement in a series of murders." Kate held up the document.

Her eyes went wide. "I'm sorry, what? No, that can't be right. Dean would never..."

"Ma'am, we can explain everything but right now we need to come inside and begin our search," Kate insisted. "If you'd like to wait outside, I or a member of our team can stay with you."

"No, uh, no, that's fine." She reluctantly stepped aside. "Come in."

As the team entered, Kate regarded the woman. "I'm sure you have a million questions, but we have reason to believe your husband may be connected to the victims who've been recently recovered from the lake."

Mrs. Crawford wore fear in her gaze. "You're wrong about this. Dean would never be involved in hurting anyone, let alone murder. He's a respected Coast Guard lieutenant."

Kate evened her tone. "I understand this is hard to accept. But we have to follow every lead. Please just allow us to do our job."

Mrs. Crawford's eyes reddened as she folded her arms. "Okay. I'll stay out of your way."

The team had already begun the search, each splitting up to cover more ground as quickly as possible. With McDaniel keeping the lieutenant distracted, the search could continue with little upheaval. Though, the brewing storm would unleash its wrath soon enough.

After almost an hour, Kate felt discouraged. Someone had called in an anonymous tip. And it was all she needed to convince McDaniel to pursue this angle, one she believed in. But they'd uncovered nothing and soon enough, Dean Crawford would get wind of this and hurry home.

She walked outside and noticed Surrey standing in the garage. He had something in his hands and so, she approached. "What is that?"

Surrey held up a small gym bag. "This was tucked inside a box at the back of this shelf." He opened it. "Take a look inside."

Kate inspected the contents. "Jesus. Looks like souvenirs to me."

"And not the kind that come from Disneyland." He peered inside again. "These look like personal belongings." He walked to a nearby work bench and dumped the contents.

Kate's heart drop into her stomach. "I recognize that." She aimed her index finger at the bracelet. "And I recognize it because Sandra Dawes has an identical one."

"It's Ashley Holland's, isn't it?" he asked.

She sensed he already knew the answer.

"Hey, guys." Duncan made her way toward them, carrying a canvas bag.

Kate turned to her, spying Walsh beside her. "What's that?"

"I'll tell you what we have, if you tell us what you have," Walsh replied wryly.

"Mementos." Kate aimed her finger at the bench. "Pretty sure these are items from the recent victims, including Ashley Holland."

"Then that is interesting." Duncan emptied the bag next to the other items. "Driver licenses, car keys...mementos."

Walsh shook his head. "Only these are a hell of a lot older than those you found."

Kate closed her eyes a moment. "The Pied Piper's victims. And Crawford's had these the whole time."

24

Dean Crawford was pulled off patrol and hauled in for questioning. He waited inside an interview room and if the team didn't get to him now, before his lawyer arrived, they wouldn't get to him at all. Regardless, the evidence they had was damning. But Kate had to know how it was those other belongings came into his possession. What was his connection to the Pied Piper?

Crawford had no idea his home had been searched. That was about to change. But he'd come in as a matter of cooperation, not realizing he was now a prime suspect.

"He has to know what we found," Kate said, standing in the bullpen.

McDaniel glanced into the corridor. "If he does, he's not acting like it. I don't think he's an ignorant man. He's protected his secret for a lot of years. That takes careful planning. So, I don't think he's expecting this, Agent Reid. I think he is under the impression our sights are fully trained on Wayne Clevenger."

"Then maybe that works to our advantage," she replied. "All

we have to do is show him the evidence and see what happens." She regarded her team. "Who wants to take point?"

"I will," McDaniel said. "He murdered my partner. This is all me now."

Kate raised her hands in surrender. "You're right. There's nothing more for us to do. Good luck, Agent McDaniel."

He eyed her a moment. "You don't want to see how it ends?"

"I think I already know," Kate replied. "Everett Knapp was a scapegoat. Convicted on the kind of insufficient evidence that verges on police misconduct. And Crawford was part of that investigation. Doesn't take a genius to think he had something to do with that." She peered beyond him toward the hall where Crawford waited. "Instead, that man in there, who clearly has some connection to the Pied Piper, was allowed to remain free. I imagine Agent Draker got close to figuring this out and that was why he was killed. Crawford's association with Wayne Clevenger, likely due to the illegal activities of the Hollands. Crawford might've played a part in facilitation of such activities."

McDaniel nodded. "Sounds about right. Listen, I appreciate all you people have done. The rest is up to me." He carried on into the hall, falling out of view.

"So, that's it?" Surrey asked. "We're done here? You don't want to know how Crawford was connected to the Jason Belgrave?"

Kate shrugged. "It'll all come out in the trial. But my best guess?" She tilted her head. "Henry Holland. There's more he knows. I'm sure of it."

"You think he was also involved in the murders?" Duncan asked.

"No," Kate replied. "I do think he's still a drug trafficker. In all the research we did on the families who've lived here for decades, I learned Henry Holland went to school with Frank Crawford,

Dean's dad. So, while I don't know how Frank Crawford connects to this, I have a feeling he does in some way."

~

The front door was open with the screen shut. Evening air in the summertime here could go one of two ways. Hot and sticky, or cool and breezy. Tonight, it was the latter, so Henry Holland welcomed the fresh air, and left the door open.

He and Jean were at the kitchen table, finishing up their meal when Ashley entered to meet them. She still lived with her folks, not like her sister, Sandra, who'd already met the man of her dreams.

"Just wanted to let you guys know I was heading out," she said.

Jean dabbed her lips with a napkin. "Going out with Jacob again tonight? You two seem to be getting close."

Ashley's cheeks turned a pale pink. "I don't know, maybe. He's nice. We're going to a movie and then to a bonfire at the lake. I'll be kinda late."

"Okay, honey, have fun," Henry replied. "Just do me a favor and don't go swimming after dark, all right? You can't see anything in that water."

"I know, Dad. Love you guys. Bye." She hurried toward the door. "Oh, hey, Dean."

"Hey, Ash, is your dad here?"

Henry had heard his name called and stood from the table. "Coming." He carried on toward the door. "Hi, Dean. What can I do for you?"

"Night, I gotta run," Ashley said, stepping outside and getting into her car.

Dean watched her leave before turning back to Henry. "Listen, uh, I wanted to ask you something about my dad."

Henry opened the door, his expression turning serious. "Well, come in."

"Thanks." He followed Henry into the living room.

"What is it you wanted to ask me?"

"You and Dad...you were friends in high school..."

"That's right," Henry replied. "Good friends. Why?"

Dean glanced over his shoulder as Ashley drove away. "I just got a job with the Coast Guard."

"Oh, that's good news. Congratulations, son. Your dad would've been proud."

"Thanks." He tucked his hands into his pockets. "Going back to my dad. He mentioned a while ago, before he started getting real sick. Something about how it was best to get recommendations if I wanted to get into their investigations division. And so, I wanted to ask if you wouldn't mind, would you put pen to paper and write something that might make the Coast Guard consider me for an investigative position?"

Henry smiled, patting the young man's shoulder. "Hell yes, I'll do that for you, son. That's no problem at all."

Crawford wore relief. "Thank you so much, Mr. Holland. I can't tell you what it means. Dad said you two shared some pretty crazy times together. He told me a lot of things y'all did."

Henry noticed Dean's expression change. His eyes looked cold. "Well, we did do some things, yes, sir."

"All right then, Mr. Holland. I'll leave you to enjoy the rest of your evening." Dean turned toward the door but stopped and turned back. "Where's Ashley headed tonight, by chance?"

"I think she's got a date with Jacob Fuller down at the lake. Nice kid. Don't know much about his dad though, other than he's some kind of shrink."

"Oh, nice. Okay then. Good night, sir. And thanks again."

Henry returned to the kitchen to find Jean cleaning the dishes. She glanced over her shoulder at him. "What did Frank's son want?"

"Oh, nothing much. Asked for a letter of recommendation for this new job he wants at the Coast Guard. Something about investigations."

"And he asked you for it?" she pressed.

"Yeah, well, Franky was with them for a while, till he got sick. So, I guess Dean figures that will help him. And then with Mike going off to war in the Gulf...and the work I did when he didn't come back...I guess that means something."

"Of course it does," Jean said. "Dean would be lucky to have a recommendation from you."

Henry peered through the kitchen window as Dean drove away.

"You okay, Henry?" she asked, seeming to notice his gaze drift off.

"What's that now?" he asked. "Yeah, fine. Sorry. Just thinking about Franky. Something he told me a long time ago." He swatted his hand. "Sometimes I wonder how far that apple fell from the tree."

25

Walking away was always the hardest thing to do. A last resort for most. And for Kate, she now faced it on two fronts. Leaving behind Ella Dawes to deal with the fallout of secrets, lies, and murder. And leaving Nick for reasons to which she'd stubbornly clung.

It was impossible to know Ella's outcome, though Kate suspected the girl and her sister would be placed with her father's parents, who lived forty minutes away.

Any connection to the Holland side of the family had been severed the moment Sandra Dawes was arrested for the murder of Shane Fuller. Having drug traffickers for grandparents didn't help either.

Fuller had his own issues, but despite his failings, his obsession with Sandra, death was too harsh a punishment for him. As it turned out, that email that set off an irreversible chain of events? Clevenger had an acquaintance who worked in the same building as Tim Dawes. Money changed hands, and voila—email sent.

According to Clevenger's statement, he'd confessed to employing the tactic to force Sandra's marriage to spiral. And so it did.

Clevenger was never going to see the outside of a prison again. Kidnapping, murdering Tim Dawes...he might not have killed the DEA agent, but he'd done enough damage to put himself away forever.

Would the Hollands ever see their grandchildren again? Well, Agent McDaniel still had nothing on them. Dean Crawford had boarded the vessel that night, murdered Draker, and dumped his body. Alex Medina still had not been found. No one knew whether he was even alive, possibly having joined the ranks of the dead at the bottom of the lake.

It was possible Henry Holland could be charged with tampering with the scene of a crime when he went with Clevenger to the boat. His claim that he'd been taken hostage had fallen into question. But that was child's play compared to the drugs he and his wife had trafficked.

Kate supposed all that was just a ticking time bomb. Their part here was done, and it was time to go back to Quantico. To go home to a future that remained uncertain.

She zipped her bag when a knock sounded on the hotel room door. She opened it to find Surrey on the other side. "Hi. Come in."

He meandered inside. "Everyone's downstairs. You about ready?"

"Yep." Kate slung the bag over her shoulder. "After you." She followed him back out into the corridor. The silence between them was broken only by the ding of the elevator as it reached their floor.

Stepping inside, Surrey pressed the button for the lobby. When the doors closed, Kate stared at the numbers as they descended.

"So, what's next?" he asked, glancing over his shoulder at her.

"Sleep," she replied with a smile.

"No doubt, but I think you know what I mean."

The doors opened in time for Kate to avoid being forced to truthfully answer the question. Because truthfully? She didn't know.

Inside the lobby, Walsh and Duncan were seated nearby. They stood at their arrival when Walsh began, "The gang's all here." He checked his watch. "Better get to the airport."

Kate kept to herself on the drive, only speaking when asked a question, not feeling much like participating in the conversation. And while they all knew her well enough to realize this wasn't her usual behavior, all seemed to give her the space to deal with the events that had unfolded. Events that they all dealt with in their own ways.

~

THE PLANE TOUCHED down at Dulles International by late afternoon. Winter was in full swing in D.C., with blustery winds and gray skies. Current weather reports predicted an early first snow tonight. It would probably just be a dusting. Annual snowfall seemed on the decline here. Shame.

The team returned to Quantico and Kate, to her office. She flipped on the light and sat down at her desk. "Now what?"

Her question was answered almost immediately when Fisher entered.

"Welcome back," he said, taking a seat across from her. "I got a call from the DEA Administrator. She wanted to personally thank you and the rest of the team for helping to bring Draker's killer to justice."

"The administrator," Kate said, nodding. "Might as well have come from the president, himself."

Fisher laughed. "That's what I was thinking. But in all seriousness, you guys did your job."

She shrugged. "Well, I'm not so sure we did what we'd intended to do. This wasn't like anything I've ever worked on before."

He crossed his long legs, tilting his head at her. "The wrong man was convicted of murdering several people. You all found the true killer. I'd say that was exactly your job."

"A little too late, if you ask me," Kate replied. "Uh, Cam, can I ask... do you know if Nick has decided anything? Has he talked to Cole?"

"I take it, you haven't talked to him recently?"

She shook her head. "Not since the other night. But this work..." She raised the corner of her lips. "It comes second nature to him, doesn't it?"

"That it does." He narrowed his gaze. "What do you want him to do, Kate? I haven't said anything because, well, you've had your hands full, but Cole's been pushing hard to get Nick back here."

She drew back in surprise. "What?"

"He wants Nick back on the team," Fisher repeated.

Her pulse quickened and confusion clouded her thoughts. "What did you say about the idea?"

He raised a shoulder. "I was honest. Said I didn't think that was the way to go. I've said nothing about this to the other guys, figuring I should come to you first. I told Nick the same thing. Given our team dynamics, I'm not sure he'd easily slide back into place regardless. I think there's too much baggage now, as unfair as that sounds. I have to consider the team as a whole, and you, in particular, because you're the lead profiler. I need you...*we* need you...at the top of your game. Always."

Her heart was torn at the prospect. "Does Nick even want to come back here?"

Fisher glanced down. "I don't think so. I think he sees the problems it could create. And frankly, nothing's set in stone. Cole would have to get Bennett's approval, and I'm not sure that would happen. I just thought you should be aware."

He set both feet flat on the floor again and leaned over his elbows. "Kate, I love you like a sister. You know that. And I care what happens to each of you. Hell, I think I've started worrying about you all like a goddam father." He laughed. "But I can see you're going through something. Something big. We all see it. So, just do me a favor. Tell me what you want because I'm not a mind-reader. I'm just a guy and so, you'll need to spell it out for me." He stood. "Take a few days to figure things out, all right? Nick doesn't have all the time in the world to sit on this either. He'll do what you want. We all know that."

∼

AN EMPTY PIZZA box sat on the kitchen counter. The television was on, broadcasting the evening news. And Kate sat in the living room with Duncan, both sipping on a glass of red wine. It felt good having Duncan there, even though they'd remained silent. She knew what Kate had been through and gave her what she needed —companionship and time to figure things out.

But when the knock came, they peered at each other.

"You expecting a visitor?" Duncan asked.

"No," Kate replied, checking her phone. "No one's messaged me."

"All right." Duncan got up from the sofa and walked to the door. Kate watched her peer through the security lens.

"Oh." She looked back at Kate. "Uh, it's Nick. Should I..."

"Yeah, of course."

Duncan opened the door. "Hey, Nick. What's going on? What are you doing here?"

He shrugged and appeared sheepish. "I was just over at Levi's having a talk. Thought I'd come by and see how you two were doing." He glanced around her. "Is Kate here?"

"Yep. Come in." Duncan stepped aside, closing the door behind him.

"Hi," Kate said as he entered.

"Hi. Glad you guys are back safely. You, uh, you doing all right?" He shifted his gaze between them.

"Just fine," Duncan replied. "You know how it goes. Just need a little time to decompress, then onto the next thing." She set her hand on his shoulder. But, hey, you know that information you gave us about the old case file, it really helped shift our focus. So, thank you."

He donned a crooked smile. "Yeah, no problem. Just one of those things, you know? Luck, I guess."

"Sure. Hey, can I get you anything to drink? Some water or soda?" Duncan asked, walking to the kitchen.

"No, I think I'm okay, thanks." He thumbed to Kate. "I was actually wondering if I might have a word with Kate, here."

Duncan did what any good friend would do and waited for Kate's approval. When she got the nod, she replied, "Yeah, sure." She slipped on her shoes that were near the door. "You know what? I think I'll go see Levi. Need to catch up on a few things, so, uh, I'll leave you guys to it." She made a hurried exit.

Kate smiled. "I guess it's just us now." She gestured to the chair next to the sofa. "Take a seat."

"Thanks."

Silence passed between for several moments until the awkwardness finally got to her. "So, uh, what'd you want to talk about?" As if she didn't know.

"Cam talk to you about Cole's suggestion?" Nick asked.

She donned a gentle grin. "Yeah, he did."

He raised his hands in surrender. "Look, Kate, regardless of Cole's efforts on my behalf, I don't think it's a good idea to come back to the team."

Relief swelled in her chest. "Oh?"

He chuckled. "Come on now. I think we're on the same page with that one." He dropped his shoulders and seemed to relax a little. "But I still have a choice to make."

"I know." Kate folded her legs under her and clasped her hands. As she looked at Nick, all the things they'd been through together...it all rushed back. The cases they'd worked. The deadly encounters they'd had during those cases. The moments of pure love for one another, grateful to have survived all those horrific things. They'd complimented each other...until they didn't. "So, what do you think you want to do? Los Angeles or Washington, back where we started?"

"Do you have any suggestion?" he asked.

But what he really meant was, 'Do you want me to stay or go?' So, what did she want? Kate felt her eyes sting. *Don't break down. Not now. Tell him what you want.* "I don't know," she whispered.

Nick looked down, disappointment masking his face. "Okay."

"It's your decision, Nick. I can't make this choice for you," she added. "You have to do what's best for you. Not me."

He looked up at her again. "You're still my wife, Kate. It matters to me what you think."

Kate hadn't yet filed for divorce, vacillating about her own choices. But it wasn't fair to Nick. "None of this is fair."

"No, but I did this to us," he continued. "And I'm sorry for that. Sorrier than you'll ever know."

She felt a twinge in her abdomen and placed her hand over it.

"You okay?" he asked.

"Yeah, it's just...a little residual nerve thing I've had ever since the hysterectomy. No big deal. It's not happening as much anymore." It occurred to her then that she'd never given Nick a chance to talk about the loss of their unborn child. Did he not have the same right as she did to mourn, to feel the pain she'd suffered as well? Maybe he did, but she wouldn't know because she'd already cut him from her life.

"I'm sorry, too," Kate said. "I know what happened...with the pregnancy...It couldn't have been easy for you to deal with and yet you had to on your own. That wasn't fair." So much pent-up anger and grief remained, churning in her gut. And the only way she'd handled it was to dive into her job. It was how she handled most things.

Nick didn't respond, yet his eyes welled and his lower lip quivered. The next few moments, they were silent, until finally, "I don't want to lose you, Kate. I have no more excuses to offer. I lost your trust, and it was all you'd ever asked of me." He wiped away a tear and stood up, joining Kate on the sofa.

"What can I do to fix this?" he asked.

Her hands trembled as she took his. "I think I've come to realize that the entirety of our situation doesn't rest on your shoulders, Nick." She glanced away, taking a moment to breathe.

Nick had been a guiding presence for her in so many ways these several years. Not unlike what Ella had experienced, believing someone was there with her, trapped in that basement, offering hope of survival. After losing Sam, and then Marshall, it was Nick who was there for Kate. Faults and all.

"Kate?" Nick asked, his tone soft.

She cleared her throat. "Sorry."

"Why? You don't need to be."

She looked into his still watery eyes and the white, salty track of the rogue tear that had fallen down his cheek. "None of this can be solved in a moment when our emotions are running high. Or a moment of fear that neither of us knows what to do without the other."

"What are you saying, Kate?"

She drew in a long breath. "I'm saying, I want you to take the job in D.C. I'm saying, we can still work on us...through counseling, or whatever. But I guess what I'm really saying is that..." Kate swallowed hard. "I love you more than anything, and I don't want this to be over any more than you do. For better or worse, right? That's what we promised each other."

He smiled, his lips quivering again. "Yep, that's what we agreed."

Broken promises aside, Kate would have to forgive him, never to hold this over his head again. Accepting who he was without compromise. It could mean of lifetime of uncertainty. Of wondering whether he'll make the right decisions. Wondering if he'll ever hurt her again. Or if she would hurt him.

But it could also mean a life filled with the love of a man who would lift her up, love her, and be happy about her successes. That was the truth in any marriage. Giving one's life to another human being, praying it will all work out. Did Kate have it in her? Was she strong enough not to walk away again?

Kate looked him in the eyes and saw the rest of her life. "Okay, then. But we're buying a house, got it? I'm not living in that condo anymore."

He burst out laughing. "Yeah, I think we can do that."

Kate didn't know what would happen, and all the hopefulness

in the world wasn't going to change that. Would they be able to mend the fractures from his recent actions? Or come to terms with a past they both struggled to bury? Time will tell. But something... or someone...reminded her that she deserved happiness. And it had been a long time coming.

THE END

ABOUT THE AUTHOR

Robin Mahle has published more than 30 crime fiction novels, many, of which, topped the Amazon charts in the US, Canada, and the UK. And most recently, she has delved into the world of psychological thrillers.

Also a screenwriter, she has adapted some of her works into teleplays, which have gone on to place in film festivals nationwide.

From detectives to federal agents, and from killers to corruption, her page-turning tales grab hold and refuse to let go. Throw in tense action and thrilling twists, and it becomes clear why her readers come back for more.

Robin lives in Coastal Virginia with her husband and two children.

ALSO BY ROBIN MAHLE

The Kate Reid FBI Thriller Series (17 books)

The Chef (stand-alone psych thriller)

The Man in My Attic (stand-alone psych thriller)

The Remy Fontaine Fugitive Hunter Thrillers (4 books)

The Det. Rebecca Ellis Thrillers (5 books)

The Allison Hart PI Thrillers (5 Books)

The Lacy Merrick Thrillers (4 books)

Made in the USA
Las Vegas, NV
09 October 2024

96543067R00164